TEX REX

TEX REX

▶ ▼ ◀

A Novel By

Marshall Terry

Dallas: Three Forks Press

Three Forks Press
P.O. Box 823461
Dallas, Texas 75382

ISBN 1-893451-07-0

Printed in the United States of America

First Edition

To all the Old Crocks and Myths
of Cherished Memory in Texas

AUTHOR'S NOTE

I am grateful for particular material relating to a sense of Texas to Bryan Woolley and the *Dallas Morning News*, to the late A.C. Greene, to DiAn Malouf, to Don DeLillo, to Ron Bradford, to *Texas Monthly*, to *Texas Observer*, and to *Rolling Stone* and the memory of Mike McFarland. I am grateful to John Nichols for the sense of New Mexico he has given me through the years.

I wrote this story in 1999 and revised it in 2000. It takes place in Dallas, Texas, and the world during the summer and fall of 1998, that is to say before history and our perception of it changed on September 11, 2001. The characters are imaginary and not meant to resemble any persons living or dead except that those who exist in the public domain are not "real" either but are meant to be the media images of themselves by which we know them. One of these, someone who may be or is like Osama bin Laden, appears in this fiction, and since I believe I caught his nature I have left him as he came to me then.

TEX REX

ONE

"Who do you think killed John F. Kennedy?"

The leonine old man peered at me from the depth of an armchair in a corner of the elegant, obviously unused leather-bound library of our host's house. I had drifted into the room to get away from the fundraising fandango, attracted by the books. In his mottled hand was the biggest, darkest glass of bourbon ever beheld even in Texas.

"I have always been ambivalent about that," I, the ambivalent Henry Rose, replied. Staring back down at the strangely harlequin figure in the chair, heavy and heaving for breath, I could not figure out, at a glance, what the glints of gold and red and purple in the man's voluminous jacket and pants and his monstrously wide necktie signified, were meant to amount to.

"McIvey," the old man said, extending his fat brown hand on one finger of which sat a huge gold, diamond and ruby crested ring. Then withdrew it, as if it were not meant to be shaken but if you jumped to it you might could have kissed the ring. "I am the King of Texas."

I chuckled, politely.

Then looked into obsidian, depthless, remorseless eyes. They were slate gray and seemed to believe the King thing, as a languorous snake believes that it can gather, coil and strike.

"Ambivalent, eh? A pro-fessor, huh? You should be. Ambi-valent. Valens. Be strong. Be dubious! 'I'm Cronkite.' 'Hello, Cronkite, I'm Dubious.' Vaudeville! You know that pathetic little shit didn't just do it by himself. Ha. I'll tell you, sir, who assassinated JFK some other time, when we have a moment. Eh? Right now, I must choose—and soon appoint—the Prince of Dallas. Do you have any nominations, sir?"

"Sir?"

Old McIvey leaned forward.

"I tried to give San 'Tonio to my daughter, if she would just marry. For a wedding present. Gave Galveston to my other daughter. She married a surly shit. Divorced. Gave Galveston back. Just as well, sir. Just-as-well." The old eyes glittered. "Went off to Santa Fe. Out of my personal domain. Once, of course, belonged to us, to Texas. I have not decided whether to buy it back. No, sir. Do you know New Mexico?"

"Yes. It would cost a lot by now. Santa Fe."

"Yes. Maybe I could have one of my daughters marry, and bring it back to me that way."

"Like Mabel," I said.

"Yes. Like Mabel," said McIvey, seeming to be quite clear who was meant, Mabel Dodge, who married the Pueblo world in Taos. He settled back, wrinkled brown lids hooding the strange, or mad, eyes, raising his glass to drink the rich, dark whiskey, dismissing me with a slight wave of his rubied fingers.

"Well, cheerio," I said, to no response, and turned to see a short, massive fellow standing by me, as if observing, as if guarding, the leonine head and elephantine, royally bespangled body of the King of Texas now sunk in somnolence in the soft wing chair. This bull rider was blocking my way, if I did not make a wide, obvious arc around him, so I patted his gristly shoulder and said, "Hello. Henry Rose, the Provost."

He had bright blue eyes and muttonchop sideburns like from the seventies or the Civil War. He laughed like that was a purty funny thing for me to say. Some others standing around in the little room smiled with him. A long-limbed, plain but pretty woman smiled at me as if she thought it was a good joke, too. I smiled back, indulgently. No one knew what a provost was, or did.

"Billy Roy," the cowboy said, grabbing my hand. He had a big grip and a big silver buckle on his belt with a Texas star inset. "Is that like a Provo'-Marshal?"

"Yes. Yes, it is. Provosts—keep track."

I had been watching the rich, elegant women in attendance through the rooms of the mansion, and I smiled back at the tall, long-limbed woman who was dressed all in some sort of silky, shimmering blue. She wasn't bad of the type. Mid-aged, oozing wealth, a jewel winking here and there. Our little university's lecture series was full of women like this. Sometimes I had the fantasy that I might marry one—replace the dear departed Myrtle Springs—and leave the hectic academic life and settle down to a later life of wealth and leisure. She had big round bluegreen eyes like some brand of a Chinese cat but turned languorously away from me and pulled *The Princess Casamassima*, in gilt leather, from the long bookcase.

"Provo'," Billy Roy said, with a snort, "jest a-keepin' track." He doubled up his fists and went into a crouch, like he was going to spar with me. I danced around him.

"That old fellow has the idea that he is the King of Texas," I said, going by.

Billy Roy smiled again, in great good humor, clapping me on the back. "I carry him around," he said. "I wouldn't bet he aint."

I left the languorous woman meeting, or reacquainting herself with, Miss Pynsent and Hyacinth Robinson and, leaving the room, passed by two thin men in silk suits who bowed and smiled but did not offer hands.

"Mr. Fuad," one said. "We come on behalf of your fine little university, to this fine fundraising event, good luck."

"Singh," said the other. "However, it is hot as ducky blazes out there, is it not? It is infinitely more comfortable for us, for him, in this pleasant room."

"For His Majesty?"

They looked at me as if I were daft, on which side of the issue I could not tell.

Where did the poor old fellow get the bourbon, I wondered.

This was Tex Flatt's place. He was letting us use it for a kickoff event for the new campaign for big-time funds for our small-time place, a campaign so illy conceived by our brash, bright new boy president.

Tex's place was in far north Dallas quite a way from our campus. Our little Highland U. was just five years old, almost no endowment, and always in trouble, Highland's small flat campus lying as we liked to joke somewhere between Mountain View and Prairie View outside of Dallas, whose interest and support had long ago been devoted to SMU and UTD and University of Dallas and so on. Somehow the founding president, idealistic old Bernard Pryor, had got hold of Tex Flatt, who then observed Bernie not doing much after the laying out of the absolutely pure liberal arts curriculum and fired him, and brought in our beamish Boy. Dear God, with a Ph.D. in Education! We knew that augured ill. He wanted to reach out to everybody in the "Metroplex" and do adult ed and recruit in Asia and be *global* and offer degrees in practical subjects like—for God's sake—Business! Dallas was already up to its materialistic ass in Bidness, what it needed was a pure place, a place of Paideia, of thoughtful repose, I mean, the bloody glorious Goddamn Liberal Arts, as classically defined. Oh—we were headed for disaster.

And were now at Tex Flatt's, our trustee/supporter/donor, who'd made his billion or so in oil when you could still do that, and bless his heart, now somehow liked to read, and *believed* in the liberal arts as he understood them, and here we were having the kickoff at his fabulous pad, at the worst possible time, the beginning of the terrible summer that was going to bake the prairie dry, a summer of drought and dread and disillusion and market down and worldwide doom.

Oh yes, we were kicking off, deep in the end zone, into the wind.

A horrible thought. Soon the Boy would want us playing football!

I had come back to Texas to be the provost, thinking that later on I'd step aside and teach a little literature at this pure new place on the Dallas prairie, enticed, seduced by old Pryor and by a thrilling, tingly dry handshake from Tex Flatt, the richest man I'd ever met. Surely we could not fail! We had a pure, fine faculty, principled renegades from East and West and especially South, not a deconstructor in the ranks! But now, after the appointment of this Boy, this pudgy boy with the lick of hair over his forehead, our values slipping away, why, it looked like a slippery slope, a weak-dog Iditarod, a house built on searing sand.

H. Rose, Provost, chief academic officer of Highland U., ambivalent about most things, was keeping track, and he was not ambivalent about this. Maybe if I got closer to Tex Flatt we could have another coup, replace the Boy. "Two roads," I might quote to Tex, for he had heard of Robert Frost, "diverged in a yellow wood . . ."

("Never saw a yellow wood," Tex said, when I tried. "Where would that be? Louisiana? Arkansas? East Texas? All the woods I've ever seen were *green*. You ever been *in* a woods, Henry? My Lord, you guys!" Tex had done timber as well as oil. The New England poem left him cold.)

Anyway, old Tex had him a pad. It was terribly impressive at night, outside, with artificial lights on artificial trees that kind of resembled the skeletons of oil wells, the tall wooden skinny kind like Spindletop. Right now it all looked like glazed fruit, and the rambling mansion like a looping big glazed doughnut in the high heat of a summer's evening with the clock set on heat, no relief, no rain, in Dallas. Now the crowd of about a hundred souls, university people including students on parade in bright smiles like Tex liked 'em and administrators and a couple of faculty, and all the potential donors strong-armed here by Tex, and the women with them or alone, the predator women from our subscription lecture series—we were bringing classical culture to the prairie megapolis—and the crusty old conservative columnist from the newspaper who was so delighted his face cracked from the strangeness of smiling for the first time in years that here was a university that was not part of the liberal, multiracial, multicultural, deconstructive revolutionary conspiracy, we were all moving outside into the heat of the evening, the sun like a fire in the blue barbecue grill of the sky above, being herded out of the hallways and big rooms of the house of eclectic architecture, rooms like barns for the cattle and sheep at the Fair.

I met John Woodcipher, in History, a pleasant, ruddy-faced man equipped with a glass of Texas Chardonnay they were serving in the hallway. John was about as near to a liberal as we had on our faculty. He wrote on the Spanish Civil War and kept a romantic fear of the Fascists and love of the Loyalists, into which camps he still tended to divide folks, and he kept a running score of the fascinating cast of political and entrepreneurial characters always at bat, getting in their innings, in the endless game of wealth and power in Texas. John devoted one day a year to lecturing his students and going on talk radio to dispel the notion that Texas still at any time could divide itself up into five states if it wished. (Why should it wish to? What folly, when it could thrive as such an eponymous powerful state, the former glorious Republic, and keep furnishing to the nation our Armeys and DeLays, our cheerleader Kay Bailey, our Motorcycle Annie, our Bushes, with old LBJ offstage pulling that hound's ears and drinking whiskey while on the phone on the pot.)

"Henry, no offense," John Woodcipher said, "but I believe I will stay in the cool of the air conditioning with the wine supply. Will you be speaking, or just standing up there by him like the dummy you've become?"

"Not speaking, John, old dear, thanks so much for asking when you know the answer. I might say something academic."

I went out into the heat of the brassy day and stood by Bunky, our Boy, our presidente, as he spoke. It was an odd configuration. He spoke from one end of a very long rectangular pool, with the people clustered at the other end of the long pool. The wind came in and rippled the blue water the length of the pool as Bunky spoke into a microphone, so that his words came out the microphone and went around the sides of the pool and either reached the people or did not, for we saw no reaction from them to the phrases as he spoke. "—merge the liberal, or should we say, conservative arts with the practical—" "—the examined life in the service of society—" "—Highland, the 'new U. for you,' takes its place of leadership—" It was like speaking to yourself on a windy day at the edge of Lake Lugarno.

Then Tex Flatt spoke. Bunky Boy jumped up and down and clapped, and we all clapped, when we thought we heard him say he would give the first two million, or some million, maybe one, to the campaign, for the Flatt Tower that would tower o'er the campus as a symbol of— Anyway he sang a pretty little nasal song as Bunky the Bunko Scruggs played a little plunk-plunk banjo in the background. . . .

As Flatt finished I avoided Bunky, who was anyway bouncing off to buttonhole and bug donors, now hurrying away from the festive scene, and shook hands with Tex. He, like his house, looked glazed, like old brown pottery made for the heat, for the outside, dry and hardglazed and enduring as the wildcat breed he'd come from. He was a fine, chaste old fellow, a Southern Baptist and a drinker of Dr Pepper, now dumbfounded it had become as Cadbury a holding of the Brits. His dry, brown old hand darted in and out of mine like a dry lizard, as I expressed our great appreciation. He shrugged back into his horribly expensive blue suit, flicked the tie in front of his blue, white-collared shirt, adjusted his gold-horsed cufflinks to his cuffs. We'd been in meetings together since his presence had helped convince me to return to Texas, had exchanged confidences about Highland U. and the weather, he'd had me to breakfast. Flicked his cuffs, his eyes at me. "All right, gubuddy," he said, in what I took to be a form of "good buddy." "Good, gubuddy, all right, good."

Flicked, nodded, turned from me to greet some old boy wearing the same blue suit and two-toned shirt and links, and gave that fellow a smile; I might as well have been the pool keeper, for all he knew or cared.

"Ole Tex," John Woodcipher said, still standing by the wine table inside, by the last bottle of the Llano wine, some ruddier of face. "I don't believe he's given anything to anyone before, let alone a university. I find that interesting. He is practically self-made, you know. His daddy didn't leave him more'n ten, twelve million, for a start. He took it on from there."

"You ever heard of an old fellow named McIvey, John?"

"No. He wasn't the one ran an ad in the classifieds every year thanking everyone for helping him make another million, was he?"

"That was O. L. Nelms. He passed."

"Well, no. McIvey? Doesn't come to me. Not known for wealth. Not active in any way I know."

We shook some hands, I did my halfhearted duty speaking to folks, the third wheel putting just a little rubber to the road. In a while we looked and saw, coming from the hallway through the barnlike room and to the entryway, old McIvey, his fat arms around the neck of his hoss, being carried piggyback out of the place, Mr. Fuad and Mr. Singh coming along then and smiling in his wake. Billy Roy carried him out the doorway and I suppose to a waiting conveyance, limo, Stanley Steamer, or carriage and four as the case might be.

"That's him," I said to John.

"Oh yes," Woodcipher said. "I do recognize him. McIvey. He's the King of Texas. Been around forever. Nice deluded old fellow. I taught his daughter, I believe his daughter, yes, as a special adult student in my Spanish War course, oh, three years ago. She was pretty bright, had lived in Spain. But then I believe she took a class from Wilson, you remember Peter Wilson, quiet little guy. Oh, you weren't here yet then. Wilson decided we would never make it and went back to Pepperdine. She took his course in Military History. I remember because, you see, Henry, she asked him out. Yes, he went out with her a time or two. Nice little bachelor fellow, good degrees, Amherst and Virginia. Scared him, Wilson said. She scared him. Thought she was a little strange. I remember her as bright, and open to ideas. This is a rather good little Chardonnay, made from grapes grown out on the Llano Estacado, the Staked Plain, where nothing grows. Gives us hope, Henry, does it not, for the tender vines of Highland U.?"

"A Fascist or a Loyalist?"

"Pardon?"

"McIvey."

"Oh. Who knows? Off in some other world, I fear. A Loony Tune. Old Herbert Pickens, bless his heart, when he was still among us, the historian at SMU, said he talked to old McIvey, a few years ago, said—"

That was enough of the King of Texas. I had my own pickle to chew on. Except I kept seeing those remarkable reptilian pewter eyes, they were so certain, sure of something. A quality of madness, I presumed. Desperate for a move from that hellhole in Alaska, I had returned to Texas and gotten myself into a fix at Highland. The faculty were losing faith. Tex Flatt did not really care, you could paint a dummy the school colors and call it provost and Tex would shake its hand and say, "All right, gubuddy. That's good, gubuddy." And the Boy Presidente knew I was not with him in my heart. It would be almost fun, a great relief, to let go and believe you were the King of Texas—the Emperor of Icecream—the Czar of Alaska—the Duke of Paducah. *"I'm going back to the wagon, boys, these shoes is a-killin' me."*

I stood outside waiting for the parkers to bring my car. I merged into the heat in my light gray suit and Harvard tie. I was not sure what colors to assume. I watched the people getting in the cars as they pulled up and the doors were opened for them, the tanned or pale enameled women, the blue-suited men, the Lexuses and bulbous-ended new Lincoln Town Cars, the Lincoln Navigators, the Expeditions and the Tahoes, the Infinitis, Mercedes and Cadillacs and the occasional faculty or staff Saab or Camry, until my old Buick lurched up and I got in and smiled thank you at the parker boy who was surely paid enough by old Tex Flatt for this service and did not need a half a rock from me.

Who killed Kennedy? My God, I'd come to think that we all did, and by now we didn't feel too bad about it, what with all we knew about what a bum the Bright Knight was, and with our juvenile Billy giving us the revolting Chapter 2 of Camelot. Think of carrying that around, the assassination riddle, still trying to solve it, what a strange, sad thing. Delusions are terrible on all levels.

Then, driving off, I remembered the last time I had thought about the assassination, the event that gave Big D its scarlet *A*, about a year ago, just after I came back to Texas and came to Highland. I was almost immediately called to jury duty, which I considered a conspiracy in itself. Called to criminal court on a murder case, got rid of quick as a professor probably unwilling to inject the lethal dose in a state with the lead in that. Had lunch in a barbecue joint down by the court and the jail and the Old Red Courthouse there in downtown Dallas not far from the assassination spot. Lean old guy in a Stetson eating with some others at a table, eating a Po' Boy, old retired detective with a leathery face looking like a withered version of one of those startled big old Stetsoned boys captured forever as Ruby came up to Oswald and Oswald cringed and felt the pain, like one of the detectives in that image caught forever, and maybe he was one of them. Telling them at the table quietly some story they seemed to know about the assassination and the motorcade and getting Kennedy to Parkland and getting Oswald, and then Ruby, and the anger and frustration of the Dallas Police.

Later in the summer new information released seemed to confirm that there was one shooter, Oswald, which, the little I thought of it, suited the clear rationality of mind which I was known and noted for.

I had no way of knowing or preparation for believing how real assassins are, how comic and human is the face of terror, how terrible in its pull is power.

TWO

On a day soon after, I beheld the woman at a symposium on campus and experienced her unexpected sharp wit, or should I say fingernail, in a class. The symposium was on the subject of how boring Texas had become in the Nineties because there were no larger-than-life characters in Texas anymore. But before relating that I'll mention Mr. Ray Rodriguez' visit that morning, in the context of interesting people in Texas; for, after all the perturbations I have seen, some large and terrifying, I yet think that the small ironies are more interesting than the large ones.

I left a message for Mr. Rodriguez on his answering service and he arrived in the same old red pickup truck to look over some dead branches hanging over the trim little house in the Park Cities I bought when I came back to Dallas. Myrtle Springs and I had lived in married bliss a street or two away in earlier times and it brought back pleasant memories of my regular life with that good person. It was also just a few streets from SMU with its beautiful campus and its gorgeous girls strolling its paths in such rich profusion. SMU was run with religious fervor by a president who exclaimed that life is too short to go to school on an ugly campus. At poor Highland we existed on a denuded strip of prairie land, treeless, comforted by our ideals and aspirations.

Mr. Rodriguez was a Christian gentleman who believed that Jesus was a friend who stood between you and God. I would have been pleased to have Ray Rodriguez there if Jesus didn't show. We had an embrazo and reminded ourselves how long we had known each other. Like myself he'd fought in Korea. We reminded each other of how the Chinese had come at us on shaggy ponies with lances across the frozen Yalu. He had relatives over Texas and in New Mexico. He had just bought his wife a diamond ring after forty years for their anniversary. How was mine? Oh, he was sorry she had gone away. Sometimes he pulled a damn old

muscle in his stomach but he was still working and we better trim those
branches off these trees over the house before the ice storm comes and
cracks them down on the roof. It was already ninety degrees as we stood
there talking early in the morning, and I agreed, excited at the prospect of
the ice storm.

Mr. Rodriguez drove away in his red truck, after telling me about
Moses and the Promised Land. He had studied Bible five years. I thought
he was remarkable, since we had taken Texas away from him and his
family, and he'd fought with us in Korea, and his cousin Willy died on
the Bataan Death March before that, and he was still willing to come trim
my trees and after all the years go buy Mrs. Rodriguez her first little
diamond ring—the "Starburst" one—at the Mesquite Mall. I asked him if
he'd seen *Saving Private Ryan* and he said, oh, no, he did not like
violence. I thought that was a damn good thing. Everywhere I walked
and drove, in the Park Cities, in north Dallas, up by Legacy, in Plano and
Allen, there were Mexican people working, constructing houses and
buildings, mowing yards, blowing leaves with their maquinas, riding in
the backs of pickups, an army, speaking Spanish, doing the work,
everywhere.

That afternoon I dragged myself to the symposium got up and
moderated by John Woodcipher on the boringness of Texas since we had
no larger-than-life characters anymore. The guest stars, the Dobie
Professor from the University of Texas, the Webb Professor from the
University of North Texas, the Ben Lilly Professor from SMU and the K.
A. Porter Professor from TCU, fittingly a woman, lamented that colorful,
flamboyant, larger-than-la vida characters had departed Texas and not
been replenished, that there were no more J. Frank Dobies, Walter
Prescott Webbs, Ben Lillys or Katherine Anne Porters. "We have done
suppressed oddity," said the Webb professor. "We finally were
embarrassed by it, embarrassed out of our roots." They pointed out that
Sam Houston, the Raven, the "Big Drunk," the first president of Texas,
was gone, and the great political individualists like Jim Hogg and Pa and
Ma Ferguson and "Pappy" Lee O'Daniel and his Light Crust Doughboys
and LBJ had long departed the scene, along with the great quirky rich, H.
L. Hunt, the billionaire oilman once the richest man in America, who got
his exercise by creeping, the wildcatter Glenn McCarthy, Amon Carter,
who pitted Fort Worth versus Dallas. Even *Giant*, starring James Dean,
Liz Taylor and Rocklike Hudson, was a film artifact, an image out of a
bygone era. The W. P. Webb professor declaimed that "the apogee of
Texas vulgar," the nadir of Texas color and comedy, the defining

moment in Texas, was Glenn McCarthy's opening of the Shamrock Hotel in Houston in 1949, and there would never be another such moment. Our own John Woodcipher led the vigorous applause.

The woman, that very woman of the library and of the shimmering by the pool at Tex Flatt's, stood the whole time in a back corner of the auditorium, as I stood across the room from her, and instead of wearing the blue silk was clad in a kind of camouflage gold and brown outfit, with pied pants and a jacket and gave off a mustardy, combat-ready effect, her large cat's eyes today behind little round blue glasses like those that Emmitt Smith and Deion Sanders wear when they are all dressed up and give post-game interviews on TV, and her yellow fedora with its bright feather in the band was much like the Boys' too. How about Ross Perot, she asked, they didn't consider him a colorful political character?

"Of course," said the Dobie professor. "I thought we mentioned him."

"And Ann Richards, pretty as a new-scraped carrot," said the K. A. Porter prof.

"Perot said the deficit was like the crazy old aunt we keep in the basement or under the hood of the car, or wherever," one offered, but added that in his humble opinion Perot was a bygone character too by now.

The woman, who did not shimmer now but undulated rather like a giant anaconda, said, "It was not that he was *funny*. He spoke to people. Dear God, you people, he started a whole movement. Have you heard of the Reform party? It is still strong, going strong, on its own. Think again, if you think you can keep Ross Perot under the hood. You academics! And how about McLaren—don't you consider Richard McLaren and the Republic of Texas fairly interesting?"

The Dobie professor, who had said no one really knew who Dobie was anymore, the old symbol of Texas-as-the-West, nevertheless toed his boot and smiled and rubbed his head as Dobie would have done as the Lilly professor responded to her question. "Well, ma'am, he was interesting all right. And certainly kind of a nut. But not larger-than-life, do you think?"

"Don't you 'ma'am' me, you supercilious little fellow!" she snapped back. "I don't know about your life. I don't imagine you'd last long in the brush. He stood for his principles, and went to prison for them!"

Genial John Woodcipher thanked her for her questions and her comments and turned to another person in the audience, an elderly woman who asked why Governor Bill Clements wouldn't qualify, with his bad plaid and malapropisms and individualism, why, he was "Texian to the toenails." They all laughed, said of course he would.

In the later afternoon I went to a meeting of the brains, the planners, of our place including Bunky Boy. It was a muddy meeting, which revolved around the same old/new topics. Bunky had found a swell new pigeon, who was making millions in the computer software biz, he was bound to be another Michael Dell like right down there at Round Rock, this fellow, Billy Kilday, was right nearby in Duncanville. He was willing to give every faculty member and every student in Highland U. a new p.c. All we had to do was put in his total software system for running everything on campus, called InstitutoSoft. Everyone around the table seemed to salivate for the coming of this savior. I pointed out that most of our professors still wrote, when they did, with pens on yellow pads; they'd never adapt to advising students by computer; we were dedicated to the new liberal arts, and to being right there with the students; that accepting this Trojan horse would let technology drive academic policy, we would be throwing ourselves on the sword of technology! Etc. My concerns were duly noted. Billy the computer wizard, he was only twenty-four years old, would be visiting us next week to apprise us of the glories of InstitutoSoft.

My heart softened a bit as it made me think of my dear departed Myrtle Springs. Myrtle Springs was always going to learn something. At one point she was going to be a computer genius and went to the community college to take a course in Word. Sometimes I regretted not getting a computer for her, she was so earnest about wanting to learn it. She and I were always going to take a course in Spanish together—each of us had taken Spanish in high school—just because we lived in a place surrounded by Spanish-speaking people and we had so little human contact with them.

I kept this pleasant aura of Myrtle Springs in my mind as counterbalance to my professional troubles as I went to my conversational Spanish class that evening on our campus. It evaporated, dear Myrtle dropped from my thoughts, as I walked in and to my amazement saw the woman, that woman, now re-outfitted in simple skirt and blouse, sitting against the wall looking plain and homely, a bit old-maidish, cat's eyes dimmed to demure, seeming to study intently the course workbook. I also sat back along the wall, several chairs from her.

The teacher, la profesora, a nice woman I knew named Emmy Wallace, came in and plopped in her chair. She looked like she'd taught all day already and with our course loads probably had. "Escuche," she said, looking at the handful of us sitting haphazardly around the musty classroom. It was a fairly international little bunch, at least our adult classes were somewhat diverse. "Who's here?" Looking at her roll. "Omar?"

"Presente."

"Bueno. Betty? Helga? Michelle? Lance? Ikbal? Craig? No? Henry?"

"Sí," I said. "Presente."

"Bueno," Emmy said, and said, "El jefe," under her breath, not very flatteringly.

I gave a quick surreptitious look at the woman. She was serenely, if not studiously, gazing at the misty, chalky erased blackboard.

"Craig es en Russia trabajando en un deal," the fat boy, Mike, whose name had not been called, said.

"Oh. Mike. Sí. Gracias. Pero, Mike—Craig está en Russia, no?"

"Yeah. Ain't that what I said?"

"Pero," she said, "*es* es permanente, y *está* es una condición, no?"

"I believe old Craig is in Russia, ma'am, anyways. Está. There."

"Exactamente. Y—" Looking around for anyone not on the list.

"Lily," said the woman, two chairs to my right, crossing her long limbs out from the chair and settling back like a lazy leopard with a little bemused smile, just a flick, toward me.

"Y Lily! Bueno. Estupendo. Ahora, miren: la pagina number fifty-eight. Y respondemas a las preguntas. Okay? Bueno. Mike—Cómo estas hoy?" Smiling hopefully at the fat boy.

"Qué?"

" Cómo estas hoy?"

"Hoy—soy—bueno. Señora."

"*Estoy*. Hoy *estoy* bien."

"Whatever," muttered Mike.

"Y Helga. Cómo estas hoy?"

"Ich bin gut," said Helga.

"En español, Helga, por favor."

"Okay. Bien."

"Sí. Y Lance—" Lance was her favorite, a young salesman. The week before he'd told us he'd been given Mexico as a territory for

16 TEX REX

whatever he sold and was going down there to try out the Spanish he had learned.

"¿Cómo estas, Lance? ¿Está contento? ¿Y qué paso en Mexico?"

"No soy contento, Profesora. Soy—ah—pissado. La clase sucke. El sucko."

His buddy Mike laughed. The teacher looked stricken. The woman named Lily, sitting just behind Lance, leaned forward to him and I heard her whisper in his ear. "Que expresiónes malas, pendejo. No nos gustan su idioma, you little prick. Apologize to la profesor, you little shit, unless you want me to cortar your—" She took a long blue fingernail and made a little cross mark on the back of his white neck.

Lance turned red in the face, then white. He did not look around to face what terror lay behind him. Instead he said, "Me siento, Profesora. See, I mean, I go, voy, down there, like I'm in Juarez—And oh hell—I'm like trying all these phrases and frases and stuff—and nobody sabe nada I'm saying, man—And these assholes come by and beat the crap out of me and take my sample case out of my car and my camera, and then the Goddamn police—"

"En español, Lance," the teacher said.

"—they viene and arrest *me—*"

"Bummer," said Mike.

"Lastima," the teacher said, and plunged us back into the workbook, to the picture on page 148 of El Monstruo Fantastico. The woman sat back in her chair, looking straight ahead and then in a moment at the Fantastic Monster on the page as if she had never uttered a word to the terrified boy in front of her.

"Y qué piensas de Monstruo? Ikbal?"

"Es feo."

"Y habla español El Monstruo?"

"Habla todas lenguas, no?" said Lily.

"Oh? Quizá. Y qué es El Monstruo?"

The answer was a bad scientific experiment or something of the sort. In the silence poor Emmy was about to answer her own question when the woman Lily sat up straight and said, "El mundo."

"Qué? El mundo?"

"Sí. Todo el mundo. Es monstruo."

Professor Wallace, sighing, giving me a look as if to say I was her boss and might have helped her out, decided it was time for the class to take a break.

Out in the hall I found her by my side and then found I was walking down the hallway and out of the building with her. "I have been watching you," she said.

"And I've seen you."

"Yep. Sure. I'm Lily."

"Henry. You were pretty strong in there. And at the symposium."

"Pooh. I'm a shrinking violet. Henry Rose. That's a lovely name. Have you been in Texas long? I mean, the Roses?"

"Oh my, yes. Sometime I will tell you that story, if we have a chance, and you're interested."

We went across the street, leaving the class to founder on, to a Starbucks and sat at a table by the window and watched our students walk by and drank strong, sweet coffee, some peculiar roast she ordered. She said the old fellow I spoke with in the library room at Tex Flatt's was her father. I said I figured so. She said he was the dearest, sweetest, most considerate man. He had meant a trust fund and a ranch and a retreat in Santa Fe to her, she said, but it was a poor attempt at casual cynicism. I could tell she loved him. She was not that homely, just plain, and had those cat-like eyes, a nice long body. I had sometimes thought— especially with a wealthy woman—as I mentioned.

She laughed out of the blue and said, "I gave back San Antonio. He probably told you that, he tells everyone."

"Oh? Yes?"

"He gave Heather Galveston, you see, and he gave me San Antonio. But just if I would marry. So I didn't, he has it back, and that's good because he adores San 'Tonio. It's his favorite city of all Texas."

"Yes. Well, that's nice, I'm sure, just to consider giving it to you. I'm very fond of it myself. San Antonio. The Spanish quality."

"You have to understand," she said, carrying on the game, "it's his to give." She smiled at me. "Daddy is the King of Texas."

"I know," I said. "He told me." I chuckled back at her. "The King of Texas. You bet your life he is."

"I have," she said. "I like it when you perk up and glow like that. You have a lot of hidden passion, don't you?"

She surveyed me, eyes aglitter, and murmured something about the depth of vitality and unbounded ambition she sensed lurking just below the surface of my apparent meekness. Surprised, I smiled and nodded back at her. Who was I to say she wasn't on to something?

Then she said, "You will have to come around to one of Daddy's afternoons. Levies, he calls them. Oh, there are always interesting people there. Daddy always has a subject, and everyone discusses it."

"Will you be there, or are these male affairs?"

"I am always there," she said.

I said that I would call the Friday next. She gave me a card that styled her as Lily McIvey, Consultant, with a Highland Park Village office address. On the back she wrote another address, a street in an old wooded section of Dallas where the unostentatious wealthy lived. I thought she was charming as she wrote out the address, with great concentration, her tongue clasped tightly in her teeth, in green ink with a gold Waterman fountain pen. Stabbing the card to pick it up to hand to me she made a little slice in it with the long sharp blue fingernail.

THREE

The prospect of going to the soiree of the crazy old man and his intriguing daughter led me to reflect briefly on Texas, the state and state of mind I had left ten years ago and come back to.

Mythology is hard to get untangled from once you get tangled in it, and Texas was the biggest web of it I knew, and always would be. My God, we had for years taught courses pointing out the myths and legends of the frontier that stayed alive even as most Texans came to live in the cities, how the frontier was so recent here we kept our guns and rode with rifles in the gun racks of the pickups and wore big hats and boots and drove, by God, *vehicles*. Sigmund Freud himself, puffing on his stogie, didn't stand a chance even pointing out such a minor instance of it as Big Tex at the State Fair of Texas, booming out his *Ho ho ho*, a big old boy sans penis in his huge hat and Western shirt and jeans. Oh, how we worked at differentiating the Old Texas and the New Texas; and how the myth transcended Texas so that all the symbols—remember, we'd come West to Texas for independence, land, wealth and freedom—the hats, boots, the bulls, the horses, the paisanos, the cactus that did not really exist in Texas, the steers imported along the Trinity riverbank for Reagan's convention, the guns again, always the guns, the Marlboro men—cowboys and vaqueros—the oil derricks, the superpenismissiles of the Space Age—were joined, yea now still are, grafted onto the nation and the world, so that the American Olympians would march in wearing ten-gallon hats and the Serb paramilitary killers in Kosovo wear Western hats and the visiting black woman ANC leader of the new South Africa coming to Dallas is hooked on the Texas myth and wants to see tumbleweeds and cowboys and hats and horses and we had only some mustang statues running in a prairie suburb alongside mock-Venetian canals and big Tex squawking his *Ho ho ho* to show her.

And Dallas, yes, dear Lord, Dallas, where I'd twice now come to live in Texas, always had its very own subset of the myth, lived by it, kept it as its image even in the worst of times. Though seen as soulless and sinister and materialistic—*ha!*—at root by other Texas towns and folks, Big D was by God man-made (of course this myth left out women and people of color but so did the larger myth, of Texas, of the West, of the Western world). It was built where there was no navigable river, why, hardly scenery or geography, by these strong men, pirates and pioneers, who stole the railhead from nearby Denton and the State Fair from Fort Worth and appropriated the great ball-less Big Tex from West Texas, and so on. And for its critics that was not the worst of it, no sir: Dallas was indeed, despite the art museums that came later to the sprawl of Houston and to Cowtown and the beauty of San Antonio's Hispanic heritage and the proud laidback nature of Austin, Dallas actually was the cultural and creative and sports as well as the business capital of Texas.

The Jewish merchant princes came early to Dallas and gave it dimensions of grace and reason never yet measured. Dallas bankers loaned money on oil underground and tied up the oil just as cotton waned. Dallas geniuses like the image guy Sam Bloom early made the city integrate and saw the business potential of the whole suburban "metroplex" and like the scientific entrepreneurs Cecil Green and Erik Jonsson saw the future for technology. Old former mayor "Uncle Bob" Thornton, who'd styled himself as being born in a mud hut on the banks of the Trinity so as to kind of parallel Dallas founder John Neely Bryan's log cabin (still kept by Dallas preserved downtown by the Old Red Courthouse and the Assassination Site), gave the horror, grief and guilt of the assassination about a month before he rose up cackling that Dallas must "roll up our sleeves" and build a Goddamn space needle taller than the one they were building in Seattle!

Meanwhile, Texas writers, poets, artists, filmmakers and creative people such as they were fought valiantly against the mythology, the Texas stereotypes, and were for the most part rewarded for their success in coming up with them again. Like, Rip Torn reverts to type, the TV series *Dallas* is dead but stays alive in our consciousness and in that of Europe, Russia, Japan and the international financial markets—mobility, greed, individuality, and then a little family loyalty if it suits you—and *Lone Star* is a great movie, right? And Dallas—and East Texas—where everything was but the image—knew their roots were Southern, cotton, corn and mule—but Dallas bought the myth, man, and rose up with the Flying Red Horse, the dragon disguised as a horse, flying high then later dwarfed and lost among all the gold and blue and green and silver skyscrapers of a skyline that was a symbol itself and was also real and was amazing—

Ah! Well—If I tend to get a bit carried away, if my pen gushes from time to time, you must consider that I write this, mostly, in haste, often on the run . . . .

Yes. Indeed. Forsooth.

Henry Rose's Midwestern background always made him skeptical of the going bullshit in Texas and in Dallas, but through the years I rode that horse, that dragon, myself, as often as it suited me. It was good stuff though, as I say, when you are from Missouri you tend to be skeptical of all stereotypes and to say, I'm from Missouri. Right? Show me. (No stereotype there, eh?)

Ten years ago, or more, when I was in Texas, first with another university and then as a quasi-administrator for the Super Conducting Supercollider, that monstrous hole in the ground outside Dallas whose bust caused me to go away, there was a mock heroic battle among literary folk over whether Texas had or did not have a national literature. Silly? Not at all, not on your tintype. Hadn't Texas after all by God been a separate nation? The Republic of Texas (the real one). Stephen F. Austin. Bowie, Crockett, Travis and the Alamo—Texas' own Greek myth, the big moral victory that proved ever after that Texas was worthy to be a nation—(though I must say, Roses usually steer clear of the subject of the Alamo).

At any rate, returning a year ago from my sojourns in California and Alaska, I found that most of this Texas stuff had subsided, that now it only lapped faintly against a more sophisticated shore. If I had been asked when I returned what was the distinctive something of living, of being in Texas instead of some place else, I would have said, not much.

Even the images, the symbols, had toned down, the Cowboys (reduced in vulgar parlance to "Dem Boys") venal and faded, newer Southern and Western places glowing and glittering at least as much as Dallas, as Houston. Of course, the world had changed. We were all just villages wired together, interdependent, in the global. And so, I wondered, how could an old fellow of even moderate intelligence, unless a real old sweetheart of a loon, find it in this day and world steady fun and entertainment to imagine himself the King of Texas? Then I came upon a report of a fellow in Russia contending that when the Romanov crown was restored, it would be his.

That Friday of my appointment with the King of Texas we had the visit to our campus of the Boy's Boy, young Billy Kilday, singing us the siren song of his software InstitutoSoft, and as I went down the hallway I heard phrases such as "cleanse the data," "migrate to," "randomness of text" and "my vision of Webability" waft from the offices, as folks began to tune in, awfully late in our anachronism of a campus, to the computer and to the unvirtuous virtual.

In the English department office I encountered Regina Singh, who would have been a feminist except that in her pride and as a Sikh and daughter of a distinguished Indian scholar she would not accept the term. She loved Texas because she thought it was like her own native Punjab. Etc.

"I was watching him on stage, this Billy," Regina said. "He is so young. He went straight into a computer science course and then quit school and did his thing, started up his company. It is amazing. Our students, with what they study here, could do no such thing. Someone said he was going to be worth one, two, three, four billion dollars. That is amazing."

I hummed a bit of *Amazing Grace*, sorting through the flyers in my mailbox.

"No. Henry, I am serious. We are fortunate that President Bunker has attracted this boy to us."

"He'll put his stamp on us, Regina. It never does not profit them, the donors, too. Old Tex Flatt and his useless tower will be an embarrassment to us sticking up in the middle of nowhere, an honor to him."

"Yes, but think of having the hook in this one's mouth, if someday he has three billion dollars. Henry! I mean, what is the worth of Africa? In my India they only pass it along. Here, Americans, even new-wealth Texans with no education, give. It is amazing."

"Yes," I said, and with amazingly ill grace left campus early, skipping the afternoon VIP reception that Bunky Boy was having for his Billy, and drove my heap back into Dallas and then out towards her wooded street called Strait Gate Way.

FOUR

It was an attractive graystone house set on a treed lot, with a long gravel driveway to the front entrance. The lot seemed to slope down behind, as if there might be a stream below. It was about what I expected, respectable, unpretentious but well-endowed. I saw an old-fashioned tiled swimming pool, a small gray bathhouse, and a gazebo around one side.

Lily McIvey, woman of many costumes, greeted me at the deep-hued wooden front door. I expected a massive lion-headed door knocker, but the knocker was something slender of the nature of a griffin. It smiled, or grinned, at you. So did Lily, in a belted tartan kilt attire, harking to the McIvey Highland or Lowland or whatever strain it might be. I'd worn a blazer, gray trousers, English loafers and a soft graygreen tie bought cheap in Scotland just to be in tune.

"Why, Henry," she said, or purred, all big cat in a short kilt now, "you did come. How nice of you. And out of those terrible chalkstripes, too. How lovely. Yes. Do come in. Welcome to my dump."

It was patently hers, all right. With the great ability to size up situations and make the best of them given to us Roses, I immediately discerned she might have tricked me. The modest house was too small to hold her father and his fantasy, I did not sense that he was lurking, hiding, resting up for it in some side room, cackling, sweating, drinking whiskey, chuckling as I had first beheld him at Tex Flatt's, ready to be carried by his bearer Billy Roy into that tasteful, low-key stone-floored living room hung with rugs and southwestern paintings. She had wanted me alone. *Ho ho*, as Big Texas croaks on the old midway. I came on in. The Rose sense failed me. I should have turned and walked away, like my Texas forebear.

"Charming room," I said. "Nice art." She had a Barbara Latham, Pueblo kids on ponies, and a Dick Mason, with the Dalmations looking through the adobe windows to the chamisa'd mountains, some Ortega weavings on the walls, and a niche for a large Mondragon-carved Saint Pascal blessing us and all with his cornucopic ear of corn.

"Thank you. I thought you'd like it. I believe you said you were a Taos aficionado."

I did not recall saying any such thing. Had she created the room just for my visit? It was exactly, so easily, the room I would have wanted.

"I'll get you a drink. Vino tinto I'll bet. Eh? Yep? A bumper of the red?"

I had been terribly careful about the drinking, playing provost this past year. I'd sipped enough Perrier to fizz my gut forever. Sure, I nodded.

She popped a cork as I looked around. Everything seemed to have been on the walls for a while, there was a bit of dust.

"You'll forgive me," she smiled, handing me the wine. It was a bumper, all right. "I usually do wine, but I need a silver bullet or two before Daddy's levies." She had a crystal clear glass of straight vodka, with a lemon peel. "Oh, don't worry, we'll go find Daddy in a minute. You don't mind spending a little prelude with me, do you, Henry? Oh, you are a nice man, I'm right about that, aren't I? I thought we'd have a little talk before we get caught up in all that other."

Leggy, she bounced and clattered around the flagstone floor kind of like a pony. She wore the kilt like a bathing suit, if not decorously then naturally. I deposited some Merlot to suffuse my system. I kind of liked her, old Lily. Her long legs were not too white and not too tan and smooth as butter. She was no spring chicken but not an old hen either. She waved me into a leather and wood chair and sat in an old carved Mexican chair she pulled a little toward me. She sat with her big blue Persian cat-eyes luminous, a tentative smile on her half-ugly Scotch mug, showing me in a straight shot through the parted skirt what McIvey women wore under their kilts. Purple silk stretched over a capacious crotch. It was excellent Merlot.

"So, Lily," I said, as if it were a seminar, "what do you do?"

"Oh," she said, "I go to fundraisers, and classes, and paint a little and write a little poetry—it's hard to find a good poetry-writing teacher, because I like to rhyme. You know?"

"'Yes, I write verses now and then.'"

"I knew it! I knew you'd understand! And go to church, Episcopal, of course, royalty has to be Anglican, right? On special days. *Love* the

Book of Common Prayer. I'm just a typical Dallas woman of independent means, Henry."

I nodded encouragingly, hoping that might be so. She gave me a purple wink and leaped to her feet, making a sour face that made her look very Mary Queen of Scots. The kilt was all green and blues and purples, really pretty deep and somber, a variation on Black Watch. I wondered if it was McIvey or something appropriated, I'd never really heard of a McIvey tartan. She made herself another bullet, chewing up the lemon from the first. Then she went to stand against the mantel, where there was a carving of Saint Francis, hands clasped, bird on shoulder. They looked down on me.

"I didn't need you to nod like that, *Pro*-fessor Rose, like some old fuddy-duddy affirming, yes, dear Lily is a Goddamn typical Dallas woman!'

I stared at her.

"How's your wine?" she barked, as if I had made it and was responsible for it.

"Excellent. I didn't mean—I didn't say—"

"Oh, yes you did! You *thought*. You thought I'd asked you over— that I was a nice broad you might have a dalliance with."

"What? Dear God, girl—Lily. I don't do dalliances."

"Ah! That's better—*girl! Girl* is good, dear dear Henry Rose. I know you work so hard at that pathetic little place, and now I'm bugging you. Well, to answer your well-meant question, I also do some volunteer work, I mean sometimes on a large scale. We have, you see, a little foundation, and I help Daddy run it." She smiled at me now, mood changed, a little girl, bright-eyed. I thought to myself, oh oh, mood swings.

"Excellent," I said, again. It was what all the students were saying. "Excellent" and "totally" and "actually."

"Do you like horses?" she said, nearly antic now. "Maybe you'd like to come see the ranch. Oh. It's about time to go see Daddy. You up for this?" She gulped her drink, as I did mine. "I do want you to like Daddy. I want you two to get along. Do you know how many of the men I've liked he's—executed? Ha! That's a joke! Yep! I don't care if you become the best of friends, but I do hope, Henry, that you two can get along. I know you'll try to be nice, won't you? We do have to try to humor Daddy along, you know. Especially now."

I was glad to hear her say that, about humoring him.

She had her glass in her hand, and waved it at me. "Do you know what you call this, what I've been drinking? Straight Stoli with a twist? No? Of course not. Daddy named it. I want you to understand he is the sweetest man. We were in this hotel, the fanciest one in London, you know the one, and the pompous waiter was being mean to a couple of American women school teachers at the next table, and lording it over them and almost making them cry, and so Daddy summoned him over and ordered a 'Squeaker.' 'Yes, sir,' the prick said, and went, and came back after awhile horribly embarrassed and confessed they didn't know exactly what a 'Squeaker' was. So Daddy told him, and it chilled that waiter's ass that he didn't know and was being condescended to, and I bet he was nicer after that, to Americans, and to school teachers. Daddy did it because Mama was a school teacher in a little West Texas town when he found and married her. She was a McAlmon. Anyway. So they wrote it down in the bartender's book in that grand hotel, and when we go there, Henry, you and I, you can order a 'Squeaker' and by God, they'll bring it to you. Well, it's Levy time. Let's go see how he's doing. I do hope he took his nap-y-poo.''

She took my arm, and led me through a sparkling kitchen and to a back door. She and I were exactly the same height, which I later learned was her first requirement in a man, none shorter, none taller than herself.

What we walked to now became magical in my eyes.

The long green slope, canopied by groups of thick old oak trees, did go down towards a river or a stream. "It's a creek, Henry," she said, "or do you say 'crick'? It's one of the seven original creeks that flow through Dallas, we had to uncover it from the concrete they put over it."

And up another slope and down and then toward the gabled redbrick front of a large house that now appeared on the next slope, or actual hill, this completely fronted by lush greensward—St. Augustine grass—in the Dallas heat, and even seeming cool as we moved along. It was shaded by now more massive and twisted old oaks. Billy Roy stood by a little table, huge in the shoulders and chest, bandy-legged, in his jeans and belt and boots, with a big flowered teapot in his hand. Incongruously he had been serving tea! A few other men stood here and there around the grassy knoll, a couple with cups, a couple of them smoking. The froglike old man sat in a large wicker chair on the grass with a large cup with a silver star on it in his fat brown hand with the crested ring on its finger, and I saw now that the crest was a Texas star set in diamonds in the dark ruby red on the heavy gold. He looked up and smiled at his daughter. Not at me. Did he see me, the blazered appendage on her arm? The slate eyes lit up in a real way, fatherly, milky eyes under the hooded lids once open and blue, I thought, like hers. I looked back to the woods and "crick," the grassy slope and lawn, ahead to the redbrick house. A proper house it would have been in Scotland for a Scottish lord. For a moment old McIvey almost looked like Old Jolyon in "Indian Summer of a Forstye," peaceful, ready to doze and go to eternal sleep; it reminded me of a scene I could not quite place in Trollope or in Henry James. It was a knockout piece of business for a middling Eng lit prof of the non-deconstructive bent.

"High Tea," I said. "How lovely."

"You met Henry Rose, Daddy. Remember, at that reception I made you go to, for the new university, at your old friend Tex Flatt's. He is the Provost, and he teaches English."

"Ha!" the old man said. McIvey appeared, in this light, to be somewhere between a ruined seventy-five and a fairly well-preserved one hundred years in age. He looked at me. " 'The Assyrian came down—' " he began.

"—'like a wolf on the fold . . . a' " I replied.

"Yes." I had passed a little test. He raised the hand, again not for me to shake but as I might wish to kiss the ring. "I, sir, am Oliver McIvey. I—"

"Hello, McIvey, I'm Dubious," I said.

"Don't interrupt Daddy!" she hissed in my ear.

But he was in a good mood, glad for the tea and to see his daughter, forgiving me for not allowing him to proclaim Himself, and he laughed. Ha! Ha ha! Remembering our first encounter when he had done the "I'm Cronkite/I'm Dubious" vaudeville bit. He did not ask if I remained ambivalent—I would have replied I did—but like a miracle stood suddenly up. I could see what a tough old wreck he was. He waved to Billy Roy, who came and bent over and received him on his back. "You missed tea," he said to his daughter.

"Yes. Sorry, sweetheart," she said, arm still in mine. "We had a nip"

"Good for you," he said, and rode Kimosabe toward the redbrick pile, we and the others following.

The house was austere, and cold with air conditioning. We went through iron grillwork doors with a Texas crest on them, down a hall and into a large den room that was a museum of Old Texas and a repository of Texas books. It had silver-embossed saddles and old Champion's longhorns set on a twelve-foot table and artifacts of cowboying and oil wildcatting; old hats and spurs and pieces of rigs and signs from

Spindletop and Burkburnett and so on. The room was walled in dark
cracked wood like out of an old barn, and it gave the feeling that you
were back there in time. It had some Ansel Adams on the walls, and
some Winchesters, Sharps, Hawkens, and a number of classic Colt
revolvers on display. But tasteful, not bad, pretty cool if you like horses
and guns and pictures of old windmills.

I sat in a comfortable chair and reflected that nobody, not neighbors
nor anybody, might know that this house, back down in its hollow and up
its hill and in its thick woods by its secret stream, was even here.

Lily did not sit by me but sat in a smaller wing chair by the large
wing chair at the head of the room into which his bull-humped minion
deposited Texas Rex. Besides the King, his daughter, his retinue and
myself, present at the levy were four other men. I had expected that Mr.
Fuad and Mr. Singh might be among us as plenipotentiaries, part of the
permanent retinue, but they were not. Instead there was—we had to go
around the circle and give our names, announce ourselves—at least the
grinning Billy Roy did not announce us, as I thought he might, as to rank
and title—a Dr. Brock, a Mr. Jackman, a Rev. A. M. Lowe, and a Mr.
Mackey, who kept working on his fingernails with a Case knife, as if he
might have gun oil under them.

"Now, Lily dear, what was it we were going to discuss this
afternoon? Oh yes, I must name the new Prince of Dallas. Or did we talk
about that last week? Little bit. Eh? A little lapse there. Lapsus
memoriam, eh, Pro-fessor?"

"Lapsus memoriae, if you will, sir."

"If I will? I will—whatever needs willing. Okay, Rose. Accept.
Except—Lapsus linguae, slip o' the tongue, eh? Thank you, Pro-fessor,
so-very-much for the correction. Okay. Lily, would you get me just a jot
of whiskey, leave out the tittle?"

She glided to the desk and poured a powerful portion straight from a
square gold-flecked bottle labeled Handmade Texas Something, put it in
his grasping hand, and he proceeded.

Princes were in short supply, in Texas, he elucidated. He had named
Henry Gonzalez, down there, Prince of San Antonio. Henry G. was a
liberal and an antsy fellow but he was a fighter, a good man, and was
retiring now from the damn Congress. Once Henry G. had walked right
in to a restaurant and seen somebody who had badmouthed him and
punched him out. McIvey was not advocating violence, there was too
much of it in Texas and the world, but that was a good quality, especially
for a Goddamn politician, to stand up for yourself and for your family.

Old Tom Lea, the writer and painter, had been McIvey's Prince of El Paso for a long time now. He never had acknowledged the notice from the King of his appointment, but McIvey hoped he appreciated it in his heart. El Paso de Norte, the Pass of the North. Tom's daddy had been mayor there. Tom wrote about the Big Ranch, that was the family name for it, the King Ranch—it was Captain King originally. That did not mean, he leaned to explain to Dr. Brock, that he, the King of Texas, owned the King Ranch. No, the ranch of the King of Texas, the Rex Ranch, was in southwest Texas, by the border in the brush country, and they were planning to teach those drug bastards that were fucking with them a lesson! Lily was fixing to take Pro-fessor down to Rex Ranch soon, maybe Dr. Brock would like to go along.

Princess Lily smiled at me wickedly. I cleared my throat, ahem, and offered an anecdote as a way of joining in.

"Last year I was teaching a course on Texas history and literature at Highland U. and I was talking about the diamond from Brownsville to Indianola to San Antonio to Laredo that was the original home range of the cattle business before the Civil War, and about the cattle industry after that, and about the great ranches and I stopped because I realized that I had a Slaughter and a West and a Kleberg in the class—all still working ranches. And I asked those boys if they would like to teach the class!"

"Inneresting," Mr. Jackman said.

"Them boys was actually in that class," observed the Rev. Lowe.

"I mean, it still goes on," I said.

Old McIvey stared at me with hooded eyes as if I was a moron who had come upon the Grand Canyon and stumbled into it.

"Why, yes," he said. "That is the point, Mr. Rose—Doctor—I suppose it must be Doctor? It still goes on."

I never did learn who the former Prince of Dallas had been. Lily told me later only that he had expired. McIvey had recently named "that one Bass" as the Prince of Fort Worth for he had given to the arts, Bass Hall and all, over there, for his civic spirit, but he had just learned something disturbing and he hoped those Basses didn't have anything to do with it.

"My God," the old man exclaimed, nearly choking on his whiskey, "over in Fort Worth, right on the square there, they put up this topiary bull. Then when people saw what a real sure-enough bull it was—why, they sheared off the bull's dick, cut off the bull's balls. Made the bull into a topiary steer! Hell, if they wanted a steer, they should have made a steer in the first place! That's about the same thing has been happening to Texas—!"

"Take it easy, Daddy."

"Well, it upsets me, Lily."

Currently there was no Prince of Houston, and probably wouldn't be, McIvey did not see any likely candidates in Houston. Who? Bill Hobby? Who suggested Hobby? My God—Jackman? Old Bill Hobby was a liberal and an Academic. No offense, Professor.

"Let's open the floor and see who these people think might be candidates for your consideration for the Prince of Dallas," Lily said to Daddy.

"Dallas is all about sports," Mr. Mackey said, clasping his knife. "You know? I'm surprised you never gave the honor to Tom Landry."

"He was a fine Christian man," said the King.

"Now you got—Who? Goddamn, not Jerry! It's a shame about the Cowboys. Maybe Troy? You think? Tom Hicks? He bought the Stars and the Rangers. He's into everything."

"The Prince should have more qualities than ownership. Some nobleness in him somewhere," said the King. Now he was upright in his chair, relishing this test of his wisdom if not his power.

"Ross Perot?" said Lily. "You can't say he doesn't stand up for what he thinks, against the politicians."

"Puts his money where his mouth is," said Mackey.

"Lot of both," said Billy Roy.

"I'll tell you, if you don't feel like recognizing Ross," said Mr. Jackman, "who the new young prince coming along around here is, his son Ross. His airport. The arena. You know? Him and Ray Hunt, H.L.'s boy, they are going to own Dallas, anyway. They are nice boys, too. They are real princes in this city, whatever."

"Do you recognize Dallas for what it is, for what it always was, a oligarthy," said the Rev. Lowe. "Then they be."

"That oligarchy has done good. What's messed it up is all the dissension—the damn democracy nuts!' said the King. 'I don't think the races will ever get it together!"

"It's too bad Dallas didn't get it together racially twenty years ago," said Henry Rose, "and get by all the bickering on the school board and the city council."

"Right," said Lily McIvey. "That's true, Daddy."

"I like the Medici, Lily. The Medici for me—tra la, tra li! Old Mayor Bob. Used to, he'd get the richest guys together, and he'd say, we going to do this for Dallas, yes or no? Called it 'Yes or No!' Should be like Florence, like Venice. I'd get me an Othello. We got an Othello here, Reverend Lowe? Any blacks come to mind for Prince of Dallas?"

"We got a black mayor, you know."

"Yep," said Lily. "Mayor Kirk. Good Scottish name. Should be a leading candidate!"

"You like anybody, there, eh, Doctor Brock?"

"Well, there are several Nobel laureates in medicine at the Southwestern Medical School. And then, the university presidents."

Oh, splendid! Bert Bunker, of Highland U., the Prince of Dallas!

"Writers? Artists? The symphony conductor?" Brock went on.

"Dallas puts up with a few creative people but does not cherish them, and so they go away," said Lily.

"Why do you say that, my precious? Because you keep showing those paintings of yours, wonderful and sexy as they are, in that gallery and nobody ever buys one?"

"Because this town is so absolutely materialistic, Daddy."

"Yes. Good. Good-and-goody-good, darling! I am so glad to hear it!"

"Stanley Marcus?" Mr. Jackman said. "The Neiman-Marcus guy. He is in his nineties, writes a column of wise words for the paper, still working, a courtly, gracious man. Writes books. Stands for everything that is cultivated in our city. I think there can be no doubt 'Mr. Stanley' should be your Prince of Dallas!"

"Well, he smiles and speaks to me," said the King. "Though I am never sure he really knows me or listens to what I am saying. Even I like Stanley Marcus."

We all agreed that "Mr. Stanley," emblem of culture and commerce, should be a leading candidate for the Prince of Dallas.

"Yes. Fuad. What?"

Mr. Fuad had suddenly appeared, with a phone, and plugged it in on a small table by the old man's chair. "It is George," he said. "You wish to take it, yes?"

"George? Yes. Hello, George, Goddamn it, where are you? Paris? Okay. Listen, are you keeping track of that arrogant bastard in Greenwich? You talked to him? We all cannot afford, we can ill afford—Oh—Thank you, everybody. That's it for today. Lily. Do the honors. George?"

"Goodbye, Dr. Brock, thank you so much for coming. Goodbye, Mr. Jackman, thank you so much for being here. Goodbye, dear Reverend

Lowe, thank you for sharing your insights with us. Billy Roy, if you will show these gentlemen back across the Avon I will walk back with Mr. Rose. Henry? Mr. Mackey, you will stay here with Daddy . . .''

I admired the room, the little museum of Old Texas, one more time, as the tightknit Mr. Mackey went to the wall and took a gold-plated Winchester '76 off its pegs and made like Jimmy Stewart and aimed it on a bead at me, as the old King, croaking on the phone like the frog or toad in the "Bud-weiser" commercial, talked to George.

"Who are they?" I said, as Lily took my arm and exited and went over the now dusk-green lawn down towards the stream in the wake of Jackman, Brock and Lowe.

"Just three guys in the city, Jewish, Black Protestant, and Catholic. They are like representative, you know? Daddy likes to try to know the views of his constituents, especially on important matters."

"Three indulgent guys?" Wanted to say, don't be silly, Lily. But it was her game, her Daddy. She certainly was loyal at it.

"You think so?" she said.

"They get a little from the old foundation, for the temple, for the church, the med school?"

She squeezed my arm. It was a lovely late summer afternoon, pretty cool here, upper nineties in the rest of Dallas. Her hand was up under my bicep as we were of a height, and I tried to make a little muscle.

In her graystone house she said, "Well, farewell, Henry. Thank you for being with us. There is always the Outer Circle and the Inner Circle, the sideshow and the main meeting, and I must go back for it. So—"

"And Mr. Mackey? Seems like I've heard of him."

"He is on the Board of the foundation, Henry. He helps take care of Daddy. You have not heard of him."

"Goodbye, Lily. You know, I think you're great. Really. You are a loyal girl. Oh my, don't blush. You are. I'm sure you must get tired of this game."

"Oh? Are you religious, Henry? I don't know if I am. I like the idea of faith in something. I read the Bible, the Old Testament. Amos. Isaiah. Boy, they had it hard. The people must have thought they were nuts— loony old prophets. I know people, you have probably talked to them, who think this is crazy, that Daddy is a joke. Maybe it is. So what, Henry? You are a man of reason, right, a basic Skeptic? I gotta tell you, the line between faith and bleak reality is not reason, Pro-fessor. It's a province, a playground. Once you find it, you are safe there. You can play God."

"Emphasis on 'play,' I take it?"

"Oh yes. Yep. Sure."

"I'll let you get back."

I turned and walked across the flagstones of her living room to the front door, satisfied with this parting note, this rather philosophical denouement to the scene. Turned to smile and say cheerio. Found she was right there, then up against me.

"And I'll let you go when I want to," she said, reaching a strong hand to grab my cock and balls within my stylish gray trousers. Actually, I was pretty pleased she found something there to grab, it had been so long. After a sharp tug, and with a smile and a glint in her cracked cat's eyes, she let go and turned and walked away, not so much like a languorous leopard but with a middle-aged trundle, trundling off dutifully to the Inner Circle.

Going out the door and to my car I beheld Billy Roy standing there. He squinched his eyes and stuck his fingers in his belt, kind of polishing the Texas star with his thumbs.

"Provo'," he said after me, as if he was pondering Utah.

Driving off, winding through the narrow Strait Gate Way and Nonesuch Lane and Hangman's Lane, I felt it click in place. I liked her. There was a ringing in my balls. They had waked up. Such a vulnerable "girl," doting on her delusional old daddy, Princess of Dallas, handmaiden, *ho ho,* to the King of Texas. Yeah. I could take old Lily, in her place.

FIVE

That little sideshow was then overshadowed by quite a more serious happening in my life.

I stand with Thucydides, the first significant historian, who happened to be the general who lost the Peloponnesian War and then wrote the history of it. If you lose the battle, why, by God, by that Truth that is the somewhat deformed, or multiformed, Daughter of Time, you have every right to define the history of it. I am a devotee of the memoir of Albert Speer, and I look forward to what I am sure will be the brilliant record of his trials and tribulations by Bill Clinton. I met him when he was a pup and had a long talk with the earnest, idealistic boy with his bad 'burns and bad '70s suit, which I may recount in a likelier place in this narrative. Or may not . . .

On that dastardly mid-June morning, Ray Rodriguez appeared with a helper to trim the tree limbs hanging over the house. The helper was a fat boy who didn't seem entirely bright, or maybe he just did not know much English.

"It's hard to get any good help these days," Ray said. "My son Aaron, he went to New Mexico, he used to help me. They don't trim trees out there, I'll tell you."

"What does he do?"

"Oh. Well, he has a little place. You know that little place hanging on the mountain side, that Truchas? Where they wouldn't let that Sundance Kid make the 'Milagro' movie? Has a horse. You know. Aaron is into that 'Earth First' movement, you know? Into that thing of self-suficiente."

"Be careful, up on that roof, Ray. You want some coffee?"

"No, thank you, Henry. I tell you what I got, two things, man: skill and patience. I got the skill of David with this little saw and this chainsaw and this long-handled cortar, and the patience of Job."

I went in for a second cup and heard them up on the roof, then heard Ray and the boy yelling at each other. Going out, I saw the boy bumping down the ladder to stand shouting up at Ray standing on the roof with his long cortar. "Throw me down some money, I got to get the bus! I ain't got no money. I need two dollars, you old—"

"You get back up here and work, I'll give you some money, you estupido—" Job had lost his patience.

"Fuck you!" said the boy.

"Fuck you!" Ray replied.

"You got two dollars?" the fat boy said to me. His pants were patched. It was Ray's business. I went back inside the house.

When Mr. Rodriguez came to the door he said, "Ran into some yellow jackets up there. Bit me two, three times, see, on the arm, bit that boy. He said he wouldn't work here any more. I said get to work, that was all. I'll just finish myself."

"You want something on that?"

"No. Drink a little coffee, maybe."

I gave him coffee and wrote him out a check for the job.

"Not that boy's fault," Ray said. "He comes up here, he doesn't have any base, no skill. Boys like that get lost in this big city. They go wrong, start yelling 'Fuck you' at their elders." Ray shook his head. "Sometimes, you know, Henry my old friend, you are a teacher, I know you will keep it as a confidence if I say this to you, a veces I think there may be something to this idea some of the people have, we should take back our place, our lands, live in the old ways, clean up the cities and the gangs, resurrect our ways. Bless Jesus. Well, I can do this by myself. I have the skill. You can forget that foolishness, what I just said. We fought together, Henry. U.S.A. forever, eh?"

When I left I looked for him to see if he wanted water or to use the bathroom. Found him out back behind the garage peeing, tiptoed back away so as not to embarrass Ray.

I locked the door and left the key under the mat for Pearly.

WE HAD A big recruiting weekend going at Highland U., students and their parents coming to the campus from over the Metroplex and even some beyond. A special edition of the student newspaper proclaimed for them "a weekend as big as Texas," with the requisite imaginary saguaro cactus and a cowboy hat and a lasso as the symbols on the page. I looked over the campus. It was just a chunk of prairie. About four trees and a ratty hedge around the main building total. Wind and dust and heat and a drainage ditch posing as a stream. A flagpole with the U.S. and Texas flags whipping in the wind where one day the Flatt Tower would stand. The two lonely dorms and the lonelier library. The Student Center, like a prefab roadhouse somebody might have dragged in from Mexia, Texas, and reassembled, leaving off the neon boot and spurs. But it was my place, now. That's who I was, academic leader of this beleaguered little bastion of the liberal arts, the provost of Paideia, Prince of Pergamum, aha! When all was said and done, I was of course dedicated to it. But all had not been said and done.

A message in my office said that the president, Bunky, the Boy, wished to see me.

Bunky's secretary, excuse me, executive assistant, had hung in after old Bernard Pryor had been fired. Now she was desperately taking a computer course though it was obvious that Word 98 had her buffaloed. She was an old babe who'd been married several times. I supposed young Bunky enjoyed being taken care of by Ms., as she styled herself, Applebaum. She was Old Guard, and we should have been allies, but for some reason she did not like me. This morning she looked up and beamed as if seeing me made her extraordinarily happy. "Go right in," she said.

Bunky was fantasy-putting on his carpet. He was playing a lot of golf these days with Tex Flatt and young Billy Kilday and others he was trying to woo to his "vision" of ruining a horn to make a spoon, taking a perfectly decent little college and trying to make it into a business/technological/serve-society emporium. He kept a-holt of the golf club, and would whick a fantasy shot now and again as he, eyes averted, talked to me. His chubby face was red and his stubby hands on the club were tensed white. I sensed tension, even animosity. His tennis racket lay in a leather chair. I thought I might grab it and take a whack at him if he took a whack at me. He had a large mahogany desk, but I must say for Bunky he did not retreat behind it. His windows looked out on a stretch of sere and dusty prairie. It was a lot more Valley View and Prairie View than Mountain View. Around on his walls he had flags of the states and nations that had students enrolled in Highland; they were Texas, Oklahoma, Arkansas, Nebraska, Ghana, Bahrain, Mexico and Russia (exchange).

"You didn't come to my reception for the donors," he said. "Tex noticed. Billy noticed. Tex said you quoted some garbage to him about going through a damn yellow wood and it was the wrong road and he didn't dig it but he understood it as a criticism of what we're doing around here. What I'm doing."

"Tell him I do apologize."

"We had a little talk about you. Tex thinks you're a regular Hamlet."

"And he's a thin, ridiculous Texas-style Polonius! Come on, Bunky—I mean, Bert!"

"—and a do-nothing and a bullshitter. What was it old George Bush called Clinton, a 'bullshit artist.' That's a good one. Tex tickles me."

"Well?"

"I don't agree, Henry. I mean, if the quality of your bullshit was better, you—we—might be better off. But you are a darn do-nothing. You think in the box. I hate to talk to you this way, Henry—" Whick. "—you being so much older and all, but you have missed the concept here, my boy.

"I'm a practical guy, as you know. Just a boy from Oklahoma. Not full-of-it like you Texas guys. Didn't you say you're from Texas, Henry? I was never sure. Anyways, think of it this way. We are on a voyage— Highland U. is on a voyage—on this ship, and it's a pretty trim ship but it's not full sail, you know? And as the new captain of this ship I need some new ideas, put some more sail on her, get some new wrinkles in the sails. Right?" Took a full whack at the ball and obviously from his pleased expression got it up on the green. Just two putts away now.

"So as I see it, Henry, my boy— Oh sorry, I didn't mean to say that, it's really like you're my Uncle Henry, I like you fine, we get along. You have been a good provost for me so far. Tex went out and got you before I came on board and is, like the fine gentleman he is, ready to acknowledge he made a mistake. Anyways, to make the long story short, as the fella says, you're the kind of guy who stands on the deck and thinks forever, as behooves your faculty roots, and draws a diagram of the rigging, and how it connects. And hell, Henry, I— I see a rope hanging down and I reach up and pull on the son of a bitch. I want to see what happens! You know what I mean?" Putt.

Then he looked up and looked me in the eye and smiled. Jovial. Little Big Boy. I knew what he meant.

"Give me your office keys, Henry."

"Right now?"

"Yes. Ms. Applebaum has it locked up by now. Your Edith is going down to train for InstitutoSoft. Okay? You aren't going to sue or anything, are you? You have tenure, for God's sake, Henry. You didn't

come over to this building to spend your life in administration, did you?
It's a salary reduction, boy, is it! But you don't have any family, do you?
Your wife—"

"Went away."

"Yes. Go over to English. They can dig up something for you to
do. Teach, I mean."

Last putt. Hole in three. Smile on face. Farewell in eye. Hand out.
No hard feelings, Henry.

I had seen poor old Bernie Pryor go crying down the hall like a
blind man, stumbling, lost, after Tex Flatt took the hatchet to him,
Gubuddy.

"You have a line on a new provost, do you, Bert?" I said, handing
him my office key.

I could have killed him. Punk! El Punko Presidente! Ruining my
place—and me! I would have liked to kill him and might have as the
Marines taught us so long ago in that terrible rocky hilly place, a chop
across the nose, to the throat, to the breastbone, all deadly blows. But.
Henry Rose was nothing if not controlled, dissembler, Stoic. Aurelius.
Rage within. Apparent apathy. I smiled as I asked him if he had a line on
my replacement. C'est la vie, dear Bunky Boy.

"Well— Sure, Henry. Thanks for asking. Bright young guy, really
digs the technology side, all you guys, you Luddites, will hate him!
We'll have a search and find him, you know what I mean. And I want to
thank you, Henry, for all you've done, or tried to do, or might have
thought you were doing, or like the kids say, whatever."

He saw me smiling back at him and held out his hand and I took it
and shook it, limply.

Going out, I did not speak to the strangely elated Ms. Applebaum
sitting at her desk. Going down the hall I confirmed that my door with
the plaque beside it saying Office of the Provost was locked. I had
nothing in there that I wanted or needed, nothing personal in there, just
some plaques of honors I had made up. I could not bear to go across the
quad to the building housing the English and History and Philosophy
departments and face my colleagues there. I had tenure and they would
dig up something, the English novel or the Myth of the West or Remedial
Writing for me to teach in the fall. Right now, I was free as a bird.

A pretty damn crushed bird.

I got in my old car and headed back toward the city and then into
the suburbs and into University Park, passing the house on Hanover
where Myrtle Springs and I had lived together those few good years. My

eyes misted and I almost wished that we were together there again. Pearly was in my little house, cleaning it. Ray Rodriguez was gone, a pile of tree limbs stacked along the parkway. Pearly was a black woman of great spirit, middle-aged, with a roving husband, five children, a new baby on the way, many problems. She beheld me stumbling in, tears in my eyes. I must confess I was not sure I could get up for this. Old Flatt had been in a hurry to have some leadership. I had eased into Highland on a fluke. It was like the last great hope for ye old peripatetic, after Irving Babbitt College and that Alaska university, dreadful places . . . . I sat in my study in my chair by my select small library of the classics and did not cry but stared into the hollow of my heart.

Pearly sensed it and stopped the endless telling of her travails and kindly brought me a cup of tea to comfort me.

I WAS STILL there in the afternoon but had switched to single malt Scotch whisky, a $40 bottle, about half consumed since noon, when Lily McIvey came roaring in. She pounded on the door. I staggered up and wavered to the front, glass in hand I did not know it was Lily. It was a good thing it was she, I might have slugged anybody else pounding on my door.

As I opened, she said, "Henry! You don't have a door knocker— "

"And the buzzer's broke. If it ain't broke don't fix it and if it's broke don't fix it either. Be 'strong . . . at the broken places'— "

"Henry! Good God! Are you all right? Henry? Dear dear, poor dear Henry Rose!"

She came in and enveloped and consumed me. Oh, the embrace was continuous. She never let go. She was strong as an ox. Half-carried me through the living room and, finding it uninteresting, back into my study where the drapes were drawn, the TV was on, and the old a.c. window unit droned, calling me "dear dear Henry" all the way, taking the glass from me, giving it a sniff, draining it down. Lily had a vast capacity. Deposited me back into my cozy chair. Took my face in her sinuously-fingered hands, ruby, emerald and diamond rings upon them. Looked into my eyes with her strange blue eyes like painted eyes on a primitive village virgin glazed and hardened in a kiln. Her face seemed strange and all glazed, too; first I'd thought her skin was buttery, then at her father's stark white; now it seemed almost yellow, like enamelware. Only her hands, holding, caressing, my face, seemed soft, soft, soft.

"Your one eye is a little cocked, Henry. Can you see me? Are you awfully drunk?"

"No, ma'am. Not one little bitty bit. D.R."

I was floating, nice. It had been a while since I really toped. Tippled. Topiary. That topiary steer . . . .

Her face like lava, dark and billowy, her eyes like porphyry, her smooth hands released me.

"Good! Because I am fixing to have one! Every once in a while, while not often, we need to let our emotions out, don't we, my dear? I see you have been crying, just a little? Dried rivulets on your cheeks, Henry?"

"I have not-been-crying," I replied, sitting up.

"Never argue with Lily," she said. "Oh, this is a jolly bottle! Good stuff, Henry. Good taste, old lad. Daddy does this, or something like it, when he's not doing the handmade bourbon, just on Scottish holidays, to preserve tradition, I believe. Here, I'll pour myself half what's left and let you have the bottle."

She handed me the slender bottle and I sat there holding it a while before, at her urging, I took a dab. I thought I'd best let myself get a little sober. It was like the fellow in the old story, gets lost in the damn desert, poor old Stoic soldier, and wakes up and finds a leopard licking him, and she's in love with him. Hell of a thing. Always loved that story.

Today Lily McIvey wore an orange pantsuit with a bright white collar, and a belt studded silver with a big silver buckle. If she'd had a Stetson on she'd have looked like a member of the University of Texas marching band. Instead she wore more hair that I remembered her having. I'd thought it was golden, or golden-brown or something of the sort, but this was higher hair, distinctly reddish. She also seemed to have freckles. I wondered, in my state, if she pasted them on. But I'd seen these Dallas women. I had been watching them. They wore distinct costumes, each accessorized, and changed them often.

Lily stood with her drink, took a gulp, looked at the TV, a soap that honestly I had not been watching, and went and got the wand and flicked it off, and stared at me.

"Henry, that was terrible. It made me furious. Go ahead, have a little more. I understand you need it. Here, down the hatch. Bravo. Henry, that little turd, that insufferable little pissant, why, he should be shot!"

"You bet," I said. "He should be shot. I'll drink to that."

I took another belt and my head began to swirl. I had to get this incredible woman out of here before she grabbed my balls again, or worse. One thing about Myrtle Springs, she would never grab your balls.

"How'd you know? They give out a news release?"

"Little turdhead! Should be shot! Right, Henry?"

"Right. Right on, as we used to say down in the trenches."

"Oh, you're a fighter, Henry. I admire that, all right! I bet he was scared to death, facing you. I was downtown, at the Dallas forum, you know, all that group, Stanley Marcus was there speaking for the Symphony, and the guy was speaking for the West End and the Arts District, and Mayor Kirk was talking for his plan of developing the Trinity River, and people were advocating the poor and the homeless and so on who were hungry, and when you are hungry, you don't care about good theater and symphony, and the blacks and browns, you know, were at it, and talking about racial relations. You would have loved it, Henry, it was up your alley, you could have told them about the great spirit of Texas, the pioneer Dallas spirit that could bring us together and overcome these things."

"Not today, I'm afraid."

"And so John Woodcipher, your buddy or colleague or whatever, was there, in the group. He is so red-faced, Henry, I believe he drinks. So-o—

"I go up to him and say that I think you are, that I think Henry Rose is, the most darling man. And he tells me what he's just heard. He was truly shocked. He is going to call a faculty meeting and get up a petition, make a resolution to President Bunker, protesting this. He says it's a violation of academic-something."

"Oh my." My head was hurting now. "He's the Man," I said. "Prez Bunky can fire me as an administrator anytime. And he had old Tex, Tex Flatt behind him. Meanwhile, Lily, I have that disease called tenure, and I will—be all right."

"Tex Flatt was in on this?"

"Yes. But he's rich and we need his money. We better not shoot him."

"You are so loyal, Henry. You are just a lovely, loyal man."

Now she looked like a girl again, winsome, as if tears might bejewel those eyes.

"Thank you for coming, Lily," I said, standing up, "for coming by. I appreciate. It's nice to have—a friend."

"Yep," she said, and took a stride to me, and reached and peeled off her wig and kissed my forehead with enameled lips and patted me on the head like I was a loyal sheepdog.

"You'll be all right, Henry. I could kill that little bastard. But it's all for the best, Henry. You'll be fine."

Trundled off and out the door. I went to the window and saw her go down the walk to a new black Lincoln Town Car with dark windows and bulbous red taillights at the curb, where Billy Roy got out from behind the wheel and opened the rear door for her.

I finished off the bottle and watched some TV—an old *Gunsmoke* and the *Wheel*, the words all blurred so I couldn't name them as the host kept patting and hugging the women contestants—and went yea early and weary to bed. I plunged into dreams of endless Alaska cold and tundra, then of being curled up into a leopard. Then it changed and I was entwined with the soft gray oozy body and tentacles of an octopus, looking into its cold acquiring eye.

SIX

"Well, H.R., I'd be careful," John Woodcipher said. "I'd be careful fooling with that woman. You have enough demons right now, don't you? She might send you into a decline. Peter Wilson said she was peculiar, and I noticed the same, just in class. She would come roaring into class all full of fire, acting like she was actually fighting in the Spanish Civil War."

"Which side was she fighting on?"

"Loyalists. The Republicans. I'll give her that."

I had talked him out of challenging Bunky on my removal through the faculty, and now he was trying to talk me out of Lily.

I had news for him. I had news for me. I was on the ropes. I loved old Lily. That is, I loved her keen and zesty interest in me. She was not gorgeous, apparently no more brilliant than the average wealthy clubwoman, and she had those scary little mood swings, but I was not exactly ageless or a great prize myself. I could use old Lily. I needed her. And, if we clicked, and settled down and her old fool of a father shuffled off his mortal coil before too long, it might be just what I had been watching and waiting for. It would not be all that bad to hang in at Highland, teach a course or two, reside with Lily in her charming graystone, maybe move over the hill to the manor house when the King of Texas and his fond delusion passed, Lily and dear Henry hand in hand, creating our own fantasies. Not too shabby, as they used to say. No, not bad at all.

The voice of my wise old Uncle Sage Rose spoke into my ear: Let the fish jump in the boat. I was sure she would. I had no way of calling or contacting her anyway. There was no McIvey in the book.

They announced, on campus, my resignation and that a brief search would be conducted for a new provost. The rumor was that this young technology wizard was coming to us from Oklahoma State. The Old

Guard faculty at once became restless. Rumors grew of the difficulty, if not impossibility, of faculty fossils learning InstitutoSoft. Four days passed, and I began to worry. But as I rose to give my talk to the Highland Lecture Series in the Faculty Club she was there among them.

She did not stand out as much as you might think she would. Of course, she was a chameleon, was my Lily. Today she sat demurely in her little white chair in the middle of the rows of them in our tacky Fac Club living room dressed simply in a one-piece dress of purple velvet or velour, wearing a simple strand of rich white pearls, smiling and nodding to everyone it seemed but me. The Princess Lily. I did not try to catch her eye but smiled and nodded to whatever other women I had seen before in the audience composed totally of middle-aged and older women and old Mr. Peabody who came to all the lectures though he could not hear a thing. I thought he probably came to remind himself of when he was vital and could get it up, for the rich exotic and erotic aura of it, all the women, the perfume, the hair colors and spray, the fabrics, the gold and diamonds, all the precious stones, the aura of wealth, the musk. You could get a whiff of it and feel intoxicated and forget what you were saying as you spoke to them.

I spoke of Mabel Dodge holding her soirees in Florence, in New York, coming to New Mexico and arriving in Taos at night and her enchantment with the chanting, the unified singing of the Pueblo, her sense that here was a place, a culture, she could merge into. Of her marrying Tony, a Pueblo man, and how he was loved for his simplicity by all the women Mabel brought to stay in the house she and Tony Lujan built, Lady Brett and Mary Austin, Cather and O'Keeffe, Martha Graham, etc. Of the luring there of Lawrence, who came for the Earth Mother and found Mabel, and his dismay and that of Frieda, and then the pilgrimage there of all the men, the New Transcendentalists, Utopians, etc., who all came to share the fantasy that you could live in tune with nature and the seasons and others and yourself in the ancient native way. It was good stuff. I knew I had her. Lily's eyes were gleaming.

After the talk, a woman came up to tell me haltingly she had owned for years a house belonging to an early Taos artist. Why didn't I talk about Phillips and Blumenschein and Berninghaus and the early Taos artists? I said that was another talk. She said she would like to hear it. She was a pretty, faded woman. She looked at me wistfully and said her husband had gone away and she lived alone in Dallas but, faintly blushing, she'd love to go and live out her life in her house in Taos there. God sent this woman to me, but I did not recognize it. I turned away from her. Lily McIvey was talking to my colleague Regina Singh, who had introduced my talk, graciously with no mention of the provost part.

"Do you know Ms. McIvey, Henry?"

"Yes."

"That was wonderful," Lily said. "I dug it deep. It spoke to me."

"I think you have the potential to be a Mabel," I said to Lily. She did not exactly blush, but a little color came into her laquered cheeks.

With a quizzical Indian look at me Regina peeled away.

"She has some interesting contacts in India," Lily said. "We haven't done much there, in India."

"She's Punjabi. She thinks the Punjab is like Texas."

"How could it be? That's silly."

"Oh, I don't know. Do you remember 'Little Orphan Annie'? Daddy Warbucks and his two henchmen, Punjab and the Asp?"

"In the funny papers? Never read—or looked at—comic strips. I could have drawn one: 'Little Orphan Lily.' "

"Daddy Warbucks and all?"

She shrugged. I was about to make her mad. I'd bet she'd heard of Daddy Warbucks. The big capitalist with hollow beads for eyes. Maybe seen the musical.

"How are you, Henry?"

"Fine. Sober as a—"

"I thought I would give you a little time to sort it out. What you may not realize is, it's wonderful. It frees you up, Henry. You don't need to be piddling around this little place. I mean, it's a nice little college, we'll keep it in mind, but there are larger things. Cosas más grandes, no? I just went to that class to meet you, did you know that, Henry? I was practically born speaking Spanish. Daddy says it's part of noblesse oblige, we need to know how to talk to them, to know what's in their mind. Daddy is not too optimistic about the whole Hispanic thing, in Texas. I saw you talking to that sweet little Doris Waltenburg, she's just your type, Henry, sweet and soft and clinging. Did you know she is one of the richest women in Texas? Patroness of the arts, my dear! She was a Schmidt, her husband was a Waltenburg. Well, do you want to come along with me, I'll buy you lunch?"

I said I was famished after releasing all that good b.s., and crossed the Rubicon. We went in her Lexus to the well-lighted, silver and crystal-glittering Café Pacific in Highland Park Village and despite my vow of abstinence had a couple of silver bullets—Squeakers—each. Lily was girlish and happy as a lark. She asked me to come again to the King's

Levy on Friday. I said I would be delighted. Lily's sharp knees bumped mine under the crisply-linened table. She smiled at obvious acquaintances seated in the booths and at the tables in the restaurant. The vodka warmed me as I warmed myself in Lily's glow, and the sole wasn't bad, either.

She drove me back to campus, and leaned across the wheel for a little hug and a buss, saying she would see me Friday, Daddy would be glad, he had asked about me. She wore black shades so I could not see her eyes. I went in my building humming "Beautiful, beautiful Texas, where the beautiful bluebonnets grow . . . ." I'd plucked that Lily, plucked her good!

Strange thing was, I liked her more and more. She had moments of lucidity.

The price to be paid was indulgence in the fantasy. Suddenly I panicked, a little bit scared of the lurching wit and Old Texas immersion of the old man, Oliver McIvey. I needed to get my act together if I was serious about Miss Lily, Little Orphan Lily, and wanted to appeal to the King of Texas. Truth was, speaking honestly, I knew Jackshit about the state of Texas. I had hardly been out of Dallas since I returned. You had better do a little reconnoitering, Uncle Sage Rose's voice said in my ear.

I went to Love and punched in my Visa card for a ticket to Austin. It was a plain plane with matronly stewardesses. I remembered the old days, the young stewardae in hot pants on blue and orange and yellow planes. Or was that Braniff? I got a van to the old Driskill Hotel and saw Laura and George W. Bush in the lobby with a retinue. That boy was the King of Texas, all right, and he looked pretty cocky. She was lovely, had been a librarian. It was some festivity or festival, and out on the street came along a big equestrian parade, phalanxes of Sheriff's Posses, Arabians, horses of all kinds, truly Texas, with riders young and old in hats and chaps and cowboy boots. Following them in the parade came Shriners wearing fezzes in go-carts just a-zipping through what the horses had dropped, and H. Rose and the spectators ducking back laughing to behold it, the carts making figure eights through the glistening horseshit in the roaring heat, the sun shining above in a wondrous blue Texas sky. A galore of balloons let go from a balloon man's cart, Texas orange and white and red and white and blue, and the Shriners zipped on down the street scattering the horsestuff far and wee, and by God, I felt Texan then, I felt *Texian*. And walked up to the Capitol and saw the real King of Texas again, the Guv, patting backs and holding elbows and shaking hands and kissing women, and went over and said hello to the statue of the Terry Texas Ranger standing there. Went to drink some beer in the evening at Scholz Beer Garden and saw the Dobie Professor and the Scarlet Pimpernel there and thought of Willie and Waylon and Steve and Michael Martin and Jerry Jeff and Gary P. and Ray Wylie and Lyle and them, and had another schooner, sitting by a guy in a black mustache and black hat and suit and boots smoking a cigar, listening to a tall fellow in boots and a belt tuning forever before he sang a couple of insipid songs. Guy with the cigar told me he was a writer and a humanitarian and a pretty noble fellow and then got up to do his gig and sang the great Texas classic "I'm Glad to Be an Asshole from El Paso."

Decided not to go there and flew over to Houston and visited the DeMenil Museum and the Rothko Chapel. In the humid heat it was oddly cool in there, and I got a scared feeling, like dreaming of that clammy octopus. Got lost driving around and around the sprawl of Houston, and flew out to Amarillo. Dome of the earth. Pitiless sky of brass. Saw an old pickup completely covered with "God Bless John Wayne" stickers. Thought of coming out to picket the plant we called the Missile Mother of the World so many years ago. Flew to San Antonio and felt how it could be old McIvey's favorite city, walking the built-up river walks, remembering the torpid river, the uncared-for paths and alleys along it, the dead rats along the way, of when I walked it as a boy. Skipped the Alamo, we Roses never went to the Alamo. Got lost in the old unfabled city, rescued by a woman who said her name was also Rose, bought us almuerzo, nearly stayed. Flew back to Love, to Big D Dallas, Texas.

Things, I reckoned, were much changed and just the same. Texas was a swarm. Amarillo and Houston and San Antonio could not be part of the same thing. Texas was a piece of work, a crazy quilt. Texas was whatever you might make it out to be. It would help to be a little mad if you were the King of Texas, like George III with some odd, vague notion of the Colonies.

But I felt better for the refresher course. I would gild my Lily now. Hell, heading back for Strait Gate Way I felt that I could gild a cactus.

SEVEN

In her Southwestern room, in a long tartan (green and purple) skirt and tartan sash over the shoulder—I guessed she always tartan'd up for Fridays—Lily bumpered me wine and built herself a large silver bullet.

"Cheers," I said, smiling at her like the veritable Cary Grant.

She saluted me and with an impish wink said, "That was a weird little trip you made just now, Henry, just flying hither and yon."

"I beg your pardon?" Holy Shit.

"I keep track, too, Henry. Don't think for a moment you can fool me, get out of my sight, you silly person! Who was that woman you ate lunch with in San 'Tonio?"

"Just a woman I ran into. You had me tailed? How flattering. Billy Roy? No, I think I would have noticed him."

"T.J. Mr. Mackey. You'd never see him if he didn't want you to. He's very good at it." She giggled like this was a rich little joke between us. "He said actually you were kind of hard to keep up with, you'd just dart around like you didn't know where you were going, like Peter Sellers."

"Lily, I think—if we are to have a relationship—"

"I hate that word! It won't begin to describe what we are going to have. Dull people have relationships, it's a dumb old word from the dull old past! Oh Henry, you sweet, sweet man. You were just getting a little taste of Texas in your blood. I understand. I do it regularly. I'll go zip out to San Angelo and see the Comanches off in the buffalo humps and hills there, or I'll think that sweet Larry McMurtry is over there at Archer City with his 'Booked Up' warehouses full of a million books, and how that's Texas too, and I'll go there and ask him to come talk to my Book Club about what he's doing there, and he'll say, 'Sure, Lily, doll, for you I'll speak for just fifteen grand,' and I'll say, 'Screw you, Mac,' and he'll laugh, or maybe I'll just pick up one day and go see all the roses growing at the rose farms in Tyler. I understand. You do the same thing as I do, because you love Texas!"

She took a swig. I nodded at her, humbly, affirmative.

"Yes," I said. "I'm glad you understand. Still, I don't like the idea of being followed, Lily."

"Of course you don't! I want to assure you it wasn't even my idea. But—well—you know—the King of Texas thing. Daddy gets mixed up in a lot of things, and he can't afford to let someone get even a little bit close and have him suddenly—you understand—take off and turn out to be a nut, or a kook. Okay?"

"So the King of Texas had me followed?"

"Surely you understand, Henry."

"I think I have been awfully understanding, my dear Lily. Because of my respect and regard for you. Understanding of this little game. But I do think there must be limits. No?"

"What do you mean, Henry?"

"A game's a game, 'for aye that,' Lily. I like a little fun and fantasy in my life, and I understand your playing this farce of the King of Texas for your father's sake. I even agree he is kind of a sweet old fellow, and he's real quick at the word games. Maybe I could work on that with him, lead him down that road? He seems to know Latin even, and literary allusions."

"Don't underestimate Daddy. Daddy went to Yale. He was in that secret club and he was a Deke. Daddy was one of them who helped George Bush get in those clubs, at Yale. You are right. Daddy can read Latin, and a lot of languages. So can I, dear Henry. I still don't get what you are aiming at."

"Let me put it this way. I mean, this is no direct attack on you and your daddy, and your fantasy. I teach literature, it's all about fantasies, forming selves, creating or adopting new ones if we're not quite happy with the ones we have. I do it me-self, Lily dear, on occasion. Yes. I must confess I do.

"Well, I had this friend in Texas, when I was here before, ten years ago, before hearing the Call of the Wild and going to Alaska, a wonderful droll chap who had come back to his native Texas to teach, Donald Barthelme. By the way, you can check this out, his father was a Houston architect who designed the Texas Hall of State on the fairgrounds here, wonderful Texas symbols tiled into it, etc., and he engraved the names of the Alamo guys on the outside of the Hall of State so going around the top outside the first letter of their names spells 'BARTHELM,' without the 'e'—"

"And you start with the 't' it spells 'Thelmbar,' " Lily quickly said. Oh, she could be quick, old Lily. "So?"

"Just a Texas reference, girl. You know how I do love Texas! So old Don Barthelme, bless his heart, he was our great fantasist, our Borges, only better, more wry, more dry, funnier. So he wrote a story called 'I Bought a Little City.' "

"And so?"

"So it was Galveston, like Daddy gave Galveston to your sister. This guy buys Galveston and looks around and decides he'll make a few changes. He tore down a block of houses and was very paternal and let everybody stay at the Galvez Hotel and made a little park for the people. Oh, he was well intended. Then he made new housing in the shape of a jigsaw puzzle. Then he shot most of the dogs in the city, since it pleased him and he owned the city. When someone protested it didn't do the protestor any good since the guy owns the judge and the jail and even the ACLU. Then he falls in love with Sam Hong's wife, but she loves Sam Hong, and you can't buy love, so he sells Galveston and moves to Galena Park. You dig?" I beamed. What a delicious little parable, how true!

Lily stared at me.

"He decides he'll leave it to God, God has a better imagination than he does. He can't compete with God. Remember you said your little game let you play God? You can't own cities, or people, play God."

"Can't? Henry, you are so sweet. I read some of him, how do you say? Bartle-me? Dull, dull, dull. I mean."

"Did you ever read the one he wrote about mad fathers? Old Don wrote a lot about fathers and their effect on you, on sons but also daughters." I was getting pretty brave, but I hadn't been connecting. "I know my own— Anyway, it says, mad fathers stalk all around us, and you can avoid them or embrace them or tell them your thoughts, or flee from them as from the wrath of God, it makes no difference."

"I dig it, Henry. Don't worry. I embraced mine. I love him. That all right with you?" Now her eyes got that large, porcelain, cracked look.

"Sure," I said. "Certainly. It's just—the game part—that it's okay when you and your gang play it, but when it gets intrusive on others it's not fun or funny. You know?"

She knocked down the rest of the bullet. "You are on the edge of not being very much fun yourself, Henry," she said. "Let me just tell you a couple things."

"It's all right, Miss Lily. Just take it I was gently demurring, from being tailed by Mr. Mackey, and all."

"You think my father is mad. Well, maybe he is. Most great men of vision, like Daddy, have been a touch mad, haven't they? Great kings and rulers, and such as that?"

"Surely." I was getting off track. The fish was about to jump back out. Was I up for this weird "relationship" or not? He was crazy as hell, but what the hell, Henry, it's just a game. Still, they had followed me . . . .

"One, Daddy may be mad, but he's not crazy. Two, there is a little bit more to the game than you think, right now, dear Henry. Oh, how could you know? So it's all right, just this one time, I'll allow you to treat me like I'm a student back at Vassar being put down by a wise-ass smirking senior professor who really doesn't know batshit beyond what's in the book, or in your case, in that silly little story. Daddy has bought and sold and bought back cities, Henry! He tried to do good things for the people in them. He owns a castle and a whole county or whatever it is in Scotland, and he owns equal to some other little states in Texas. We have this foundation that I mentioned to you. We are pretty active—in Texas—in the world—with it. Does this interest you? Or are you just interested in the incredible sexual vibes that I put out?"

"I am fascinated," I said. "By both." She was putting out those vibes, undulating like that giant snake, moving around the room, glaring, pouting, smiling at me. Then she came over and put her face an inch from mine.

"Good," she said. "I have hopes for us, Henry. I am furious at that terrible little man for firing you, but I am so glad that you are free. Well, it's—damn!—already Levy time." She backed away just before I could reach for her, grab her ample ass, cram myself against her tartan'd bush. I stood, a bit shaky. It had been a shaky cocktail time.

Taking my arm and leading me out and once again across the quaint bridge over the stream and up the greensward to the redbrick pile of the King of Texas, Lily murmured to me that we might could be a team, if I was interested in the foundation work, oh, it was totally about helping people. We could be a team like Ted Turner and Jane Fonda. They had bought half a million acres in New Mexico, did I know that? The principle was, you had to control something, corner a market, make a profit, but then you could be a benefactor to those that needed one. Of course it would be fun to think so. I nodded, kept my damn mouth shut. I was sure the old K of T was going to give a billion dollars to the U.N., match Ted Turner's gift! Lily's arm held me tight. Well, all I could think was that Myrtle Springs went to her Church Circle, studied depressed countries, migrant and refugee peoples, hunger, and came home happy, thinking she'd had a part in saving the world.

"So what is the subject for today?" I asked.

"You are," she said. "Daddy wants to get to know you better. And the drought. Have you noticed there is a drought in Texas, Henry? Folks are suffering."

When we entered the Texas Room, late, the old man, in his great wing chair, was already in conversation with a character with the Texas name of Weatherford about the number of days of consecutive heat over one hundred degrees in Texas, the drought, the plight of farmers and ranchers. Every county in Texas was like to be a disaster area, the fellow said.

"What can I do? Doody-oh-doody-oh-do?" The Rex, old McIvey, was dressed today in black and silver boots, silver-buttoned cowboy shirt, voluminous black-and-gold flecked shirt with a massive old-turquoise bolo, and wearing about a twenty-gallon Rancher Stetson hat. Billy Roy stood behind him, looking very serious. T.J. Mackey perched on a stool nearby. He did not give me a flicker of recognition as he whittled on his fingers with his Case knife. Some fellows in the costumes of farmers and ranchers were gathered before the King, grouped around the Weatherford fellow.

"This is a grave situation, Pro-fessor," the old fellow said as in an aside to me, motioning me to come stand by him.

"Make it rain, I reckon," the fellow said, with a little laugh and that Texas half-nod of making the best out of the worst.

"We done tried," said Billy Roy. "We tried that scientist, seeding with them crystals, and we tried that Indian, that Navajo guy. Nothin'. Clouds drifting in today from New Mexico, just hanging there, over Amarillo."

"Mac, I want to tell you, this is serious. Half of us are going out of business, giving up, if this goes on."

"I understand, Homer. What is your greatest need?"

"Feed, sir. We are about to lose our herds to lack of hay and grain, not just West Texas but East Texas, too. Right, boys?"

"State of Texas needs help. Even when it's a disaster, we'll give loans, get the Guv'ment in it. Won't help the ones who are going under," said Mr. Weatherford.

"Okay," McIvey said, his ginkie Scot's eyes alert. "We'll see what we can do. Billy Roy, where can we get it, hay and grain? A shitload of it?"

Billy Roy said Kansas, maybe, or the Northwest. The King said for the group to get organized to receive. They seemed to take him seriously. He waved his hand, dismissing them. They tipped their hats and gimme caps and left. He smiled at me. "It will be a donation, from the farmers and ranchers of the Midwest to their Texas cousins," he said, beaming at me. And when I read about it a little later it was, a noble gift from brother to brother, region to region, delivered over Texas in trucks furnished by a benefaction from the T-Rex Foundation in Dallas. Still, in the moment it had the feel of being staged. The farmer-ranchers looked like they might be actors, saying lines.

The old man said now that that was done, it was just us. Why didn't I set down by him, we could have a little talk? Here, in this old bullhide chair, it was from the ranch. I set, and said how much I admired his boots, his hat.

"Hear you been antsing around Texas like a damn roadrunner," old McIvey said. He rested the fat brown hand with the King ring on it on the other, in his lap, over his paunch; every so often the great stomach would rumble or quiver, or the hands seem to jump, like frogs on a pad.

"Yes, sir. Took off on a little jaunt. Gettin' restless, sitting around Dallas . . . ."

"Unemployed. Eh?"

"Well. Underemployed, shall we say?"

"You shall. I will. Goddamn shame, I'd say. Not that I know a Goddamn thing about 'em—universities."

"I hear Yale is pretty good."

"Used to be. Did history of the West. Howard Lamar. Then went to hell, liberal. Before the Bass gift, I reckon. Like all of 'em –"

"Not Highland. At Highland –"

"So I've heard. Yas, yas. So where did you go to school, Professor?"

"Amherst. Princeton. Duke." Lily smiled at me radiantly from her lesser wing chair nearby. "Did you know I was a Deke?"

"Say! No! The devil you say! Here—"

McIvey's paw tic'd, came alive, rose and leant itself to me. I grasped his hairy hand girdled by the ring and managed to insert my fingers into it in the secret grip of the good old Deke fraternity. I'd paid a down and out fellow a C-note for that in earlier days, noting all the Dekes in American literature, figuring it might come in handy.

"Lily! Lily!" he croaked, not letting go. "He is, he is a Deke! By Godfrey! Lily, do you know who else are Dekes—besides George Herbert Walker—and young George—"

"Gorbachev?" Lily laughed. "Yeltsin? Jiang?"

"No, you impertinent pup!" He let go, then again crowded our fingers back through the fraternity grip, just in case I had fingered my way by some sort of divine luck. "Gerald is! Ford. He's a damn liberal, of course. And young what's his name, Quayle, couldn't spell 'po-tato.' That's how he got him, George did, for V.P., asked Gerald who was a good young Deke could keep his nose clean, and he said *Quail*, eh? *Bob-white—bob-white*."

He pulled out of the grip, thrust my hand away. I might be a Brother, but I had touched the King long enough.

"Say, Pro-fessor—Bro'—Henry—Señor Rose— Since you are a Goddamned Deke, I suppose you will join me in a drink-of-whiskey! Unless Lily has got you skunked already. I do not appreciate you children coming in late to the Levy."

Billy Roy brought me a large round glass of the Texas Handmade sourmash whiskey, by appointment to the King.

"I was feeling some depressed. This drought is terrible, it is like to ruin Texas. Depressed. Maybe just dyspeptic." He took a sip of his own. "Ah. Disheartened, discerptible, disabled, discouraged, disheveled—Pro-fessor?"

"Discombobulated?"

"Yes. Just diz. But am feeling better. We have to feed those herds, damn it, Billy Roy! T.J., what are you doing sitting there with your head up your rear, man, get on the horn. Call Kansas City. We'll buy all their Goddamn hay! So you took a little trip, did you, Brother? Henry Rose? Just to get out of Dallas, eh?"

Never did anything so attention-getting in my life, I almost said.

"To get his heart beating in tune with Texas, Daddy," Lily said. "Henry just loves Texas!"

Billy Roy cracked his knuckles. "Hung out at Scholz' with Kinky Friedman. Went to San 'Tonio but didn't go to the Alamo," he said, as if these were matters for grave suspicion.

"Kinky Friedman is a Jew," said McIvey, as if imparting to us a deep revelation. "Are you a Jew, Rose?"

"What difference does it make?" Lily cut in. "You admire Netanyahu."

"I do. Think he is on the right track. Tough hombre, Netanyahu. He will probably be killed for it. We met. He did not quite understand who I was . . . ."

"No, sir," I quipped. "Your Royal Texas—"

He swiveled his head, winked a slate eye at his daughter dear.

"This is the one guy I let get smart with me, eh, Lily? Liked your pro-fessor bullshitter from the start, I did. Oh yes! Okay, Rose. I'm Dubious—"

"I'm Rose, Dubious. Henry Rose. I am not Jewish. I am of French heritage. And Roses never go near the Alamo, since my kinsman Moses Rose left it."

"Jesus God! Moses Rose! You are kin to Moses Rose, the guy who left the Alamo?"

"Yes. My great— Uncle. Something. Yes. Travis drew the line. Nobody stepped over it—except old Moses Rose. He was older, he'd been in the French Army under Napoleon, came to Texas to make a new life. He thought he had done it already, the fighting and the sacrifice. So he stepped over that line in the sand and said adios and was over the wall and away that night. Either a yellow coward or a pretty smart guy, depending on your point of view."

"Why, that's terrible. I would have fought from my bed, like Bowie, to the last!" Lily cried.

"Bah! Bah-bah-bah. You can fight Henry to the last in your bed, Lily. He he. Goddamn, sir, you son of a bitch, I want you to know right now, I would have been over that wall with old Moses Rose in a heartbeat! Lived to fight another day. Yessiree, Bob! Told that tinpot imported Colonel Travis, this Alamo is not worth goatshit as a fort, this whole thing is a mare's nest of monumental proportions! That is a remarkable credential, Señor Rose, being kin to Moses Rose, the only s.o.b. that got out of the Alamo alive! Congratulations, Lily. You done good in bringing him to us."

T.J. Mackey, in the corner by the racks of frontier rifles, whicked his knife shut and looked at me. He had deadly pale eyes. "Your birth certificate, and all, say you were born in Missouri," he said, "not in Texas."

"I never said that I was a native."

"No, he never," Billy Roy agreed. "He never had to."

"Where were you born?" said Lily.

"St. Louis. Most of the Roses were born there, set out along the Santa Fe Trail, to the West."

"Moses Rose is a myth," said T.J. Mackey. "He never was. That is a made-up story. I studied Texas history."

"No. He's real, my Uncle Moses. Personally, I admire him Like His Majesty here, I probably would have done the same. Anyway, Mackey, he is documented. If you will look in the best little book on the Alamo, Lon Tinkle's celebrated *Thirteen Days to Glory*, you will see—"

"Hold it," said the lovely Lily, going to the shelf of Texas books in the Texas room, looking, pulling it from the shelf.

"Yep," she said, after a few tense moments. "This says he was. Dictated a statement years later, when he was an old man living in Nacogdoches. Louis Moses Rose. Came to Texas in 1827. Buddy of Jim Bowie. Etc. At least one old feller said he was, believed the story, testified later. This writer, Tinkle, says in here. Hey, this Lon Tinkle's ancestor, Lin Tinkle, came to Texas with Davy Crockett!"

"My whole family says it's so. My old Uncle Sage Rose even had memories of—"

"Oh yes! I'm sure he has. Your uncles, Sage and Moses! Yes! Splendido, bandido! Pour me one here, Billy Roy. I decree that Mr. Rose, the Pro-fessor, has established his credentials as far as I am concerned, in regard to Texas. That is terribly important, to me. I am the King of Texas. All right! I am a little tired. I have to hook up to that machine. Next time we'll discuss philanthropy, as our subject, try to edi-cate the Pro-fessor here a bit. Lily, could I have a word with you for a minute, Love? Oh, thank you so much, my dearest beautiful girl. Mr. Mackey, I told you to get on the horn. Billy Roy, will you walk the descendant of the Hero of the Alamo out, there, boy, and don't let him get lonely while he waits for Lily? Thank you so much, my friend.

"Thank you for coming, Mr. Rose. Henry. 'Friends from the heart forever.' Eh? Fellow Dekes? Splendido, Rose!"

Lily gave me a little just-a-mo' wave as she sat up close to listen to what her father had to say. She helped him take off the huge hat. He rolled his head and neck and shrunk up as if it had weighed a ton. T.J.

Mackey walked up and took me lightly by the arm, his other arm extended. I thought, my God, he's going to stick a shiv in me until I found he was offering to shake my hand. I took and shook it.

"He's the Man," he said. He had a blank map of some regions of the world I had no clue to for a face, as if he'd had more face lifts than Evetts Haley. "I serve him, Mr. Rose. No hard feelings. You ever been in the service, Mr. Rose?"

"Thank you, Mr. Mackey. Korea. Came at us with lances on shaggy ponies across the frozen Yalu."

"Yeah? I wasn't there. And you weren't in Nam. I'd know if you were there. Probably opposed the war."

I took my hand back. "Opposed the hell out of it," I said. "You may ask my former students."

He shrugged. "Things get mixed up. The Big Bullshitter was off at Oxford smoking dope, wasn't he? We do know that. Anyway, no hard feelings. Just checking up. The Old Man is strict about security. By the way, sir, do you know that woman you met in San Antonio, that Rose, she's an artist, and she is a member of the U.H.F."

"The what?"

"United Hispanic Front. Right? The Hispanic revolutionary movement. I would avoid her. She is kind of like their, what you call it, La Pasionara."

"Never heard of it. The U.H.F." I meant, like, I had never heard of it.

"Take care," said T.J. Mackey, eyeing me like he hoped I would not be a problem. Goodbye, I said with a nod, no hard feelings, you hired goon. I suppose you have to play your role too. Moved outside. Turned to the slope-shouldered, bound in muscle from toes to head, court jester, smarter-than-you-think good old Billy Roy.

"So what's your last name, Billy Roy?" I said amiably. "Since I'm confessing all, I'd like to know exactly who all my buddies are."

He had a little Fu Manchu mustache. Danced a step or two before me. "Crockett," he said. "Billy Roy Crockett. Davy Crockett was my Goddamn great-uncle." Danced back a step or two, eyes also dancing. Nice guy probably. Big heart no doubt. Probably also very loyal. Suspected he adored the Lily girl. Put out my hand to him.

"I'll be darned," I said. "Put her there."

He had to laugh. We shook. He had a grip that made T.J. Mackey's seem like old McIvey's. It was Grip Day. I had no idea where to go from there. I started walking towards Lily's. He took me by the shoulder and easily thrust me down into a lawn chair by the table on the rolling grass where he'd served the tea.

"She is a great girl," he said, popping his knuckles. "That is what I do, you know? I take care of her." He danced around like he was dancing to a one-man band, or was one. "I don't know. I don't know about you and all how you love Texas. It would break her heart. She has saved it up, you see." He said it sadly, for whatever reason.

I tried to think of something along an earthy vein to reassure him about my deep love for Texas.

"There's a lot of Texas," I said. "There are a lot of Texases. I remembered that on my little trip yesterday, the day before. I am a bit out of touch, to tell you the truth, but I mean, I truly do love Texas."

He stopped and popped his knuckles. Professors were naturally suspect to these boys.

"So what is your own favorite thing about Texas, Billy?"

"'Billy Roy.' That is my name my daddy gave me and that is what I'm called. I ain't 'Billy' and I ain't a kid. I came up mean and hungry as a snake along the hardscrabble country, central Texas. Got to Sam Houston State, not no Deke and Princeton, became a peace officer. She seen me riding in a rodeo. We can ride, and sometimes we ride together, her and me.

"The music, I guess. The damn old country music that tells the story of my life."

"Ah yes. I was just down there, you know, sitting on that very bench by the Terry Texas Ranger at the Capitol in Austin where E.T., old Ernest Tubb, sat after flying from El Paso to Austin and going there in the evening, and thinking of Texas, and he sat right there and in a sitting he wrote 'Waltz Across Texas.' 'When I dance with you, dear, da da da da da—I could—' "

"Yeah, I heard him tell how he done that, on the record. Can't stand that damn 'Waltz Across Texas,' it is 'most as worst as 'Yellow Goddamn Rose of Texas.' Me, I like Willie—and the Cherokee Cowboy—'Lay your head upon the pillar—' "

"Those were great days, drinking and smoking a little dope over there in East Texas with Willie and Ray."

"You know them? Willie? The Cherokee Cowboy? Hell, I was just a boy when they was doing that. What other adventures did you have with those boys, those old Texas country musicians?"

I rifled my mind for something. "You ever heard of the Dripping Springs Reunion, on that ranch in Hays County there, Billy Roy, in 1972? 'The Armageddon of Country Music'? Had almost all those old boys there, to that. They said they were trying to bring cowboys and longhairs together. It was the first big outdoor country music concert."

Billy Roy's eyes bugged out at me. He looked like I had taken a leak on his daddy's tombstone. "Dripping Springs? How d'you know about that?"

"I was there."

"Ah, you were never! Goddamn, I was there. Had old Tex Ritter and Roy Acuff, and Willie and Waylon, and Charlie Rich and Bill Monroe and the Blue Grass Boys, but nobody came. Loretta Lynn—"

"Kristofferson. Hank Snow. Roger Miller. Except, you are right, nobody came. It was a triumph and a disaster."

"Damn straight! What was you doin' there?"

"My cousin Billy was one of the promoters. He lost his ass and never got it back. It was damn sad. I came and lay out on a bale of hay and listened, and then we had to sneak Billy out of there because they couldn't pay the talent. What were you doing there?"

"Ah, you are just bullshitting me. You were never there. You just heard about it. I was a guard. Just a boy. Rode shotgun around the perimeter. There was about forty of us, with rifles and shotguns, those crazy bastards really had the security. I was a damn teenager."

"Called you 'pig-fuckers.' "

"Beg pardon?"

"Called you guys, the horse guards, that. Nothing personal."

"That right? I just got one thing to say about that," said Billy Roy. "Balls. So what was the name of the little café there in Dripping Springs, if you was really there, Mr. Bullshit Artist?"

"It didn't really have a name. Everybody called it, from the sign, the 'Have-A-Pepsi' café. And the gate you all guarded, we called it 'Checkpoint Charlie.'"

"Well, hell, that's what we called it, all right. That is real interesting, that you was there, Provo'."

"No more."

"Okay. Henry. So who else do you remember bein' there?"

"Oh, Charlie Walker, Dottie West, and Pearl Beer. He was there big-time."

Billy Roy nodded, laughing. "Billy Rose," he said. "I think I heard of him. Well, you take care, there, now, Henry." He drifted back kind of under a great oak as Lily came along.

"That was fun," she said. "Daddy says you're in. I wish I could go celebrate, have some wild abandon! But I must go back to him. I'll be in touch. Go home, Henry, dear, and I will call you tomorrow. Now don't you go roaming around . . . ."

I said okay, adieu and adios, received a peck and a pat and departed.

At home got a drink from a new bottle of the single malt and settled in my den, pretty pleased. It was a damn fine Levy. Had I not shone brightly, with Lily, with the King, with the goon, with Charming Billy (Roy)?

I had the remote in hand switching from local news to *Washington Week in Review* when the TV told me that Bert Bunker, the young president of Highland University, had been shot and killed.

EIGHT

I did not sleep all night. I deadbolted the doors. At 5:30 I furtively ran out and grabbed the paper. It was in the Metropolitan section. Bunky had been whiffed in his own house the evening before. Shot once in the head. There were no signs of forced entry, nothing missing, no fingerprints, no clues. I staggered to the campus, driving like a drunken person.

Ms. Applebaum was guarding Bunky's door. She looked at me as if I'd done it. I raised my arms in a sign of supplication. She sniffed and pointed down to where I had officed, the Office of the Provost. I found John Woodcipher sitting in there, bemusedly masturbating his Guards necktie.

"Good God, John! I'm shocked! It's terrible! I had no idea."

"Of course not, Henry. Don't be silly. Sit down, man."

He told me a few more details he had heard. His wife had found Bert Bunker in his study where he had been writing a speech for taking the Highland U. campaign to Houston. Woodcipher had it on his desk. It was a string of phrases, the Well-Rounded-plus-Skills-in-the-World cliches with which we were familiar, titled "Highland Takes the High Ground." It might have been suicide except there was no gun or reason for Bunky to take his life. Mrs. Bunky had been watching television in their bedroom. Now she was in Presbyterian Hospital recovering from shock. There was not a lock or a window or a lamp shade disturbed. It was some terrible form of black magic, Woodcipher, the rational historian, opined.

"I am terribly sorry . . . ." I could not say that I was scared to death. "He was going to ruin us, change our very raison d'etre—our reason for being—but—"

"Cuidado, Henry. Let not trash escape our lips. We must be seemly, now."

"So what's with Highland? Why are you in here?"

"Might be you, eh? The big if. I'm Acting President. Last thing I wanted to be. Won't be long, I hope. The wizard from Okie State, we are going to tell him not to come. We'll name a provost from the ranks."

"Who's in charge, John? Who is dictating all of this?"

"Tex Flatt. Called in late last night. Who else do you think it would be?"

"Oh. Tex. Of course."

"There's visitation tonight, funeral tomorrow at two at Restland."

"Can I do anything?"

"Sure. Get out of here. I'm just sitting in the saddle. Everything is frozen, the campaign, the new curriculum, to do. Go get hold of yourself. You look haggard. You look like you waked up at Jarama. Or like you'd seen a ghost. I don't blame you one bit. This is right peculiar. I mean, who in God's world would want to—have the least interest in—offing the poor pompous little peckerwood?"

I drove back in to University Park. I thought I'd get some groceries, cook up some eggs and toast and bacon. I had not eaten breakfast, or lunch or dinner the day before. I went to the neighborhood Tom Thumb. I had chewed every mouthful of Scotch whiskey twenty-eight times and was tired, achy, hung. I had to get a-holt. She said that she would call. Sweet baby Jesus—

Stumbled around in the Tom Thumb like a Lilliputian. Checked the large eggs in the gray A1 carton, two were cracked. Bacon was full of pepper. Out of Country Wheat. Maybe some spaghetti? A pile of hothouse tomatoes from Canada, there were no Texas tomatoes this summer. Picked one from the pile, a bunch fell. Tomatoes bumped to and rolled on the floor. Crouched like a crab, scuttling to pick them up, came up with 'em, hit my head on the scales in the produce aisle . . . . Left my empty cart in the aisle and exited the store . . . .

She called about eleven, casual as a bird flying from limb to limb.

"Henry!" she said. "I have news, oh some great news for you! You'll have to wait 'til I can see you. I want to see your face! I'll pick you up, for lunch. Did you like Café Pacific? We could go to the City Café on Lovers, it's always nice and quiet. We could go to the Mansion on Turtle Creek, but there are always celebrities there. Not that we aren't celebrities!" She giggled.

"Listen," I said. "Lily. Did you hear? Bunky—President Bunker—of Highland—"

"Oh yes! You poor dear! Isn't that terrible? Why, it's just terrible"

"Yes. It is."

"Are you thinking—? Oh, Henry, you sweet, silly man! What a terrible, nasty thought. I know we said—you said—he should be shot, but you don't think for a minute, do you? I mean, he was a vile little man, and he deserved it, didn't he? But we would never— Good Lord, Henry Rose! It's a terrible coincidence, I gotta tell you. You know what I'm saying to you, Henry?"

"I think so."

"Good. Noon-ish. I hope you are good and hungry. I'm famished, just had oatmeal for breakfast. I am a growing girl. Trying to stay on 'Sugar Busters.' At least we can eat meat! I'll pick the place, I don't mind making decisions, you'll see, dear Henry Rose. Dress up. Look nice. Ta-ta!"

All right. You bet, Lily. Click. I recalled that after Caesar crossed the Rubicon he was out of dice. He'd just had one die, to begin with. I shaved and showered and put on a Burberry blue and white-collar shirt just like Tex Flatt's and my Brooks Brothers blazer and shod myself in Church's English shoes, did not touch the bottle. I was pretty hungry. Wore an Oxford tie, the red ox at the ford, silver university tower, blue background, from the men's store on Turl. Murmured, Be Calm, My Soul. It was a terrible coincidence. We didn't really want poor Bunky dead. Lordy. They were a bit strange, but Lily and her crazy father were game-playing, they were not in the business of whiffing people. Lily had good news, did she? Well, a bit of cheer would be quite welcome, actually, as the students said.

Lily came gliding up my street in her blue Lexus with gold signature as I went briskly out to greet her.

WE HAD RACK of lamb at the City Café. Lily nodded smugly at several people, elegant people, at the other tables, like she had returned from safari and had bagged me. I smiled generously around. We had Merlot. Lily wore a blue suit with lots of piping, a kind of military garb, and a hat with a long radishy feather in it, kind of like Myrna Loy or Claudette Colbert. Her foot in its low heel came up my leg and wiggled on my crotch. She murmured something like she hoped my mind was at peace and my spirit free, and I murmured back they were, shrinking back into my chair. The waiter asked if we'd have dessert, and Lily ordered rich chocolate cake and the foot came in again. I ate like a Marine, devoured the meat and crunched the bones. We never mentioned Bunky.

"So what's the good news?" I said.

She did the anaconda about to strike and hissed at me: "Daddy has decreed you are the Prince of Dallas!"

"I beg your pardon? Lily? Dear? How can that be?" I sat back, academic, bemused, Woodcipherean. Actually, I was relieved. It was all a game again. She looked across the table at me, cracked-eyed, pouty that I did not leap up and yell Hurrah! attracting the attention of the elegant clientele of ye City Café. "I mean," I said, "how can that be?"

"What do you mean, how can it be? It just is, Henry. Daddy named you, out of all the candidates, the Prince of Dallas. Aren't you thrilled? I am absolutely ecstatic."

"But the others we discussed. They had—qualifications. You know? This is—arbitrary. No?"

"Oh my.   Here, Marcus, another bottle of this stuff, por favor? Henry—" She looked around the room, saw she was attracting interest, lowered her strange, mellifluous then twangy voice that went up and down the scale so quickly, and said, "Being King is arbitrary. I mean, it is singular damn bidness. Why, Jesus, my sweet, if you are the King you can name anybody. You need to go study up on kings and what they do and how they act. Daddy can name anybody, and he has named you! I am thrilled, as I thought you would be."

"Why, I am honored. Flattered. Pleased. Indeed. And—"

"Yes?"

"I want you to know that I understand."

"What?"

"He did it for you."

"Well." She looked around the decorous room. "What's wrong with that?"

"Nothing. Nada y pues nada y nada y pues nada. Not a thing. It pleases me."

"The thing is, though, Henry, you have to believe in it. Daddy is the King of Texas. He named you. You are the Prince of Dallas."

"Okay. I will try to live up to it. I believe. I do."

I put a twinkle in my eye, as old Mark's King and Duke came to me.

"Yes, ma'am. 'I am the rightful Duke of Bridgewater, and here am I, forlorn, torn from my high estate, despised by the cold world, ragged, worn, heart-broken—' "

"Are you being funny? Don't be smarty, Henry Rose! Oh, are you serious? You may be a little down now, but you're not despised. Oh,

Henry. I'm sorry if you're ragged and heart-broken, but Lily will take care of you." She snaked her head, hat and feather on it, across the table to me. "And you will take care of me, won't you, Henry, dear dear sweet sweet Henry?"

I stared back at her; nodded in a kind of surprised, dog-like way; her eyes glittered hypnotically; it seemed to be enough.

I made to pay, but she simply signed the chit. She smiled imperiously at the people as we left arm in arm. "Stand straight, Henry," she said in my ear. "You are the Prince of Dallas now."

Who would know? I thought. Would it be in Peppard's or Bryant's gossip column? Mr. Stanley Marcus would be amazed. I would have to tell him it was not my idea. Ho ho.

In the leather seats of the Lexus, barreling down Lovers Lane, she said, "Since you're in –" It was like I had been dealt into a poker hand, jokers wild. "– I have to tell you, happy as I am – I am happy as a skylark, can't you hear my heart singing, Henry? We have a little problem. We're going to my other place. That's where my art is anyway and I want to show it to you. Daddy has been real worried about the Market, the N.Y.S.E. Also he is worried about the markets in the world. Daddy and George have gone together to stabilize the markets. They are getting after someone they all call 'the Hedgehog' up in the East who is playing Russian roulette, thinks he's smart. And bin Laden is truly a terrible man."

"Bin Laden? What's his name, Abou Ben Laden –"

"'May his tribe *not* increase.' Not funny. This is not *literary*, Henry. So anyway, someone, probably one of the international characters, has put a hit man on Daddy. It makes me furious! We've had to call up the King's Guard. We've made a safe ring around Daddy. They made my little house a Guard House. So I moved out, over to the other one."

"Come on, Lily," I said from the mind-numbing torpor of food and wine, my senses occupied with dazzle of sun on the windows, the deep leather seats, the gentle air-conditioning. This was getting out of bounds.

"But they think maybe they found him down in Waco."

"The hit man? Dear God, Lily, there aren't any assassins in Waco. The poor Branch Davidians were enough on the plate for Waco."

"Yes! I hate that terrible Janet Reno woman. Sent in tanks on women and children!"

"Well, they seem to have pretty well torched themselves."

"Every time," she said, thumping the leatherbound steering wheel, "you put a woman in power she thinks she has to act like a man only more so. Look at Hillary. Look at that old Albright! She'll have us in a dozen wars all over the world before she's through. Billy Boy Clinton, the adolescent retard, should put his pecker back in his britches and control that lady! No terrorists, hit men, in Waco? Oh, it's a wonderful quality, only a failed academic could have it these days. Henry, you are the most naïve person! You just stay tuned, and keep track like you say you do, not of your world but of the real world. There are a shitload of shadows flickering on the walls of our little cave here. You'll see."

A failed academic? Holy Hegel. I supposed she meant it was why I was so sweet.

Anyway, the old man was playing Besieged in his Castle, and we drove to Lily's other place.

"I got this for under two million," Lily said. "It was a steal."

The house was on a bluff, actually very like a protected castle, by itself, on several acres, in an old section of the city. Electric gates activated by the car phone opened to a drive that wound through landscaped grounds complete with topiaries of amorphous animals and painted wooden cutouts of a cattle herd which I imagined had been designed and done by Miss Lily herself. We parked under a carport by an enclosed three-car garage. We passed by several waterfalls by a series of turning stairs to the main entrance high above the driveway. We went in at treetop level with the afternoon sun so white and hot it scalded us. Karastan carpets lay on the teak floor, and all was marble and white oak. We stepped from the entry room to a formal living room into a library room with oak bookshelves going from the floor to the top of the ceiling. I looked up.

"Fourteen feet," said Lily. "You like it? I thought you'd like this room."

The Franklin and other leatherbound book series had been bought several times to fill the shelves. Around the corner was a wet bar.

"Let's go downstairs," she said. We got in an elevator and went down to the lower level, a master wing of bedrooms, bathrooms and exits to the pool cabana and garage, and a long gallery where Lily's work – her own paintings, drawings, crayon and pencil scrawls – were hung upon and stacked along the walls. A sheet of bulletproof glass and security devices separated us from an outdoor living room circled with trees.

"How interesting," I said.

"Yes. It was a steal."

"No," I said, as if I was used to multi-million dollar houses. "Your paintings, I mean."

Lily's actual oil paintings were all of large women, sometimes chasing, landing on or riding men who looked kind of like a naked Billy Roy if he had a hairy body, hammy buttocks and an ugly little red dick. The women were large, with long arms and legs all akimbo, cobalt eyes and purple-nippled akimbo breasts, with great orange and red and purple patches of bush and underarm hair. They were climbing, falling, levitating, floating and whatever. They were on the move all right. Lily herself began to clatter up and down the gallery like a pony in a stall.

"Never sold a single one," she said, but not sadly but with pride, as if, of course she hadn't, who could run with this? They weren't pretty and they weren't ugly, as my Uncle Sage used to say, they were pretty ugly. She looked at me, sweet dear Henry, eyes shining, for a judgment. Man, it was no time to say "interesting" again, or "what vigor" or "remarkable."

"I wish I knew the woman inside of these," I said. I was pleased with that. It was true. This Lily, she was something. The paintings did have vigor, strong color and line, and were shameless. I had an intellectual reaction, tinged with irony, and a visceral reaction, i.e., a hard-on.

"I don't know if you have ever seen them, but yours remind me of the paintings in the hotel on the Taos plaza that D.H. Lawrence painted there. Large men and women, with big breasts and butts, along the river, in the red rushes there."

"Well, I went in that hotel once, years ago, and tried to see them, had my two bucks out, and this weird old man was very rude to me."

"Oh?"

"They were in his office, and he said I could see them free if I would go upstairs and make the beast-with-two-backs with him. He was an *old* kind of a heavy man!"

"Lily, Lily, that was old Saki, the Greek guy who owned them. That wasn't rude. It was a compliment."

"Oh? Good. I'm glad then that Daddy didn't have Luther kill him. Everybody said they were awful, rude and crude and terrible art. Is that what you are telling me?"

"They had power, Lily. They were part of D.H. Lawrence's thing. You know?"

"You mean that they are sexy? Oh yeah?" She clapped her hands. "Oh, I'm so glad! I loved *Lady Chatterley's Lover*! I love to play 'The Lady and the Gardener!' Come on out here, I want to show you something. It's all right, everything is secure down here, and Billy Roy is on guard up in the rifle tower. Come on."

She took my hand. Hers was just a bit larger and stronger than mine. Led me to the door of the garage, beeped it unlocked and opened it, switched on the lights. In the garage were an antique '57 T-Bird, a squat, ugly Hummer and a gleaming big silver Mercedes.

"It's an original. Daddy used to drive it, then I did," she said, pointing to the T-Bird. "The first, little one. Can you imagine Daddy in that? Oh, he used to be so slim and handsome! He was a dude!"

Then she pointed one long arm at the Mercedes, and bowed to me, taking off the feathered cap and pointing with it, like Maid Marian saluting old Robin in the forest.

"A gift for you, my Prince," she said.

I went over and ticked the massive silver machine on the windshield, tried to see inside the tinted windows. She clicked the Unlock on the key remote. I opened the door. It was all executive suite in there, airplane console, black leather cocoon. I felt a sadness.

"Oh, Lily," I said. "I'm sorry. It's not for me."

"What do you mean? Are you crazy, out of your gourd?"

"No. I'm in my gourd. It's not my style, Lily. I'm sorry. I hate Mercedes."

"Oh. Henry. You mean, because it's German and you're Jewish?"

"No. I told you. I'm not Jewish, I don't think."

"Your ancestor's name was Moses."

"Well, he was a wanderer, a mercenary, like."

"So what are you saying, Henry? This is a beautiful, very Goddamn wonderful, expensive car. It is judged to be the ultimate road car. What is that old piece of shit you drive? A Mercury? I thought you would be *thrilled*." Lily was getting pissed.

I thought I better be straight with her. "Buick," I said. "I don't care for foreign cars. I don't think we should be buying them."

"Bullshit! Everything is international, transnational now, Henry! Daimler and Chrysler, everyone is going in together."

"I'm surprised that you drive Japanese. Your daddy has a Lincoln, right? Anyway, I have a special thing – actually a horror – of Mercedes. You see, when I was a boy in Ohio – in Missouri, I mean – my father took me to see a friend of his, this was actually after he moved to Miami,

I think, and I don't know what this fellow did, if he was in the Mob or what, but he had this classic Mercedes in his garage, I believe it had belonged to Hitler."

"Uh huh," Lily said, looking at me pouty-lipped, bug-eyed, hat in hand, feather tickling the floor of the garage. "So?"

"So this fellow leaned into the front seat, showing us this great old car, and caressed the seats with his hand, and looked at us smiling like a salesman, and said, 'Jew skin.' My father was horrified. He took my hand and we got out of there. I was five years old. 'What does it mean?' I asked him. 'It means there is a lot of evil in the world,' he said."

"Well, that was a bad experience. And there is, a lot of evil. Oh my yes. Did that really happen, Henry? I can't imagine a person, in this country, *keeping* such a thing. Never mind. Obviously you don't want my gift. We'll get you a nice old Roadmaster station wagon."

I shut the door on the rich-smelling interior of the gleaming car. She clicked the lock and clicked off the garage lights and went back in the entrance to the gallery, leaving me to stumble along behind.

Inside she stood in a ballet stance, one foot on the other, dejected.

"Lily, thank you."

"I thought the Prince of Dallas shouldn't go around in that old heap, that's all. I'll trade my Lexus for one of those Cads with Northstar in the morning if that's how you feel. I tried to think of other things. You know? I thought I'd give you a Chair, fill it with roses and make you guess, but I thought that might embarrass you."

"A chair?"

"Sure. Endow you one. Just two mil, Henry. 'The Henry Rose Professor of English.' Then when you retired or died, your name would go on, and meanwhile you could have a Chair with your own name on it. But I know you would be too modest to want that."

Oh? Now that was a damn good, a brilliant idea! Go, Lily!

"Lily, my dear girl, you don't need to give me anything. I don't need a present. Thank you for the kind thought, but I am honored by the – honor – that your father has done me, unworthy of it as I am."

"But I wanted to give you something! Goddamn it, Henry!" She stamped her foot.

"Lily, dear, all I want is you."

Eyes glittering, she came towards me and when she reached me grabbed my belt in one hand, my rear in the other, and put her homely mug to mine. I took this as acceptance of the proposition.

"Would you like to play 'Monica and Bill'?" she said, undoing my belt, going for the fly.

"I am constitutionally opposed to that," I said.

"You are some weird guy," she said, stepping back, licking her lips, starting to undress. She led me by all the forms of the wild surreal women with pubic hair prancing and dancing and contorting on the walls down the hall to the master bedroom and to the great playground of the bed.

Lily had a sweet long body with a rounded rear and little cup of belly. Her calves and thighs were muscled from riding, her inner thighs soft as cocoa butter. She had sweet nipples, as she had never given suck to child, the color, texture and taste of ripe plums when they rose. The hollow of her throat was tender, her mouth thin and irregular but smooth as pecan pie inside. Her long limbs were none too gainly and off-putting in the preliminaries, but finding her you found a smooth tunnel, sensate, liquid and ferocious as a turtle.

After that first random bout and a gentle kiss on the ear, Lily confided she usually liked a little structure. She had a set of sexual fantasies, of which "Monica and Bill' was just the opening of the door. There were in the girl-part of her mind, some, like acting out sex moves to funky Elvis songs, untried yet in fact. She confided she had not had sex for a long time, she did not wish to demean herself, or Daddy, or what they stood for, and I believed her. I told her I had not had sex since Myrtle Springs, and she believed that too. She was no goddess, and unlike Bill, the distinguishing characteristic of my privates was that they were not distinguished; but we were not disappointed. I felt happy if not peaceful in her arms. She asked me what sex fantasy I had in mind that I would like to try.

I said, oh, I had always liked Maupassant's "A Passion in the Desert," the leopard who finds the soldier and fiercely guards and loves him. Now there was a movie of it. Oh, we'd have to go and see it. Sounded cool. Lily would be the leopard. All I can say of that, she had a leopard's tongue. Hours later, as we stirred again, she said I could be the leopard. She was a hell of a French soldier, too. I felt the spirit of my old kinsman, who'd left the Alamo, for all I knew, so that I might be here on a blistering July Texas day in Lily's bed, look down upon us with pleasure – C'est bon – and approval.

"Just stay here, Henry," sweet Lily said as I crawled up finally from the vast Loch Ness of her bed.

"I need to go to Bunky's – to our slain president's – visitation," I said.

"Oh, that," she said. "You can take the Hummer."

This seemed to amuse her greatly. I left her uncoiling from the bed, tall, right regal, naked, laughing, heading up to the wet bar.

I DROVE THE Lexus out along Greenville Avenue to Restland Memorial Park. There were several chapels and other buildings from which the straights and diagonals and squares of tombstone lines radiated out, and no one in the information booth. It was coming on to twilight as I parked and chose the nearest building. I came into a hall with a crowd of people ahead and many colorful urns of flowers. I wondered who in such numbers would have sent flowers for Bunky. I saw not a soul from the university. In fact, these were all Hispanic people. I began to pedal back.

"Ah, Señor! My friend Henry! Emilio, this is Mr. Henry Rose, a friend of many years . . . ." It was my tree-man Ray Rodriguez who had me by the hand.

"We appreciate very much your coming, sir. He was our great compadre, a valued leader of our movement," said Emilio, a man of very dark eyes and much mustache. "They say that it was suicide, but surely it was not!"

Ray Rodriguez moved his hand sideways, in a deprecating way. "It is the little movement in which my son is involved, which I mentioned to you, Henry."

I saw the placard on the wall before the room with the closed casket said: Oscar Hernandez.

"I must confess, Ray, that I have made a mistake. I am here by chance."

Emilio nodded and walked into the crowd. Ray nodded and said, "Perhaps fate brought you here, amigo. Qué va."

"And who was he? Señor Hernandez?"

"He was the secretario of the U.H.F., the United Hispanic Front, a man of gravity, someone who seemed wise, to be playing at this game, eh? Perhaps it makes us feel important, do you think? It is a nice coincidence, any-way, to see you here, Henry. We fought in the same war, for the U.S.A. We must remember that." Ray turned to make his way to the casket.

I went out of that building and into the one across the way. There in the outer room the placard read: Bert T. Bunker.

Old Professor Lumpkin, of Philosophy, and Ms. Applebaum and Regina Singh and two people from Economics and three from the sciences and John Woodcipher were standing in a circle around Bunky's wife Patricia and their two small children, murmuring to them. A picture of Bunky looking very young sat on the closed casket. I had expected him to be smiling horribly at me; but after all he had been shot in the head. I approached the little circle.

"My God! My God!" the woman, Mrs. Bunky, screamed. "You killed him! Oh, I know you did! You killed him, Henry Rose!"

"Now, now," John Woodcipher said, patting, trying to soothe her, but she flung away from him as I turned and headed for the exit.

I passed Tex Flatt coming in. He flicked me a hand. I made a tragic face. He looked like one grim old gubuddy.

I drove home and checked the phone and mail. There was a card in the mail slot from a Homicide detective who wanted to talk to me. Lily was on the voicemail. She was cooking *veal*. She would open an aged French bottle for us. I locked the house and got back in the Lexus and drove around, before too long heading back to Lily's pad on Bluff View. The car was hers, and I thought I had better get it back to her, didn't want her coming after me in that Hummer.

I flashed and the electronic gates came open. I drove up the winding drive to the lit-up castle where Billy Roy was standing rifle-guard in the tower, the Prince returning to his princess.

NINE

"What do you mean, she went away?" Lily said. "Is that a euphemism for she died? I really don't care, but I certainly do hope so, Henry. You just say, 'Oh, she went away' or 'she departed.' Do you close your eyes and see her when you're hosing me?"

"Not hardly." I laughed. We had been enacting the sex fantasy of Elvis's "Are You Lonely Tonight." The chairs in her parlor had stood lonely and bare as she looked at her stairway and wished I was there and then I came creeping in to the actual music, and she looked shocked to see me, looking over her shoulders on the football field-size bed with pillows under her and I entered her from behind and Elvis crooned—it was a song that broke him up in one version of it—"Are you lonesome tonight?"—and Lily screamed in answer, "No!" I don't know what made her think of Myrtle Springs, except during sex Lily let herself get down to the level of "Are your eyes open or closed? What are you thinking of?" I supposed it was something denied her in her youth. She rolled over and took me in hand and ticked me with that razor-sharp long blue fingernail.

"Yes. She departed. 'Went west,' as they say in Texas, Lily. Actually, she went away a good deal during the time we lived here in Dallas, on trips, mostly east."

"Where did she go?"

I thought the question deserved a precise reply. "To Elysian Fields, in East Texas," I said. "It was home. She would go there to visit her friends, Ada Taylor, Marshall Henderson and the others who lived down the road from her. She was a good and loyal spirit."

"So am I. You'll see, Henry. Elvis—Elvis. What else is there to do of Elvis?"

"How about a little slow dance, all Elvis aside?"

She fell asleep. I thought of Myrtle Springs. She was a pure person and came back to me from time to time. Now she clucked at me, like a hen chastising a bad old rooster. Myrtle Springs cherished the Bible, which said never to call a person a fool, but I could tell she was close to it. Raca, fool. My father, Aaron Rose, always told me to cherish life for it is short. When I was a boy he walked out with me into his fields of corn, his tangled berry bushes, his splendid grape arbors flourishing on his Ohio acres. "Cherish life, Henry," he said, "for it is fleeting, and beware of it." It made me not wish to believe in death. Always I avoided death. I pretended that grim cold rocky place we were sent to fight some strange foe was a vacation, a play, a movie in which I was an extra. No one died in my Korea. It was like watching cinema now, like watching *Wake Island* and *Corregidor* with my father before that. I stood aloof from death as an absurdity, handled it abstractly, philosophically, as per Camus in a story. My own scant writings were Aurelian, pre-Christian, for I also did not believe in any of the given solaces for death, certainly not that we rattled around up yonder ever after. In that I am quite Jewish. This is it, old dear. Mainly, of course, I played out life and death through my surrogate world, my "field"—just as my father Aaron had his field of blooming things—literature. It was a game even richer and more engaging than that which Lily and her ridiculous father played.

Poor Bunky was a spirit or a memory now, depending on which view you held. I went back out to his grave, having been so rudely chased away from the visitation room and then not caring to attend the funeral if I was going to so upset the family. It was one hundred degrees. The wind blew in south from Bunky's native Oklahoma, I supposed. The Lakota tradition says the wind comes to visit death. It danced around his gravestone, bits of dust and motes of heat arising from his already parched little carpet of new grass. On the prairie at Highland U. they would place a plaque on a bench for him. Mr. Bunky, he dead. Whatever, as he himself said the students say. Like the Lakota poet, I could only tell his story, the part of it I knew, and admit that I despised him.

Sam McGee, the Homicide dick, was black. He came to see me, did not call me in. Came easing around to my office on campus, where I would go to sit and read the classics between bouts with Lily. "Lotta books here," he said. "You read all of these?"

"Yep," I said. "Yep."

"No leather books," he said. "I like them leather books."

"Yeah, it's nice to feel of them. You can kind of oil 'em while you read 'em. Most folks don't read 'em much though."

"Speaking of which—it is Doctor Rose?"

"Yes. I am a veterinarian."

"Hah. That's cute. She, the wife, is obsessed you had something 'r 'nother to do with it."

"I am terribly sorry."

"He fired you."

"I am basically a teacher, a professor. We come and go in these administrative jobs."

"You didn't get along."

"Philosophical."

"That is dangerous shit, that philosophy."

" 'The Most Dangerous Game.' True. But our wars are—"

"Academic."

"You got it. I—"

"Oh man, I just have to ask you, for the record. Right? I mean, this is some ace pro job, man. This is a professional. We are still trying to figure how the shooter got in and out. It's like magic. I mean, it obviously wasn't you." Meaning an obvious vague, bumbledicking academic fellow. "You never killled no one, did you?" He looked around the office at all the books.

"I was in the Marine Corps."

"You and Lee Harvey Oswald." By which I took it he meant he doubted it, that I was a Marine. I should have kept my trap shut. He looked at me with new interest, Sam did. He had a big gold tooth and a gold earring in one ear. If I lied about one thing . . . Then he said, "We will never know *why*."

"Maybe he felt he was in over his head. He had an awful lot going on. He was on the line to raise millions. Is there any chance you haven't found the weapon?"

He put his finger, like a barrel, to the back of his head. "You mean like he shot himself in the head and then went and hid the gun? Sorry to bother you, Professor."

If I'd kept my yap shut I could have been rid of him. A few days later, checking into my University Park pad, I noticed the small random displacements that meant my rooms had been gone through. They checked my accounts at the bank, in case I'd paid out for the assassin. I did not use my deadbolts so it would be easier for them to get in the next time, but left the alarm on so Sam wouldn't think anything was fishy. In

my private time I was rereading *The Good Soldier*, which I much
enjoyed.

But there was little private time. Miss Lily McIvey had me over her
fender and was showing off my points, in the heat of damn July plunging
us into the endless Dallas social whirl.

"Summer is so slow in Dallas," her friend Gloria, a babe about
Lily's age with highly stylized hair who would always pat you on the
rear with a strangely detached look, told me. You could have fooled me.
"Just wait till September, there's the Cattle Baron's Ball and, oh, a whole
buncha fun things! Lily, did you see what I got me for the Cattle Baron's
Ball? It's getting to where you can't hardly wear anything distinctive to
stand out anymore!" Gloria stood out about a mile in front, so that her
bust and voice preceded her. "I got me a big black beaver with old-
turquoise silver conchos for a band, Lester got it for me in Santa Fe, isn't
that sweet? It'll show up real good in the photos, last year I was so
furious, that dumpy little Doris Waltenburg got in the pitchers of the
Cattle Baron's Ball, and I didn't!"

Lily told her she'd had a concho hat like that for years. She loved to
gig poor old Gloria, who was on the climb from over in Paris, Texas.
Gloria's Lester, you had to admit, was an Armstrong and had played
football at Texas A&M back in the Dark Ages. Lily had this circle of
older, Old Texas friends but for now insisted on taking me, as a proper
trophy, to all the Dallas hotspots and Dallas "foodie circles." We plowed
through the soaring heat with the ultra-hip to mondo cool gallery shows,
drank straight Stoli at the Art Bar, where women smoked cigars, watched
the casual cool cats and birds at Aqua Knox, ate tapas and drank Vino
Toro at Café Madrid, where I told Lily of my sojourn in Spain, and
luckily I had really been there for of course she'd had a year in old
España too, had English roast in the gold-walled Barclays and steak at
the Palm, huge luscious steaks with creamed spinach on the side, oceans
of Merlot. Lily kept us on the Sugar Busters diet, so we could eat endless
amounts of meat, drink endless wine and just so we did not eat corn or
potatoes or pasta stay slim, healthy and sexually vigorous and inventive.
Several times our pictures, Lily and me, appeared with those of other
calm, bespectacled men and smiley blondes with firm clefts and shining
eyes and teeth in the society pages of the *Dallas Morning News: Teeny
and Al Beck, Lily McIvey, Henry Rose*. It was amazing how many people
saw and remarked these tiny photos of us amidst the swarm of social
bees. John Woodcipher clucked at me, said, *otra vez*, "Cuidado, boy.
You in control, Henry?" Ms. Applebaum, now his loyal assistant, smiled

at me forgivingly, even coyly, in tribute to this new and unexpected fame.

ONE NIGHT with the Becks, Teeny and Al, we went to dinner along Turtle Creek at the McDuffs, old McDuff being a friend and associate in various ventures with Oliver McIvey and Victoria McDuff a famous former beauty and collector of—stuff. "If I like it, I buy it," as she said. Old Duff McDuff had built her an Italian villa with high ceilings and dark rooms, jam-packed with a jumble of stuff from around the world. We ate on gold plates with gilded forks and knives and drank from silver goblets chased with gold. I sat at the long Georgian table under a tapestry of saints among a former ambassador, a retired general and an admiral and their bejeweled wives. There was a bit of awkwardness until the admiral, ambassador and general decided I could be addressed as "Professor." They talked of the Good Old Days in Dallas, meaning when the Oligarchy clearly ran it and before the Republic and the First National and the Mercantile banks crashed and oil and real estate went bust more than a decade ago. They cherished the quixotic figures from that and the farther back past, old "Uncle Bob" Thornton, the mayor who ran the "Yes or No" Citizens Council and said, "Let's roll up our sleeves and build Dallas" after the terrible faux pas of the Assassination, and old H. L. Hunt, the frugal, unpretentious right-wing billionaire who carried his lunch in a paper sack and drove an old Pontiac car, and who brought his second family over from Shreveport when his first wife died.

"He was a true gambler," old McDuff said from the head of the table, leagues up the way. "All the Hunts are gamblers. Old H. L. won his first oil well in a poker hand over there in El Dorado, Arkansas. I heard it from Albert Lakey, who was over there then. Then Herbert and Bunker—" General laughter. They all knew what the Hunt brothers had tried, to corner the silver market. "Damn near did it, too!"

Down at our end Victoria, the hostess, said in her cultured Texas-cum-Smith voice and tone, "Mr. Hunt came here to dinner once. I believe it made him most uneasy. He left early—though they said he always did. He did admire the red Turkey rug in the entryway."

They looked at her expectantly. "No," she said. "He did not crawl about on it. He was an eccentric, not a fool."

Lily's sharp fingernail dug into my thigh, like, That's the point, you catch that, Buddy Boy? "Professor Rose is like that," she said aloud to the table. "He is so modest of his accomplishments, why, he has taught at

Oxford, and everywhere. And Henry—" Looks around the expectant table. "—drives an old—something—just like Mr. Hunt did."

"Buick," I murmured.

Old McDuff raised his gold-chased goblet to me, as the conversation quickly shifted to a less boring topic, the collection of Asian art which a Dallas entrepreneur owned and for which he was furnishing a new downtown museum for displaying it to the public. They had kept it for years, unseen, in their private home. Mr. MeWhinny, a young artist in the community and admirer of the family, whose name was Crow, now took the ball and galloped happily down the field with it.

"It is glorious," he said, "a fabulous collection! What civic spirit to share it with us! It is rare, priceless, sui generis. They are putting it in the building in the middle of downtown, renovating it just for the collection, leasing the space for fifty years!"

"What happens after that?" said the general, whom I had seen on television as an analyst during the Gulf War crisis.

"Why— Why, surely someone will buy the building before then, and donate it!" he exclaimed, looking right at Lily. I was beginning to think she really had a buck or two. "Anyhow, I have seen the collection, and it is mondo marveloso, of course on a smallish scale. There is a jade Tong horse, a China lacquer piece carved with endless dragons, a hardwood, hardstone and jade carved throne that went behind the Imperial screen—and then, the *screen*—"

"Think of ripping off all that stuff and keeping it just for yourself," I whispered to the sweet Lily. I did not know how much that upset her until we had said our good evenings to the McDuffs and their guests and their villa and she was driving us in her Lexus SUV—she had not traded for a Cadillac with Northstar but had upgraded in the Lexus line—on Preston Road up from Turtle Creek and by the estates that sloped down to the creek of Governor Clements, the oilman Ed Cox and Cowboys owner Jerry Jones.

"What the hell's the matter with you, Henry? You sound like a nut, like a Communist or a radical! I sure am glad you didn't say that *aloud*!"

"Damn straight, Lily. I mean it. They should give it back to where it belongs. To China, Japan, wherever they took it from."

"Listen here, Henry Rose. Let me give you three damn reasons why not, you hear? Don't you be sidling your hand—quit!—while I am talking to you!"

"Yes, ma'am."

"Don't you see, this is *wonderful*, in the first place, for all this big population of Asians we have in Dallas now. It will appeal to them."

"They're going to like it that they were robbed of all that stuff?"

"Absolutely! Sure. They all left those places and came here, didn't they? Second—quit pawing around for my sexbud, I am driving, Henry—where would it all be if the Crows hadn't relieved them of it? Answer me that. This kind of collection is a *service* to society, to humanity, Henry. You should realize that. Most museums are tied into your universities, aren't they? And, in the third place— Oh, Henry, not *that* place, oh Golly—It *belongs* to the Crows. They *bought* it. It's *property*! They are tremendously generous to restyle this perfectly good business building and give it to us, to the public to see, free! So shut up. Ahhh! You are a terrible person, Henry Rose— That's a bad tendency you're demonstrating— Oh, no, not that, that's f-f-fine— Oh shit! A bad tendency, to think like that, for a prince, for a king—"

Later, in bed, she said, "No kidding, Henry. Don't make me worry about you. You aren't going to turn out to be some sort of kook—or nut—a socialist or something, are you?"

"Oh no," I said, "never fear," the pearl of great price once more between my fingers.

I SUPPOSED that kings have their paranoias and that regicide is a major one of them. There were no Levies, and we skipped several Inner Circles in July, and cancelled the session for me on philanthropy, since they were playing the game that a "contract" had been taken out on Daddy because he and the character called "George" were trying to stabilize the international markets and supposedly had upset several people including the notorious Osama bin Laden, hiding over there in Afghanistan. Lily slipped me a clipping one morning stating that a hitman for him had been found and arrested by the Texas Rangers in Waco. She simply sniffed, as in, See there, Smarty! In August, then, our embassies were bombed in Dar-Es-Salaam and in Nairobi. Something was going on in the world, but certainly beyond the bounds of the little game being played by His Majesty Oliver McIvey, self-styled King of Texas.

His own Texas was in no great shape that terrible summer of 1998, either. It was, truly, a cataclysmic time for Texas, as for the nation and the world. As the editor of *Texas Monthly* so aptly summed it up early in September, it was a time of clear blue sky, no rain, thirty days over one hundred degrees in Dallas. The damnable drought. Driest growing season of record in San Antonio. Second-driest in Austin, Dallas and Fort

Worth. Giant cracks in the dry earth. More than a hundred deaths from the summer heat. Illegal immigrants dying from the heat after crossing the Rio Grande. 106 degrees in Dallas in August, sky over the famous skyline turned black. Shifting ground broke the main water line in Fort Worth. Train derailments from "sun kinks" in the tracks. A $5 billion loss to Texas agriculture and agribusinesses. A horrible high pressure mountain that would not move away. The Dry Rock would not crack. God was angry. As Lily and Henry cavorted and played their way through the summer months.

TEN

Then on a Thursday the old boy summoned us. This was startling, for he loved his Thursdays, called them each "Sweet Thursday," his day to pleasure and to please himself. He read—he really did read those leather books from the library in the baroque Texas Room where he held Levies—Marco Polo, Winston Churchill and *Travels in Arabia Deserta* being among his favorites. And he would watch his favorite movies, *Doctor Zhivago*, *She Wore a Yellow Ribbon*—he loved the scene in which Quincannon, the master sergeant, old Victor McLagen, laughs and drinks and knocks down nine lesser soldiers who try to take him to the guardhouse, exclaiming all the while in Irish brogue, "Ah, the old days are gone forever!" And on Thursdays he liked to play endless games of easy seven card across and five down Solitaire at which he found ingenious different ways to cheat and never lost.

"There is something special on his mind. He has never ever wanted to see us on a Thursday," Lily said. "See, what he does basically on Thursday is rest up for Friday, for the public time."

We drove from Lily's over to Strait Gate Way. I noticed a car parked down on Lily's street start up and follow us. It was a plain tan Ford and I imagined it must be Sam McGee seeing where I was going, who my contacts were. We had not been to Daddy's since Sam got on my case. I mentioned it to Lily. She slowed down so Sam got right up behind us, flipped him the finger, and accelerated. He came right on behind. We passed into Lily's graystone house's driveway, now barricaded and turned into a guard house by the King's Guard, and they stopped him there. He turned around and went and parked on down the street. I thought it must be boring for Sam, unless he enjoyed speculating on what was going on with a bunch of cowboys in big hats and boots and carrying automatic rifles, on what they were doing manning the entrance to an apparently simple little house in this pretty, meandering treed part of Dallas.

They had a lot of guys on duty, some electronic gates, an expensive game. Guys with rifles in scabbards on beautiful horses rode the perimeter of the King's redbrick mansion. The creek had been made dry and the little bridge removed so no explosives could get up under it. I saw what I took to be mortars and bazookas and machine gun emplacements on the grassy slope leading from Lily's to her father's house. The grass had been let go brown. At the command tent in front of the King's place stood a giant of a fellow, about six foot eight and 300 pounds with a strangely scarred face and agatey eyes. Looking down on us, he smiled at Lily as we approached arm in arm.

"Miss Lily," he said.

"Oh, Luther, you sweet thing!" she said. "Henry, this is Luther. I've told you about Luther? Colonel Luther McLuther. Luther, you know, is captain of the King's Guard, whenever we need him to be. Actually, he is foreman of Daddy's ranch, the Rex Ranch. And he is Daddy's—nephew."

"Cousin, removed, Miss Lily. My granddaddy was brother to your mama's sister. McAlmons, from Angelo, out there. How do you do, sir?" Huge hand, shaken loosely. "I am pleased to meet the new Prince of Dallas. Eh? Sure do hope you fare better than the last one. Eh, Lily? Little joke, sir, just a little joke 'tween me and Miss Lily here."

"How is Daddy?"

"Doin' fine. Restless, I think. Was tryin' to walk on canes. Stubborn old cuss. Fell. He's all right, tho'. I got holt of a copy of *Saving Private Ryan* and we watched that, he didn't like it all that much. Said he preferred *The Longest Day*, that D-Day film, to it, still." One side of his scarred lip turned down in an aside to me. "Likes the Scots coming in over the bridge with the bagpipes playin', I think is the reason he loves that one so."

"Like in *Gunga Din*," I said.

"Yeah. Likes that one too, though as a field commander I think it is durned silly. Climbing up on that temple dome with a bugle. But the Old Man likes a little melodrama, he doesn't mind a bit of bullshit, eh?" Looking at me as I had been mentioned in those terms.

"Everything secure?" said Lily.

"No sign of anything or anyone. No approaches, even, except that unmarked police car just down there now."

"Following me. I seem to be a suspect in a murder."

"Yeah, Prince. Right. He has been following you, we been following him." He grinned crookedly again, as if this was another little joke—though it was news to me.

"Thank you so much, Luther, for all you do. Daddy and I do appreciate it. It's so ridiculous! It's terrible! They should be shot for threatening Daddy! I mean—" A look at me. "Are there any leads?"

"There's a fellow come to town. We are watching him. Right over here in Arlington. Working in a tire store. I reckon the Feds will pick him up. We don't need to shoot him yet." Another little laugh. Either Luther really enjoyed playing this elaborate game or he was getting paid real well. They let us through the cordons and we entered Daddy's dark abode.

Billy Roy was back over guarding Lily's Bluff View place. T.J. Mackey was sitting oiling a rifle in the Texas Room.

"You wait a minute here. I'll go on in," said Lily.

"How they hanging, Prince," said T.J. Mackey to me with a slight sneer.

"They hanging pretty low," I replied. "Hanging pretty low."

He smiled grudgingly at my good-naturedness.

"You kind of like guns, do you?" I said to him.

"No more, sir, than knives," he said. "I do admire knives."

I nodded, fingering the dull Oldtimer in my pocket, remembering him whicking with his Case knife.

In a while Miss Lily burst out upon our soundless sea, smiling happily. "He wants to see you. Alone," she said, giggling, or more like the snorting of a filly. Oh my, I thought, LSAT time. I gave I was now sure the quite evil Mr. Mackey a cavalier salute and betook H. Rose into the presence of the King.

He was chuckling, chortling, snorting, chuffing, snuffling like a hog as I approached.

"Oh, hello, my boy! My dear Pro-fessor! Prince! How do you be? Howdy-do-do-do-do-do-do! Oh, this is rich! Look at this, Henry Rose—this is really rich!"

Today he was modestly dressed in a kind of drab Mao suit with a banded collar, no signs of myth or rank on him except the garish, gaudy ring of kingship. He was in a leather chair with great carved legs heaving with mirth like a tickled Jabba the Hut. He reached his arm out for me to receive a newspaper clipping, to share in this wonderful source of mirth.

I took and looked at it. It was a story in a West Texas weekly newspaper, a story repeated from being in the paper a hundred years ago.

I read it as the King of Texas sat heaving, snorting, applying a handkerchief to his nose, recovering from its terrible humor. It read in full: "Sheriff A.T. Lilly states that in a fight at a dance last Saturday night on the Shimerda farm near Thalia, one Negro shot a pistol at another and the bullet struck the Negro squarely in the forehead, tore a hole in his hat and pierced the skin, but when the bullet struck the skull, it turned upward, traveled between the skull and scalp and came out the top of the hat. The bullet did not kill the Negro."

"Oh, my. Oh, my. Luther brought me that . . . . Wish I could find me one, a Ne-gro, like that these days! They don't make 'em like they used to. McMurtry made a good one, in old Deets—"

I wished Sam McGee were here to share the moment. I was sure he would appreciate the humor or the parable, as the case might be, of the story of the tough-skulled Negro. "I'm amazed they would reprint it, these days," I said.

"Ah? What? Yes! Multiculturalism! Exactly! Let the Negro be the Negro, I say! Some things you just can't change, eh, Rose? Don't get me wrong!" A royal decree. "We are not being racist here. No, the thing is the bullet—you see? It's like that crazy bullet that supposedly went through Kennedy and turned and went in and out of Connally."

"The first time we met you mentioned the assassination—asked if I knew who killed JFK. You haven't mentioned it since."

"The assassination? Who mentioned the Goddamn assassination?"

"You said you would tell me who did it, sometime. Didn't you?"

"Did I? Oh, my. Yes. Why—Mr. Mackey shot JFK. Right, Mr. Mackey?"

"With a little help from my friends," T.J. Mackey said with a short laugh. I had not noticed that he had slipped in behind me and stood by the wall, no doubt on guard against the possibility that I might be after all an enemy agent and try to assassinate the King of Texas.

The King ceased mirthfulness. Said with terrible seriousness: "What I will say to you, dear boy, is that you—everybody—can understand the Kennedy incident better now, in the light of the profligate Clinton monster, that Boy who is shaming us now. Kennedy, in his behavior, brought shame. It was a *moral* act. But it was not a *Texas* act. It was not a Texas thing, I want to assure you of that. That was what was so bad about it. Maybe one day you and Mr. Mackey can have a chat about it, it was a real complex thing." Mr. Mackey shrugged, as if that would be a long day coming. "Thing-a-ding-a-ding! I do want to assure you that my old friend Lyndon—LBJ—had nothing—nada—to do with it. Well, now, Henry, look at you—getting to be a dude, eh? Eh? Wearing a bolo. And that bolo looks familiar. Don't it look familiar to you, Mr. Mackey? Old blue turquoise, old Navajo silver. If I didn't know better, I'd say that once belonged to me! Lily gave you that, did she, Professor?"

I nodded that he had me—and her—dead to rights. He motioned to me to sit in the smaller leather chair next to him. He motioned for T.J. Mackey to leave the room. The fellow raised his eyebrows, supercilious in the literal sense, got a vigorous hand motion like a whack to the head, and left. I was trusted. Actually in the moment I thought of reaching over, taking the old man's windpipe between my fingers and crushing it; but I knew it would displease Lily. I sat and let the pointed ostrich toe and shaft of my new custom-made Lucchese boot protrude from the cuff of my charcoal trouser as I crossed my princely legs. The old toad licked his lips and ticked his hand on the boot toe with a child's delight.

"Now, Henry," he said, "there is a learning curve for you, so you can begin to understand this endeavor which I govern as the King of Texas. Now, you see, we have the foundation and the Fund. Both are called T-Rex, though both have other names as well, in various places, in various countries, etc. We are active in philanthropy, but the essence of our being, and I know this is not very Texas, Henry, my boy, but it is very necessary for effectiveness and protection of our interests, and ourselves—threatened in this very moment by that monster, that old bearded, turbaned Sammy—Is that we do it very quietly. You understand. Not like a Turner or a Gates. I was reading that they call that young fellow, Bill Gates, the King of the Rain City. Well, good for him! He has a foundation, though it is only worth eight hundred million— while he is worth fifty-sixty billion. His partner is like our young boys here, Perot, Hicks and Hunt, he owns the team and owns downtown Seattle, a terrible place to have to live, you would be wet-soaked all the time though I will say we could use a little of it now here in Texas, it's so bad the Baptists are postponing and the Methodists are just licking. Anyway, it's the same philosophy, whatever. Which is this, Rose."

He explained to me the basic principles by which he, and Gates and Turner in their domains, and all of them—Soros in his world—operated. It was a sacred principle. You must make a profit as you give. Your giving and your goodness, on whatever scale, must set up a future profit, or at least add to or strengthen your position, practically or philosophically, above the ground or under it, like the brilliant old banker boys in earlier Dallas who loaned money on oil under the ground. Tex

Flatt was willing to give a million or two to Highland U. to perpetuate his name—the Flatt Tower—but also because Highland University was not deconstructive, multicultural and feminist, students would learn the basic things in the good old ways, their ideas would not be subversive to everything he had himself done and believed. (I wanted to say, look out, the old liberal arts can be pretty damn subversive, but I quieted the old Socrates demon in me and did not interrupt his doxology.) On a much larger scale George Soros was a huge and beneficent investor in a world he wished to influence to his vision and his politics and his profit. So it was with the King of Texas, as he looked over his realm, and beyond, to the interests of Texas in the world. His slatey old eyes settled into clear, gunmetal gray and he looked more solid, less a caricature, as he spoke. I wondered what my wise old Uncle Sage Rose would have said about him. Not much, I reckoned, for I doubted Uncle Sage had ever met his like. He peered at me to see if the Pro-fessor understood.

I thought I should reply so as not to appear uninterested, ambivalent. I asked him if he took a hand in the affairs of Dallas, or if he anticipated that I should do so, as the Prince of Dallas.

No, he said. There was no need. The King of Texas had no real need to meddle in Dallas. The developers ran Dallas just fine. Everything went according to the King's philosophy in Dallas; he left it alone, it was in perfect equation with his own values. Right now he was taking a hand in Texas. As I had noticed, it was a rough time in Texas. Been drought, and flood was coming on. The farmers and the ranchers and the little people needed help. But then, in Texas, everything looked good for the election in the fall. Texas would be a Republican Republic, a Fortress Republican. Lily would be working on some of the campaigns, for young George W. and them. She was already lining up most of the West Texas sheriffs to do TV ads for young Rick Perry, he would be the governor when George W. went off to be the President and restore honor to the nation and bring new glory and clout and profits to Texas! Meanwhile, sir, there was the Goddamn bloody world—!

Highland U.—universities—museums—symphonies—these kinds of things—were easy. Lily had some idea about our little university, Highland, what Tex Flatt was doing there was no more *relevant* than teats on a boar! A university or a museum was easy to lift. But all the poor suffering screwed-up nations trying to get their systems right, to be capitalist nations without the capital! America and everybody was suffering from strained systems—from finance to football to ethics. The fellow that said that institutions don't fit the problems was right! George

Bush the Elder in his wisdom was right! It was a Goddamn New World
Order, all right. You had to be a Point of Light in the world! It had to be,
Lift it, Keep it up, do whatever to make capitalism and democracy, or our
form of it, Henry, dear boy, work world-wide! Volunteerism, on the
largest scale! Philanthropy in hitherto unheard-of ways! Grab it! Don't
let go! Ahh—

The volume had risen high. Lily poked her head in. "Are you all
right?" she said. "Henry, are you exciting Daddy?"

"We were talking about that Bill Gates fellow, Lily," Daddy
wheezed.

"Oh, he's sweet! He married a Dallas girl, you know."

"Give us just a minute more, precious. I am telling Rose—Henry
here—a few things he needs to know."

"Okay. You sounded a little wound up."

There were eight million wrinkles in his forehead, cheeks and neck
as he cradled his head to me: "We must not allow assassinations." His, I
presume, included. "We must not be subject to terrorism. We must
subvert it. We cannot have disruptions! We must find a way to—placate
them. We must buy them—own them—oh dear God, let them own a
little—the Sammies."

"The Muslims? Bin Laden?"

"Yes." Deep sighing whisper. "The embargo is not working. We
must shower them with apparent kindness. Stuff their mouths with dates
and honey, it is our great weapon, to have, not to have not, every Texan
who has inherited, who has worked his way knows that. Get them in the
tent—and then—control them! It is the only way. Bombs beget bombs,
just as bombs have e'er begat—"

He looked around the room, its serrated shelves of books. It seemed
to soothe and calm him. He rolled his great chair backwards so he could
look, beam, at me regally.

"Lily is some chick, eh?"

Nod. Yes. Oh yes.

"I have dreamed that Lily might one day end her—restlessness.
God knows, I know where she gets it, my own killed her mother—certes,
sir, oh certainly. And marry, and be—content. Oh, I never dreamed of
such a one as you. Though a kinsman of Moses Rose I suppose will do,
will have to do. She likes you. I can tell. You get her all aglow. Lily ain't
glowed in years! So, if you were to really capture her heart, I'm
postulating—pontificating—in the sense of building this here bridge to
you, sir—punting under the pons, to make a pun, pons-factoring, as I

hope not the *pons asinorum*, the Bridge of Asses—that if you and Lily, my Lily, sweet little image of my dear dead Doreen who died so dolorously and untimely, why—"

"You would give me Galveston?"

"Galveston? Be serious, sir, you scoundrel! Why in hell would I give you Galveston? Who wants it? I take it you have more sense than that! No, sir. Nor San 'Tonio—don't try for that. While I live perforce of necessity here, that sweet langorous city, San Antonio, is the King's own sweet place. No. Better. I will give you Texas, what is left of true Texas. I will give you Rex Ranch!"

"Well," I said. I had some recollection that Lily had said a while back that we would be going there. "That is mighty big—kind. Actually, I—" *I can't ride a horse* came to mind.

"Oh, I have been thinking of it. I am getting excited about it. Haven't been there for a while, Henry. It's been McIvey land since land was claimed. It is where my soul dwells, on that ranch. Why, I think I will go there with you and Lily. Yes! It is time to go there, to the Rex Ranch. *Lily!*"

Col. McLuther and T.J. Mackey came in with Lily.

"I am going to the ranch with you," said the King.

"We got security?" said Mackey.

"We got security, there."

"How get there?"

"Helicopter to Love. Jet in to the ranch."

"All right."

"Yes, sir," said Luther. "That will be fine, Oliver."

"Damn straight. I'm going. Oh, I'm so excited!"

"We are taking delivery on that new bulldozer, there, next week," Luther said.

"Oh boy, I'll get to ride it!"

"Yes, sir," Luther said. "It's a dandy."

"Well, now, Lily darling, pull up a chair, set down by me and Henry. I believe Henry gets it, he don't seem too bright at first but I expect he is catching on. Ha. That is a joke, boy! We might rawhide Henry up. That Moses Rose was a smart son of a bitch, to get out of there. The Fleeing Frog, they called him. Ha. No offense, Pro-fessor. Well. Shall we have a little session of the Court. Thank you, Luther. Go check outside. We must be vigilant—vigilans—vigilante— American Patrol—"

"I have a petition for the King," said Lily.

"On behalf?"

"On behalf of Highland University. You know, Daddy, it is just blowing away out there on the recent prairie."

"Yes. Why shouldn't it?"

"Henry believes in it, after all is said and done, with his wonderful forgiving spirit. It's a real conservative place, with good values. They are trying to build Texas virtues, to build, you know, like, character."

"They built one in Henry here."

"Yep. In every sense of the word! That is why I adore him so."

"Cut to the chase, daughter."

"Twenty mil."

"What for?"

"Endowment. Scholarships. Make it pretty.Plant some trees. Couple new buildings. It's a desolation. Has no endowment, now."

"Ten. Cut it five and five."

"I vote against it," said Mackey. "It's pure indulgence, Mr. McIvey."

"Right. Ten."

"Fifteen, Daddy. Ten endowment. So they'll get half a mil a year for operating on, for programs, and put five in grounds, salaries, scholarships, student stuff, right now. Would that help, Henry?"

I felt, strangely, half offended. They were either joking with my place or under-valuing it. Universities with $500 million were struggling.

"Henry hesitates."

"He feels this deeply."

"Okay. Make it twenty. For a start. See how they do with it. Who is going to run the place? Henry?"

"Oh no! Henry doesn't want to do that, do you, Henry? Henry is going to have much more important things to do, isn't that right, sweetheart?"

Oh no, oh yes, I nodded. Why would Henry want to do that? My Lord.

"Right. One thing is, Rose, you see, it's all confidential. That sneaky little Spaniard did it, old Anonimo. Just leak out a little news of anonymous gifts along the way—two, three, five years—small goals that get made, you sabe? You checked this, I am sure, with G.K. Chambers, Lily. We have that many beans in the Edu Fund, for this?"

"Yes, Daddy. Thank you so much, Daddy."

"It's a deal then. Keep Tex Flatt as head of the Board. Tell him he's stuck with it. It'll make him look good. Huh? Get another president in

there, Lily tells me the guy who's doing it now is a liberal, though Tex
says he's okay, he really is not a card-carrying one. Shit, take care of it!
Henry, you pleased—you copacetic on all this?"

"Sure. You bet. Why, it's wonderful!" It was. Highland might really
make it, now. That is, if this were not some Midsummer Dream that we
all might wake from, the game over, reassuming reality. Meanwhile I
said, "Thank you, Daddy."

Old Rex beamed, and winked, and chortled, happy as ever the King
was on the raft with the Duke with real water underneath and the puzzled
Huck and Jim aboard.

"Lily," I said, "is this for real?"

She was offended. "I told you we had a little foundation, and tried
to do good things with it. This is for you, Henry. And I'm going to throw
in that endowed chair for you and name it the Henry Rose Chair in
Literature and you can go sit in it whenever you want to, and it will be
there in your name after we are dead and gone. And I have a perfectly
wonderful idea of who should be the H.U. president."

Who it should be was Regina Singh. I looked at Lily with mouth
and mind agape. It got a lot of attention, more than the announcement
that anonymous gifts to Highland University were allowing the building
of a new sciences building and a new language center. President Singh's
mother and father traveled from the Punjab to her inauguration. I am sure
the winds of wonder blew over Bunky's grave. The plaque on the back of
Bunky's memorial sidewalk bench grew worn and polished from the
backs of students sitting there.

"YOU KNOW, I am getting tired of that detective fellow, that damn
blackamoor in that unmarked car, following us," said Lily on our way to
somewhere else. "Aren't you tired of him, Henry?"

"For God's sake, Lily," I rejoined. I had come across the line, as my
ancestor had not. I believed. "For pity's sake," I said.

She smiled, laughed, fingernailed her way along my leg. "Oh, don't
be a poo-poo," she said. "You have such a noble nature, my dearest. Do
try to have a little talk with him, and tell him to stop following us, you
hear? I give him to you, sweetie. His fate is in your hands."

"HOWDY, stranger," John Woodcipher said upon one of my brief visits
to campus. "So what have you been up to?"

"Not much," I said. "How about you? You been enjoying being out of the Prez's office?"

"You bet. Been reading Burke. Kenneth, not Edmund. Do you read anymore, Henry? Burke is an interesting critic for these times."

"Oh?"

"Yes. Here is a quote from him I just read." Woodcipher looked to his book and back up at me over his Ben Franklin-style reading glasses. "'The cult of Kings is always in the offing.'"

Good one, John. Emphasis on the "offing." If you only knew, dear boy.

WE WENT down and over to the Rex Ranch, 300,000 acres in the heart of the Brush Country in southwest Texas facing Mexico, by jet, landing on the runway Oliver McIvey had for his convenience right by the Big House. Looking down from above, Lily said, "Here's the beginning of it, the whole cluster of buildings, there. And that's the Rex River, the Rio Roy. I was baptized in it—oh, not into Christ—into Texas—swimming in that river."

"But that's not a ranch, is it?"

"Of course not, dummy! Those are highrise apartments, in gated communities, the Rex Ranchland Homes and the shopping center, the Rexland Plaza. We ain't stupid, Henry. Lots of ranches are doing that now. It is kind of weird, and sad, isn't it? Oh well."

As we got over the real ranch land, just before landing, the grass below glowed under relentless sun like old parchment.

"Not been a drought like this since 'eighty," Luther said, feeling of the network of scars that made up the terrain of his face.

"Where is my new bulldozer?" said the King. "I want to see it right away! Is it red?"

"It's Japanese," said Luther. "It's blue and yellow. It's being delivered over from Eagle Pass mañana."

"Oh, pooh," said Daddy. "Oh poo-poo-pooey-pooh!"

The Big House had, literally, a moat and a drawbridge leading to it. It was an incongruous French chateau sitting in a sea of scrub and mesquite, the terrible hermit brazada, dust and sunlight. The ceilings were very high inside the house. Lily and I were issued a bedroom together by Luther, who lived here through the year when not on assignment here or there by the King. In the plain high study were wooden and glass cases of books and guns. Over them hung old portraits of McIveys, McAlmons and other Mc's. One portrait I swore was the standard Spanish painting of Mary Queen of Scots except actually it was of Lily. I remembered that in the portrait of Queen Mary she looked mean and like a rat. In this oil rendering Lily did not look like a rat, she did not really look like Mary except that she was plain and dressed crazily like her in a kind of jeweled ruff and had a narrow-lipped and cruel mouth. I knew how strong that mouth could be, and how sweetly soft also sometimes it could be. (If I digress, Lily had been for me a long digression.)

We ate at a long formal dining table in a high-ceilinged, stark dining room. Old Oliver drank bourbon with his dinner, as we others were allowed wine. Billy Roy had come along, happy as ever I had seen a grown man to be, off guard duty and with us and at the ranch; he carved and served the roast and roasted spuds and pinto beans and hot bread the kitchen provided for the midday meal and poured the red and white wine to our little family of six, including Mr. Mackey and Mr. Fuad, who had also come along.

"Drink up, Prince, and be somebody," said Billy Roy to me. "You need to be oiled up, and limber, Prince. We got just the horse for you!"

"None of that, Billy Roy," said Lily. "Don't you bring him out Diablo, now."

"Can't we have us a little fun with the tenderfoot, Lily?"

"No," she said, protecting her interest. I had told her I was the equestrian equivalent of a rigid, ill-rhymed sonnet.

After the meal, needing a nap, we took a walk around in the penetrating heat and pervasive dust.

"If we get hitched," Lily whispered, "*if* we ever decide to do such a foolish thing, which we could only do if we prove ourselves absolutely true to each other—I could not bear disappointment at this age, this point in my beleaguered life—but *if*, which is a real sweet thought to let in, like, in this moment— Why, all this, my dear, would be ours! Daddy says he'll give it to us if we marry. He told you that."

I sneezed from the dust stirred up on our path, thinking I would much prefer being given an air conditioned library. "I'm not much of a cowboy," I said. "Won't you get it anyway?"

"Inherit it? Oh no. I already have what I get when Daddy dies, pray God in Heaven it will be a long, long time off! No, Luther will inherit the Rex Ranch."

"You mean I have to worry about Luther, if—?"

"Oh no, silly. He won't be upset. He'll get another ranch, Daddy would give him the Tejano. It's closer to Mexico, and smaller. Luther would like that fine. This is a lot to keep going, the big old Rex."

"How in the world do you keep it going, Lily? I mean, it's—"

"It's an anachronism? Of course it is. But it's ours, you see."

"I haven't even seen any cattle."

"Oh, there's lots of cattle. My God. We'll take a tour over it later, in the helicopter. And you will notice those black metal things, Henry, that look like blackbirds pecking at the ground, they are called oil wells. It doesn't do much good right now, with the price of crude so low, but it's necessary to have some of those pecking away, to help a ranch keep going. So all in all—we keep it. Because it's ours."

Because she did not want me to break my balls a-horseback, as she so delicately put it, I was exempted from the great Rex horse show that followed in the afternoon. I was privileged to sit and sip and view it from the porch of the Big House in the company of a neighbor and old friend of the family who came over from where he lived in Laredo to visit and who owned a 90,000 acre spread in the vicinity, a big Rock Hudson-like fellow by the name of Redwine Walker.

We talked of the pioneer ranching families, including his, Anglo and Hispanic, who had come and taken the land here and remained and furnished the nation the basic mythology of Texas: Storey, Yturria, Gifford, Allen, Jones, Perez, Walker, McCan, McIvey, Davis, Koontz and Captain King and his Kleburg descendants, including Miss Alice Kleburg East, granddaughter of Captain King who lived her long spartan life at Zapata near the Rio Grande on the San Antonio Viejo Ranch and was presumed to be the basis for Luz in *Giant*. I liked this fellow Redwine. He was so easy-talking and so much how I supposed an authentic Texas ranch figure to be that I almost felt as if I had created him to meet my model. He seemed so much more valid, somehow, than these crazy McIveys I had got tied up with. But since I was, I asked about them, for they were real. They were parading past us out there on beautiful horses now.

"I'll tell you," Walker said. He had been telling about his own father, who had killed a man in a knife fight in Mexico and had never been able to go back over the border, which saddened him, for he loved Mexico, and sat on a porch like this one forbidden drinking by his doctor and drank Scotch whiskey till he died, and about his Uncle Bob, who went down to Mexico to oversee the acres his family had there until Mexico took them and Uncle Bob came back to join his brother on the porch. Now Redwine tried to keep together what was left, the wealth of land with little cash, from town. Now, as they paraded by, Oliver McIvey un-resplendent in faded jeans and old rancher's side-creased Stetson and Nocona boots, tied onto his Arabian steed by Billy Roy, who rode a black stallion by his side, Redwine turned to telling of his lifetime of knowing the McIveys.

"I came back from college, and I nearly married Lily," he said. "She kept coming down here to the ranch. Might have, if it wasn't clear she loved the society life in Dallas. No, I don't think we ever would have married. Soon as I got halfway ready and serious she lit out of here like a dose of salts through a widow woman. Wouldn't have lasted, I do know that. Why? Well, because my marriages don't last, Rose. Four 'til now. I am a little like Lily, and her father, I suppose, and our whole breed: soft-headed, hard-assed and horny as a goat. But Lily, I want you to know, she was a lovely younger woman. Some people would say plain—but a woman that a Highland chief could come home to.

"Old Oliver, too. The wreck you see—of course, he may be near a hundred, you understand, tied on that horse is not the man he was."

"Well, he rides like he was born on, not tied on, that horse."

"Yo. Still, not what he used to be. Lord, Oliver was a real Texas figure, like my daddy was, once. Why, he and Miss Doreen would come down here from Dallas, when Lily was a girl and her brother O.T. was a pup, and they'd all take part in the round-ups, and Miss D. would help to brand the cattle! Society lady in boots and jeans working like a man. And so would Lily, of course. Then Oliver and Miss Doreen would go back up and get in formal clothes and she'd put on her diamonds and pearls and they'd be the sponsors of the Cattle Baron's Ball and all the rest of it. So they bridged these worlds, you see. But speaking Texas, Oliver was the genuine article, in his prime. He was authentic, before he got to be a character, and living in a fantasy."

"You mean, the King of Texas thing?"

"Sure. I only see him down here. Struts around, acts like he really believes. Luther plays along . . . ."

"So you do think he's playing, acting out a fantasy, with the King bit?"

"I have a Master's in psychology," Redwine said. "Doctorate in geology—for the oil—and another in religious studies. I spend half my later life meditating, don't you see. Yes. McIvey is a megalomaniac. He creates his world. Lily is sane as hell, like women are, able to function in both worlds, play the role. Needs ballast though, I reckon. You do that for her? You really have been let into a remarkable circle, for a—"

"An academic?"

"If you want to put it that way." Walker put his hat down a little more over his eyes and shuffled his feet on the porch railing.

"Not as a scholar but just as a student, I admit I am fascinated by them. He may be crazy, but he really does have this."

A gorgeously mounted, crisp-khaki, big-hatted Sheriff's Posse paraded by, followed by a band of sombrero'd vaqueros who made their horses dance and the silver in their saddles shimmer as they passed.

"Yes," said Redwine Walker, himself one of them. "There are some left. Old Wat just died, in his nineties. He was one. Wat Matthews was a remarkable figure who fit the myth, the mold, and transcended it with puredee integrity living on his land and so made it more real. Went to Princeton, and came back, you know. Old Oliver is an eccentric, in his megalomania just the opposite of Wat. He'd die if you flew away and left him down here on this ranch for a week. So how about you? You serious about Lily? Where do you fit in? You could move down here and we could start a college. There's a rancher Rhodes Scholar right over the way, at Cotulla."

I smiled. Probably be a pleasant kind of college, the kind that professors dream of, all faculty and no students. "Just a stranger passing through, podner," I said, with a shrug.

He laughed, shook his head negative, lumbered up and into the yard, got an old branding iron from a rack there and came back and, making a hissing sound, mock-applied the *RR* Rex Ranch brand to my cowering ass.

"Good luck, old hoss," he said. "With our Lily, I mean."

I knew what he meant. He handed me the branding tool. I stood there looking at it, then out to them as the horses and their riders came back around.

ELEVEN

In the morning Redwine departed and some other visitors came in from around and about that Lily and McIvey had to pay attention to. We postponed our helicopter tour until afternoon; Daddy was chafing at the bit to try out his new blue and yellow Japanese bulldozer. Billy Roy got up early and roasted a few goats and we had cabrito and much cerveza for the midday dinner. Lily and I had a silver bullet, our Squeakers, just before it and groped a little bit before she had to play hostess to the visiting ranch people. She greeted them at table with a glint in her cracked, glassy eyes and two buttons undone on her blouse to let them know that we were active.

These were interesting people. The men were weathered and the women were not made up or bejeweled for this informal get-together. The men were tall and lean or short and lean and the women tended to be dumpy but spirited and bright-eyed. They had honey voices, while the menfolk had strange accents—several had clipped English accents, the Hispanic ones of course warm guacamole accents, and one guy I thought was just over from Germany but learned he'd had his spread a hundred years, or his family had. One fellow had a high, piping voice, I didn't know if he was the Pied Piper or Peter Pan. A couple of the men, in their crisply starched khaki shirts and pants tucked into their boots, were massive. One old man was so mean, Lily said, that his wife ate herself to death to get away from him. She told me other odd tidbits about this or that one. I thought she liked them though, and for sure Lily did not play queen, or royalty, among these folks. One old gal, upon learning that I was the incumbent Prince of Dallas, which Lily offered up I was sure only because she could think of no other distinction for me that would impress her friend, replied she had been a few years ago the Duchess of Del Rio.

"My God, Betty," Lily said, "that was twenty-five years ago! That's for the San 'Tonio Fiesta," she explained to me. "They have duchesses from all over."

"Well, Miss Lily McIvey," Betty said, responding to this putdown before going off to join her husband talking cattle, "it's better than being the Prince of Dallas. At least it's *real*."

"They say they have a *mariage blanc*," Lily said wickedly after her. "I don't believe Betty has had sex since she was duchess, if she did then."

But mostly she enjoyed these people and was open to them and natural with them and only whispered about them to me. As for H. Rose, the Prince of totally another place in Texas, I had nothing to say to them. My conversational output shrank to the equivalent of a deformed haiku. I hoped they thought me wise, if mute, but doubted it. This old hoss was off his feed. I almost yearned to be back in a Highland U. fundraiser with the eager Bunky. Ah yes, Bunky. The air conditioning was not turned on in Daddy's ranch house, he bragged that it was thirty degrees cooler inside because of the thick walls. That made it, I believe, just ninety-three degrees inside. Lily said that sometimes the old boy would run it but certainly not with these visitors here, they would think he had gone soft. Even inside, I sneezed from the dust and heat, began to think my eyes were going bad from the motes of light and dust that floated in them, began to have a low, terrible feeling of totally drying out. I drank some whiskey. It burned, made me feel weak and sick.

Looking down from the helicopter piloted by Lou T., Luther's large son, the shimmer below made me feel even stranger, sicker. Down there trucks were hauling feed to the cattle, which were starving from the drought and came running crazily to them. The limp landscape shone under the terrible sun like polished goat, sheep, horse and cattle shit. It wasn't that, but just the brush, tumbleweeds floating along like dry pages of Egyptian parchment. "We do the roundup by helicopter now," Lily told me cheerily.

Then: "Originally, Henry, the Rex was about the size of Rhode Island. Can you imagine that?"

"No." Rhode Island with its lovely water.

Later then: "You're not going to be sick, and puke up here in Rex Two, are you, Henry? Here, take my cup." The wine fumes from it almost made me do so.

"Here, set down, Lou T.," she said. "I think Henry has a little air sickness."

"No–" I said.

"Here is a nice little grove," she said, just about pushing me out the door as we landed. "We'll be right back. I want Lou T. to take me to check on something. Here, you sit here and rest a minute."

She smiled and shut the door, and the bird whirled its prop and lurched back up and away south from the way we had been coming. My God. I looked around. There was a stand of pygmy umbrella-topped trees, as I imagined there were for Hemingway in Africa, or in Isak Dinesen. The country was absolutely scabrous, colorless. Lily had left Jesus to reflection—or madness—in the desert. I staggered and sat at the base of one of the dusty pygmy trees. I looked up at the sun. It had burned a hole in the sky and was burning one through me. Utterly still. Maybe she had arranged for the real leopard to come and love her soldier.

Lily was either truly just off to check something, or was teaching me something. My sickness turned from heat and motion strain to the existential nausea of Sartre, or that feeling of sickness that first intruders into the great West felt when their Romantic sensibility abandoned them and they knew for certain there was no God, these stunted trees, these rocks, this terrible brazada, the sun and earth were not one with their transcendental spirit but truly did not care, were quite and entirely indifferent to them. This country had been settled on, then fenced and claimed, parceled out in large enough bundles to sustain some human life and commerce, years ago by the ancestors of those I had just so unsuccessfully mingled with. The land was hard and desolate, the trade was the hardest work in tough conditions, real work that produced pride in accomplishment, but when, like Daddy, you were cut off from it and just had its tools—guns, hats, boots, whiskey—in your Texas Room, the pride turned to something bad, false, a craziness. Old Larry in one of his best, most valid contributions, caught it, the craziness of old Uncle So-and-so cut off from civitas, lone and lorn, on his ranch—while old Oliver McIvey, cut off from the ranch, the reality of it, pompously posed in the circus shell he built around him. But this—dear God—this was the reality.

And to me it seemed not just deadly but horrible, truly Hell.

Nada, y nada, y pues nada . . .

There was some movement. Terrifying. Then some wild turkeys wandered a way off through the brush. I thought of all the Western movies I had seen as a boy and man, and forgave myself for that feeble part of me. Waited for the sound of the solitary horse *clop* coming, the

Mexican with sombrero and pistols and bandelier coming to smile and say, "Hello, Señor, howvar ju?" and smile and kill me . . . . Waiting for the huge rattlesnake to wake and coil just under my leg where it had been napping as I sat here. Heard a slight rustling in the tree above and jumped out from under it, rolling, sure the snake was inching down the tree like the snake in the tree in the original little grove.

The Texan John Graves wrote the one best story of the lament for all this, the fleeting cattle kingdom and the horrible heroics of fighting with the Indians, what became the narrow civilized bridge over the American Western experience, in "The Last Running." The strangely named Comanche chief Starlight brings his rackety warriors when it's all over to his old antagonist Tom Bird Tejano to claim a buffalo bull to run, for they have never run one. It is the restrained Hemingway-like story of the running of the bull—Milton or Shakespeare these old stoic well-read ranchers always named their bulls—and its meaning. A lament for what is dying, what is gone, the little left. I loved that little story, read it aloud to classes; and now sitting by the weird tree, imagining the snake, it made me sicker just to think of it. The character old Tom Bird Tejano who gave "Starlight" his last bull was just as crazed with it—the romantic sentimentalism of the supposedly stoic Anglo men—the Scots—as old Oliver McIvey. Daddy was just down the line a bit farther, still hanging on. But there was nada really left. This Hell in which I sat and now lay back in to let Sol take my soul was what was left. The land, and dispensing it, possessing it, fencing it, skyscraping it, had crazed us all. There was nothing to lament, except our loss of humanity together, our mean and petty differences; no pity. I felt the terrible dread again, and the sense of the insignificance of my existential self and my schemes and weakness and put my hat down over my eyes and sat up under the tree which did give some shade, and bounced up with a shout, a wave, as the helicopter came zigging down to let me in.

"Well, that seemed to do you good," said Lily. "Here. Here's some water, Deja Blue, it's cool, I got it at the checkpoint for you. We used to ride out to hunt turkeys here, Henry. Did you see any? I shot my first turkey down there when I was nine. Guess where we were? It was interesting, but I thought you might get really sick, riding further to where we went. Head back now, Lou T."

"I couldn't guess." I was irritated. She was, among other attributes, a controlling, vicious woman. But she had come back. Had not left me there, like Canavan, to die of heat and dehydration. That was good, for I was no Louis L'Amour, no Canavan. I could not eat lizards and let the bees lead me to secret water and scrabble back and kill them all. Of course she had not. For a moment I'd forgotten that she loved me.

"Oh, we flew over to look at where that Mexican goatherd, I mean he was an American Mexican, was shot right on the river by Redford. Did you hear about that? He was shot and killed by our own Marines dressed up in their stupid ghillie suits so he thought they were wolves and took a shot at them, thinking he was protecting his damn goats! his War on Drugs just is not working, Henry. We have our own patrols against the drug guys, but we have to hide up in the hills at night while the Marines and all the other morons flounder around in the dark spooking each other. It's ridiculous! If they'd just leave it to Daddy— leave it to Luther—we'd have it cleaned up in a couple months!"

"Stake out a few of them bastards over anthills like the Comach' used to do, cut off a few hands," offered Luther's progeny Lou T. His name made me think of a similar one.

"Redwine Walker said you had a brother," I said to Lily. "O.T.? I never heard you mention him."

Lily froze beside me as the 'copter with the Texas star on it gulped its way through the thin sere air, whipping us back over the hard parchment earth below.

"He died," she said. "Ten years ago. Thrown and trampled on by a young stallion he was riding in a July Fourth parade in Santa Fe. O.T. hung out in New Mexico a lot. So did I, but I hated it after that. He was a ne'er-do-well."

"I'm terribly sorry."

"Why? He was a little prick. He never took Daddy or his own responsibilities seriously. God, he was over thirty when he died. My little baby bro'. That stallion was too jumpy, too young, too green to be riding it in that parade. It spooked and threw him, then cut him to ribbons with its hooves." Lily seemed to relish this detail. "Since he did ride him, he should have been able to do it! Even Daddy said so—though of course he shot the stallion."

"I see. O.T.?"

"Oliver Texas. Daddy is Oliver MacLean. He named O.T., like, romantically. He was supposed—"

"To be the heir apparent. But—"

"That's right." Lily reached and grabbed my dick for solace. "But, as you say, it turned out we didn't need him. Hey, your response time is getting better! We should leave you out on the desert more often! Right? Did you see any snakes by yourself out there?"

"There are some big old rattlers out there, that's for sure," said the jolly boy-man Lou T., dipping us down and cradling us on the wide driveway by the Big House.

Billy Roy came running towards us from the house.

"Jesus, something is wrong!" yipped Lily. She shoved me back and climbed over me getting out of the helicopter, then loping to meet Billy Roy. "Is it Daddy?" she said to him.

"Yes, ma'am. He ain't dead, but he's had a pretty bad fall. It was my fault, Miss Lily, I let him do it. You weren't here—I tied him on that damn old bulldozer and he went riding off on it, and into the field, and lowered the scoop and hit something— Oh hell, I'm sorry! I never would of thought it could just turn over like that— But he's not dead, just all black and blue. Luther took Rex One to town to get a doctor. Mr. Mackey said we shouldn't take him in there, my God, he pulled his gun and nearly shot Hermano and Pedro, they been on this ranch all their lives, T.J. said they might be agents of the U.H.S., the damn Hispanics. Hell, for a minute there, I thought he was going to shoot me. Luther and I got your father out from under that damn Jap bulldozer. He is pretty bunged up, black and blue, but I don't believe nothing is broken. Oh God, he was excited as a little kid, Miss Lily—"

"Shit," she said, striding past him on towards the Big House. "You were damned lucky," she said, pointing her finger back at poor huffing-puffing Billy Roy.

"How's that, Miss Lily?" he called after her.

"That he didn't shoot you. I think I would have shot you."

"She don't mean that," said Billy Roy to me shaking his head. "But it's true I let him—"

"How is he?"

"Don't know, really. Took a mean fall. Thing rolled on him. Had him tied on there good. We carried him in to bed and he drank a bunch of whiskey. He is sleeping now, snoring like a banshee. He is a tough old man. God, he has got scars all over his body, from accidents and being sewn back up."

"Where is our friend Mackey?"

"Inside. Luther has him under House Arrest. He ain't too pleased. Says we are all a squad of dumbass, romantic amateurs."

"Where did he come from, Billy Roy? T.J. Mackey?"

"Don't know. Lily brought him in, to guard her father, but the Old Man never had too much truck with the fellow. I believe he is primarily loyal and responsible to her, to Miss Lily. Not that he ain't a cool dude.

He is. Scares the shit out of me, I'll tell you, Prince. I'd rather have him with me than on the other side."

He turned, and blipped back in. I stood there wondering what this meant. Would Daddy bounce back up? If he didn't, would the game go on without the King playing his grand role? I looked off toward the horizon of Rex Ranch: the sun was so hot you could not see it in the sky, it was like it *was* the sky, a blur of horrible heat. Almost made me wish I was back freezing my ass off in Alaska. Even there, than here.

Ride back with us to the gallant days of yesteryear . . . .   Hi ho, Silver, away . . . .

Knew that if I turned and walked over and got in that pickup over there and drove away, she would find me.

Walked on in the house. Two of Luther's guys were at the door with rifles.

Lily was in Daddy's room kneeling on the floor by his bed, holding his limp old hand. I took one peek in, waved at her. She looked up at me glassy-eyed, motioned for her boy Billy Roy to shut the door. In the dusty den room Mr. Fuad was on the phone making arrangements to take the King for special hospital care back up in Dallas, even as Dr. Northway, a renowned border physician, arrived by helicopter with Luther McLuther. In the corner, totally at ease, sat T.J. Mackey, apparently just neutralized, not supervised. He had no expression on his non-face whatsoever, looked at me as if he were seeing me on TV. His hands were clasped. It was the first time I had seen him in repose, not playing with a knife or gun. It came to me with deep certainty that he had shot poor Bunky, and a host of others, or knifed them or blown them up, that he was an assassin, that he reported to my sweet and loving Lily, and that it might be my fate to be slit or shot by him. His eyes merely flickered like a lizard's as I stared at him.

"Dr. Northway is kin to old Dr. Northway that was the chief vet on the King Ranch for years," Billy Roy offered. He was standing in the doorway to the den by me with his stomach stuck out and his arms crossed over his massive chest. In my mind's eye I could see him carrying the old Oliver in from the bulldozer accident. He seemed terribly downcast and full of guilt.

"What's going on?" I said. "What are we doing, Billy Roy? Who's in charge?"

"Why, Miss Lily is in *charge*. You'll see."

In that moment it was very clear to me that I needed to get away, to get out of it. The fun and romance, the intrigue and titillation of it had waxed and waned. I felt no claim of love or honor as a character in this drama, I saw myself completely in the moment in terms of irony and pity. Let Lady Brett, with her appetites and quirks, her sexual drive and drive to power, be; let me take a cleansing swim and not go to Madrid to the Hotel Montana. I almost thought I'd try to bribe Billy Roy to get me out of there, but what was I to bribe such a fellow with? An honorary degree? He stood beside me, breathing heavily, sweating, planted deep in the hope that Lily would forgive him for letting Daddy ride the blue and yellow Asian tractor.

"Sit down, Prince," he said, pointing into the den, and I realized that he was also guarding the door, precisely against the possibility of any defection.

I sat down in a rawhide thing across the room from T.J. Mackey. "Hot enough for you?" I said to him.

He regarded me with implacable antagonism for a second, then clicked back into his personal internet. That was it, he was like a computer, totally binary. He was like a machine.

The curtains were drawn across the windows. I could hear the come and go of the helicopters, then the arrival on the runway of a small jet. Cars and jeeps circled around. Mr. Fuad left the room. McLuther poked his head in, made the peace sign to Mackey, who stared at him. Pretty soon Billy Roy reappeared, said, "Lily says you'll want to come and say Godspeed to His Majesty."

I got up, went into the hallway, leaving my good buddy sitting in the corner. Daddy was being wheeled out by medics in starched white. His mane seemed sparse and limp. His visible hand and face had yellow and blue bruises. His eyes were closed. He looked nearly dead to me. Lily trotted along beside him. She grabbed my hand, pulling me along.

"Oh, Henry," she said, "dear sweet Henry! I'm so glad you're here," as if I had just arrived. "Daddy looks fine, doesn't he? He is going to be all right. Isn't he a terrible, stubborn old— coot. You'll be fine, Daddy."

She stopped, let go my hand, as they wheeled Daddy to the medical airbus, and lifted him in. She zoomed back in the house, and back out and on board. I thought she was going with Daddy, but she calmly climbed back down, long legs in jeans and range boots, and smiled, saying again that he would be fine. He was being flown to a full security suite at a private Dallas hospital for x-rays and such, though Dr. Northway did not think there were any broken places or internal injuries. She said she did not completely trust him, Northway was somewhat of a homeopath. Maybe we needed the other Dr. Northway, the veterinarian, for Daddy! I was a bit startled by Lily's little joke. Then T.J. Mackey, in business suit and dark shades, emerged from the Big House with a black briefcase that I was sure contained some black tubular up-to-the-moment killing device and with his Glock and silencer I was sure strapped under his arm under the suit coat and nodded to Lily and boarded the medical transport. He was going to guard the King of Texas against further attempts upon his life, like this had been one. The small silver jet took off.

"Thank you, Fuad," she said to the little pin-striped man as the wind and dust and heat swept over us. "You did well."

"Yes. The others will be arriving soon."

"We are having a meeting of the board, Henry," she said, looking at me keen-eyed, very much in charge. "You are on it now. Okay? I am going to take a bath and a nap. I suggest you do the same. If you hadn't gotten me out on that wild goose chase of a tour I would have been here and Daddy would have been all right! I never should have left him!"

"I beg your pardon?"

"Yes! By God! You should!"

On the way in she put her arm around Billy Roy's shoulder and cooed something in his ear. He straightened up and brightened hugely, and went off to barbecue the supper. Manuel, the main house man, showed me to another room, a small, spare single with bath down the hall from where I had been cohabiting with Lily, who retired into herself. I was glad. I didn't even mind being blamed for Daddy's fall, ironic and ridiculous as that was of sweet, demented Lily. I'd been afraid that Daddy's accident might have spurred some strange new sexual fantasy in her. I sat and read a tattered copy of *Horseman, Pass By*, or *Hud* as it was called in this paperback version, that was lying on the bed stand. I was on the board now? Oh boy. When old Homer Bannon, symbol of the Old Texas, had his accident out on the ranch road his nephew Hud had shot him. Just showed how civilized these folks at Rex Ranch were . . . . I dozed over *Hud*.

Manuel came and got me. We had a big evening meal, served by Manuel and Cisco and Teresa and Josefina, barbecue and all the fixings. Lily was all dressed up in silver concho belt and bracelets and all but a silver and turquoise crown. She was reigning. She ate like a horse and drank some draughts of wine. I recalled that after a good hanging or a burning of a Protestant at the stake, Mary Queen of Scots also enjoyed a hearty meal. McLuther was at table, with his son Lou T. and his other large sons Luke and LeeBoy. I met Mr. G. K. Chambers, the financial man, who had flown in, a dumpy nondescript figure who however sported, like a footnote to himself, two-toned alligator shoes and was very quiet. He sat in the command center, a now-revealed room full of computers from which the ranch was run. The inestimable Mr. Singh had also arrived in a private jet and seemed quite excited by the whole turn of events.

"It is hot as ducky blazes here," he said. "It is hotter than the hottest part of India. And these cattle—those bulls I saw out there, they are passing strange. What did you say you call them, those funny ones with the big necks and humps on their shoulders, my dear Colonel?"

"Brahma," said McLuther. He said it, Bray-ma.

"Bray-ma? Brahma? Oh, shuttlecocks! You Texians! Surely you are joking me?"

After supper we repaired to the den, Lily, McLuther, G. K. Chambers, Mr. Fuad, Singh and myself. Lily ran the meeting, quickly and informally, sitting at the head of the circle buoyed up and weighted down with all that turquoise and silver, her plain or ugly as the case might be face earnest, a little secret touch and wink and smile to me, as if she had remembered our deep love and attachment, to begin with.

"Well, this is, like, a meeting of the board of T-Rex," she said, "and I am calling it to order. We gotta make a few decisions here, amigos. You know what I'm saying to you?"

"Oh yes," said Mr. Singh, a lilt to his voice. "Russia."

"You betcha," said G. K. Chambers. "We have to go ahead and get over there. We are very vulnerable there. It's collapsing there, in Russia. I talked to George. George is freak-out. Thinks all of us, all the interested parties, should go and talk to them, those morons."

"Russia?" I heard the voice of Henry Rose inquire.

"Yes, Henry. I was saving it for a surprise! You and I were going on a little trip to Russia, just to Moscow, I believe. I was going to represent Daddy. Mr. Singh is going to talk to those bums, and I was going to represent Daddy, the King of Texas and the T-Rex Fund. You know?"

"I had no idea."

"Of course you didn't! Like I said, it was going to be a surprise, kind of like a honeymoon trip for you and me. I speak a little Russian, you know. I certainly hope you do, too!"

"Yes. I do. A little. Why?"

"Because now you have to go alone. Or with Mr. Singh. That's pretty much like going alone, isn't it, Singh?" Singh kind of giggled a Ducky Blazes giggle. "Oh, and on second thought, I think I will send

Billy Roy along, to take care of our precious, irreplaceable Prince. Mr.
Fuad, would you ask Billy Roy to step in here to the meeting for just a
mo'—"

"Lily, I don't think this is such a redhot idea, my dear."

"Oh now, it will be all right. Billy Roy can go. Hi, Billy Roy, you
don't mind, do you, doing this for Lily Girl? We'll get Daddy out of the
hospital real soon, and secure him in the Mansion, at home, and Mr.
Mackey can take care of Daddy and me too. I can let you go for just a
week, Billy Roy, but then you better hurry back, you sweet thing, you
hear?"

"Goin' where, Miss Lily?" said Billy Roy.

"Russia! It will be a nice change for you. Haven't you ever wanted
to go to Russia?"

"I been to 'Nam, and I been, then, to China, but it never entered my
pea to want to go to fucking Russia," he said.

"You will be going with Mr. Singh and Henry, on a mission for the
T-Rex. I want you to watch out for Mr. Rose, and see that he gets back
here safely. I know you do that usually for *me*, but this is a very special
request. Okay? I was going, but now I have to stay with Daddy. So
Henry goes to represent the King of Texas personally with these people.
Henry, we will have to make you a Prince's ring, with the star on it, to
wear over there. And wear here too! You are part of us now, Henry. Oh,
thank you so much for agreeing to do this, Daddy will be pleased when
he wakes up and knows. And your Lily will have a very special reward
for you!" Her homely face flushed at the thought of the pleasure that lay
ahead. "Those Russian sons of bitches are still autocratic as hell, you
know, they lap up royalty and authority, miss the one and crave the other.
Right, Singh?"

"My goodness, yes, Miss Lily! Not bloody democratic like us!"

"All right. Are the arrangements made, Mr. Fuad? When do they
leave? You cool with this, you understand it, Billy Roy?"

"Yes, ma'am," he said. He teetered on his black red-threaded boots,
exhaled and gave me a look that conveyed that I had betrayed him
deeply.

I dived into the reservoir of my mind and found that I could say
"Hello," "Goodbye" and "I love you" in Russian.

TWELVE

Sam McGee was sitting in my office reading Terry Eagleton's intro to literary theory and picking at his gold tooth when I stopped by the university to touch base. Talk about the fish jumping in the boat.

"You enjoying that, are you, Detective McGee?"

"I have wanted to try to understand somethin' 'bout this theory business," he said. "So how are you, Professor? Not pro-fessing much these days, huh? Been kind of scarce, have you? Done been gone down to roundup, and now getting the old pasoporto renewed, are we? So where you off to, Rose? That is some bunch you are tied up with, you know that?"

"Russia," I said. "Just a brief jaunt to Mother Russia."

"Hey," he said, pulling on the gold earring. "Russia. Of course. Russia. Where the hell else would a scholar of English damn literature be going off to in the damn dog days of summer? Be nice and cool there, I reckon, in Russia."

"Speaking of being cool, may I inquire as to the status of your investigation of the death of Bert Bunker?"

"No leads. I mean, like, it's over. It certainly was not you. I'm just still interested in you—well, Henry, to tell you the truth—because I got interested in you. You know what you been playing wit', man, and what is the game they're playin'?"

"How does it look to you, Sam, I mean, from the outside?"

"It looks like they think they are in a movie, or something." His intelligent dark eyes lit up and he smiled.

"Listen," I said, "I'm not sure myself, but I do know I need some help. I need someone to look out for me, just like you've been doing . . . . You know? Any chance I can hire you away for a while from the force, from the DPD? Watch my back, check up on a few of these characters—work for me. I think I could arrange for you to be well paid."

"I got some time coming. What we talkin' about here, Henry?"

"Oh," I said, off the top, "I'd put in for ten thousand a month."

"What you getting?"

"I'm just along for the ride. Just getting fringe benefits, so to speak."

"I might could do that, for a spell. That's way too much bread, man. Make me feel like I was being set up for something."

"May be. I may be. May be dangerous. I mean —"

"Yeah." He smiled. "Of course, may be dangerous liaison for you all, too. I'd still be working for the force, you know."

"There's that." I shrugged. I suddenly desperately wanted Sam McGee to be with me, wherever we were going, I didn't care if he'd be double-agenting or what. I though H. Rose needed a little protection around here. I asked him if he might be able through his sources to find out some background on a character named T. J. Mackey. He said he maybe could.

"Keep the book," I said. It was a paperback we used in most of our lit courses.

"Thanks," he said. "It's interesting. This is like what I do, you know? Deconstruct shit."

When I told Miss Lily I had hired Sam McGee on leave from the Dallas Police for an outrageous sum she never batted an eye. "That's your prerogative," she said. "That's clever, too, Henry. Gets him off your back. He can be your guard when you get back. He can drive you. That will work out fine. We'll have to get you a car, won't we? That old clunk of yours is not reliable. Yes. Lily-girl will get Henry-boy a nice new car, for him and his black Sammy boy."

When I asked if I couldn't take Sam McGee to Russia with me and Singh in place of Billy Roy, she said *no!* Emphatically, eyes flashing. Billy Roy was set to go. We didn't know how good this Sammy McGee really was. Billy Roy was good. Billy Roy was loyal, capable. He was even warming to the idea. He would take good care of me and Singh. Billy Roy had been a Marine. Billy Roy was imbued with the philosophy and values of the Rex and the T-Rex interests. Thus, as I reflected and rationalized later, it was she, Lily, who signed his death warrant.

Before we left I took delivery on a monster new Lincoln Town Car, *Cartier*, leather seats, white with those enormous taillights, tinted glass just like a Mafia car in the movies. I turned it over to Sam McGee to drive while I was gone. He didn't think it was too cool, said it drove like a boat out on the lake. I hated to admit it, but I loved that car.

Also before I left I went in and had a talk with Daddy. He seemed alternately confused and lucid, which wasn't too much different from before. He lay in a canopied bed fit for a king in his Victorian bedroom and opened his eyes and swiveled them around.

"Well, Daddy," I said. "Rex. Sir. Oliver." Not thinking that anything but croaks would come back my way.

But he said, "G-going to R-Rooshia, are you? Eh? Prince? How's your Rooshian, boy?"

"Vash tu lublu," or some such, I replied.

"I love—you too. Ha ha! Hope—can do it, boy. Rose. Moses. Moses into the Promised Land, eh? Not hardly. Not hardly, Henry. Prince. Lily says can do. You can do. Hoo-hoo-hoo! What you gonna do, fella—how you gonna do-do-do?"

"I will, sir, be guided by Burke's admirable admonitions, as stated in a major work. 'When in Rome, do as the Greeks. When in Europe, do as the Chinese.' When in Texas, do as the Yahoos. That one is mine, not Burke's. When in Russia, do as the Texans do."

"Burke? Who is Burke?"

"Billie Burke. You remember her in those films."

"Yes. Cute as hell. That's cute about the Greeks and the Chinese, too. I even agree about Texas and the Yahoos. I'll take my spirited handsome horse friends over most duck-billed inhabitants of Texas, and you-may-quote-me-on-it, Henry. But you yourself—you, sir. You are, I noted, hardly an aficionado—a fan—of Houyhnhnms, of horses, are you?"

"Oh, I'd bet on the sorrel. And I have ever, in my life and guises, chiefly truly wished to avoid controversies, wranglings and disputes." This I thought a nice sally, a true quote from old Jonathan, and true of me, to boot.

"Ah, but I thought, as you said at first, that you were Dubious!"

This was a sally of his own, of memory and wit. Then he became not silly, quite lucid, staring at me from his propped-up position in bed with those baleful slatey eyes. "So go. Do it, Prince. Tell 'em— Tell 'em stability. Tell 'em George—me—all'a'us—we'll rip them loans off, take 'em back like peeling panties off a whore. Mean it! Comprende, Henry? And—Prince—

"Keep your nose clean. Diplomatico. Powers that be, Henry. Don't' fool with Dissidents. If you can't see Boris, that's okay. See Anatoly. Right? Give the message and come back. Do not fuck up, Henry. Come back safe, dear boy."

With a wave of the mottled hand I was dismissed; he was snoring before the great-ringed hand fluttered back to his heaving chest. I went out into Lily's embrace. She had obtained great shaggy fur coats for us. We wore them, naked, doing the fantasy of "The Mating of the Russian Bears."

Flew in to Moscow, our happy little trio. Billy Roy barely spoke, while "Ducky Blazes" Singh prattled incessantly. Surely, I thought, he must have a sound head for finance, or politics, or something, for on the surface he played like, or was, a perfect Peter Sellers playing the silly Indian at the party.

I remembered flying in to Madrid at dusk with the forbidding orange Guadarramas all around it as a similar experience. Coming down into Moscow was like entering a large fuzzy gray area of boxlike nothingness dimming down on the TV screen. The lights from above were dull and somber. There were streams of those changeless black cars and gray trucks. There were lumpy gray people pushing and shoving in the airport. It was strangely warm, I mean, it was very warm, over eighty degrees. I carried the Shearling coat Lily had mis-bought me for the occasion over my shoulder. Sweat glistened on Billy Roy's wide, puzzled face. The Russian folk in the airport, dressed like New York or Peoria, stared at him: his hat, his big silver Texas belt buckle, his belly, his boots. We were met by a slim, young, student-looking fellow who, as it turned out, was a double or triple agent, a government subaltern, a dissident idealist and God knows what else in all the boiling intrigue there. I shall call him "Razumov." I liked him very much; he reminded me of certain earnest students of mine through the years with a taste for scholarship and a gift for intrigue who went for second-rate Ph.D.s and ended up as professors or administrators in Wyoming, Idaho or Texas.

"I am so happy you look like Texas," he said to Billy Roy. "We are loving Texas. Oh, of course Texas is also elegant and sophisticated, as you are dressed, sir. I see you have the ring with the star of Texas on it. Are you the person known as the King of Texas?"

"No. Just the prince. We kind of follow the Chinese system. Old guys pretty much keep the power in Texas."

"Ah, but that is not a negligible honor, to be the Prince. I would like to come and see Texas—its vastness, its space, its proud people, its resources, its courage, its wealth, its great Idea of itself—so much like Russia. Except, of course, we are under a bit of a strain right now."

"But of course, oh my, the Russian people are so indomitable," says Singh, whose squeaky voice had led me now to think of him as "Ducky

Bub." Rasumov looked at him with his dark, hot little eyes like where did you come from, why is this one along?

"Well, you would be mighty welcome!" Billy Roy says, whacking the kid on the back and shoulders, relieved that this damn Rooshian spoke English and was agreeable and held Texas in the proper regard. "We'd be proud for you to visit!"

"Meanwhile," the kid says, "you are in great good fortune. Uncle Vodka is in town and he is fairly well, but heads back to his dacha tomorrow, and with great urging from Anatoly he has agreed to see you. And Anatoly, of course, will visit with you. The investment and support of the great T-Rex Foundation is much appreciated."

"Things got to shape up, buddy boy," says Billy Roy.

"Razumov" looked at him, startled. H. Rose also looked at him, startled, as we sped through Moscow streets in the dark limo. I hadn't reckoned Billy Roy to be in on the policy end of things. The kid looked at me, the Prince in pinstripes carrying my great bright yellow chamois fur-trimmed gift of a coat. "We have a serious message to deliver," I said.

"I understand. The atmosphere is nothing here if not serious. It has surpassed 'crisis.'"

"Of course," chirped Singh, "we are very anxious to—"

There was a long silence before the fellow I am calling Razumov said, "And then, I have arranged for an Evening, here, in the famous Café Momus, with—various—individuals. Who will be happy to hear from you, as you will no doubt be appreciative and burdened to hear from them."

"Exactly," said Ducky Bub.

"Doubtless," said I.

"Goin' to be hard to get these old boys up to the salt log," Billy Roy muttered to me. Young Razumov heard, but I doubted the idiom, salt or log, was in his ken.

That evening before retiring to our very nice chandeliered and bugged hotel room we met and exchanged toasts with Anatoly in his silk suit and a heavy-set sack of potatoes I'll call "Primo," soon to assume a very large role with a lot of Communist support. He was of the opinion that things had to even out for Russia to make it, not to go absolutely belly up. The robber barons had to be curbed, the State had to retake some ground here, boys. You know? Even in Texas the federal and state governments fixed what was broken, insured rights and needs, and regulated commerce and industry. At the same time he and the others all appreciated the significant investment T-Rex had made in their country. We must all now just hold tight. I delivered the stiff warning that we would withdraw, were on the verge, if things didn't stabilize. The elegant one and the lumpy one knocked back their toasts and politely withdrew, and sent in a beefy boyo by the name of Ivan to beat our carpet. This fellow lectured us, using Soros as the foil to our selfish message just delivered. Soros was the great investor and philanthropist in Russia, supporting all good democratic causes through his Open Society Institute. Two years ago the U.S. had invested just $95 million in Russia, Soros had put in $500 million. Now he had about $2.5 billion in Russian businesses, and he, unlike the relatively feed-for-the-chickens T-Rex Foundation, was not threatening to pull out in this regrettably bumpy time. Uncle Soros wished every good for Russia, its military, its literacy, its schools, etc.

Well, so did we, so did the King of Texas and T-Rex, I countered politely. Unfortunately or fortunately in this world today, as we all well knew, the markets, not governments, set prices and allocate resources, and there must be real value in the market.

Oh, like your internet stocks, for example, Ivan sneered.

Oh my now, that is not quite exactly the whole truth, our dear Mr. Ivan, said Singh, sailing in from whatever tranquil bay his mind had been in repose in. The fine and estimable Mr. Soros, in whose debt we all were, so to speak, idealistic as he might be, also followed the first rule of investment, even in the form of philanthropy, that it must have profited. Recently had he not warned Russia that it must go beyond the robber capitalism that had so perverted and crippled their economy and struggle for true capitalist democracy and an open society?

"Yes," said Ivan bitterly, "for a billion dollars he has bought our telecommunications industry."

"I believe you have done forgot the tune you were a-singing," said Billy Roy.

"I believe the message has been delivered," said Razumov, looking at Ivan.

"Yes," he said. "Consider it so. And, if you get to see Uncle in the morning, if he is here and well— Well, I would not bother him with this—negative—message, or in any way bring clouds into his already gloomy weathers. You must know, he is subject when greeted with such negativities, to fits."

"Oh my Maxwell's-silver-hammer-great-goodness," said Mr. Singh. "He is subject to seizures? This is most interesting, and something not generally known?"

"Apoplectic fits," said Ivan.

In the morning, then, we met him, old "Uncle Vodka," the burly, still peasantly-handsome old bear of Russia, who had led them firmly to the present "freedom," the present chaos and corruption. "Hall-oo," he said, beaming, lurching, shaking hands with us. "Halloo, hall-oo, hall-oo. You tell my bood-y Bill hall-oo—"

We gave him greetings and murmurs of support from Texas. He smiled and nodded. He reminded me of an old NFL player that had got hit in the head one time too many. He seemed a nice old guy, like a throwback, like our Pitchfork Bens and Huey Longs and Pa Fergusons of another era, before the corporations had yoked us and pulled up the grassroots of America. Then I realized what the old bear reminded me of was Oliver, old Oliver Rex, the frigging K. of T.

"I kind of liked him," I said to Razumov.

"Ah," he replied. "He is irrelevant. Russia has—has always had—a great destiny in which the circumstances of its leaders are irrelevant!"

I thought of mentioning Stalin, but didn't. Instead I said to the young idealist, "My God! What the people here have put up with! What they are going through now!"

"Ah," he said, more gently. "I am surprised, and pleased, to encounter such empathy in you—in Texas."

Having a beer in the bar instead of lunch I said to Billy Roy, "You know what fascinates me?"

"Well," he said. "Lily, I reckon. I know she fascinates me. I wish I had her and you had a wart on your ass. Which I wouldn't bet against you. Just remember, Provo'—Prince—the sun don't shine on the same dog's ass all the time."

"True," I said, for it was on the general theme of my thoughts. "Lily, not the wart. She is an interesting, not to say amazing, woman. Person. Woman person. A true princess, worthy of esteem. What I was going to remark though, was, given she is something, I am fascinated as I go down the road by the absolute commonness, the banality of people who are 'special.' My God, 'Uncle Vodka' rules Russia!"

"Well, you got your George Washington with bad false teeth, and your Thomas Jefferson keeping him a black wo-man, and your Honest Abe. Jesus, Prince. And your William Jefferson Clinton can't keep his pecker in his pants right now, I mean when he is the *president*. Just all real common folks, good 'Mericans, if that was what you were meaning."

"In a way it was. But I was thinking of the old bear we encountered today, what a 'common' fellow he was. And, sure, Clinton. Yes, Billy Roy. You know, I met him when he was a boy still, in Dallas, one evening. He was running McGovern's campaign in Texas. George McGovern was glad to meet a few professors, since he was one, and a couple of us went down to the hotel and chatted him up. Weren't more than ten people, total, about how many voted for the fellow in Dallas County, and I got to talking to this earnest, idealistic young guy, his campaign manager, this Clinton boy. Had a real bad suit and kind of muttonchop sideburns and you would not have bet he would ever be president! Thinking, Billy Roy, of the inevitable commonness, the banality, of the people who are 'special,' specially these days, in the 'New World Order.' 'Commonality' was what Myrtle Springs would have called them."

"Well, that Bill Clinton is the banality of our existence, all right, Prince. I bet he slides through, too. He sees the lie of the ball, lies right out of it. On the other hand, you see, he is not some prig of a spoiled boy done eased through life. No, sir. Which is why we ain't goin' to blame him too awful much. Why, you know, he came in to Dallas when he was a boy, he remembers, eleven years old, on the bus. Stopped in Paris, Texas, and a bunch of other places, it was in 1958. He was just a boy, like you or me, or me anyway. Went to a game at the Cotton Bowl, didn't remember who won—always had that 'selective memory,' I guess. Played miniature golf, went to the show—*How the West Was Won*. First time he'd been out of Arkansas. Big D Dallas, Texas, was the biggest place he'd ever seen. You got to kindly love a boy made his way up from that. I do, leastways. So who is this Myrtle Springs you mentioned?"

"My wife. She went away."

"I didn't know you had no wife." Billy Roy gave me a quizzical, exasperated look as if wondering how such a thing as my possessing a wife could have ever been.

"She is long gone," I said. "She went to Elysian Fields."

Billy Roy raised his glass of dark beer in a poignant little gesture to the dear departed.

That evening the fellow "Razumov" led us to the Café Momus in a flickering quarter of Moscow I am sure I would never find again, to the Evening he had arranged for us. A number of people came and went and others came so it was hard to keep track of who they were, my ear for

Russian, particularly thick vodka'd Russian patronyms, being dull. We were engaged in talk—I mostly nodded—and subject to speeches, speeches sotto voce or loud, reasonable as pie and impassioned as pitch. It all had much to do with the so-called "Russian mentality." "Solzhenitsyn was right, you will see!" one young fellow shouted at me. "Your freedoms are absurd." "You must temper all this steel with grains of salt," young Razumov whispered. "Actually most of these people are anti-Communist, actually they are quite religious." This did not tend to reassure me. "We will root out this crime and chaos and confusion, this corruption," Razumov whispered to me. "You will see. Mother Russia will emerge. Only Russians can understand Russia. Russia is—"

"Superior?"

Razumov, hot-eyed, knocked his vodka back and poured some more. I had heard of this, 'twas called the "Russian Idea." They would come to their own system, their destiny, from their own roots, religious and philosophical. They by God needed tyranny, or at least strong order, solidarity. The old Tsars and Stalin, they knew that. I just hoped that what they came up with had some vents of reason, some need for trade bucks in it. Were we going to deal with another whole mindset different from ours, like the Muslim world? Then I wondered, bin Laden, he was a player, why weren't we trying to talk to him, as an investor, a capitalist? If we could talk to the Bear, why not him? I quaffed the Stoli, suddenly missing Lily. Wouldn't she coil and strut and gleam among these cats? I felt like I was set down in a smoky, hazy, bluish pen of chained, snarly dogs who had been whipped, of Yahoos who would rise and kill the horses given half a chance. Then I thought again: but what an amazing people. I wondered how Americans would get through what they were going through now. I staggered up from the table, as a fellow shouted at me about Dostoevsky, did we read in U.S. the great *Crime and Punishment*? Yes, yes, I waved at him, of course, dear sir, four and four is nine, or two and two are five—or what the hell was it? It was the irrational sum in *Notes from Underground* that seemed the relevant Dostoevsky to me. Disjoint, it was, the equation, anyway. A man dressed all in black carrying a gold-headed cane motioned for me to sit down by him. He had mad eyes, a mad old man. Introduced himself as M., head of the Chechen Mafia. Was I this wealthy Texas fellow who invested? They could use some money, man, they would give us high interest on our investment. He offered me what appeared to be a long dark Grozny joint.

A woman came in with several young men all in dark doublebreasted suits, dark neckties and burr haircuts. These were the Democrats, I heard. The doublebreasted suit seemed to be a symbol of being a Democrat. Razumov pulled me to her. She was from St. Petersburg and was a person of great courage. She had criticized some old fart of a general for his classic claim that what was ruining Russia now was an "international Jewish conspiracy." Her party was called Democratic Choice. We exchanged pleasantries. She seemed saner than most of the fanatics in the place. I met her young companion or bodyguard, he said was Texas really like they said it was? I said, absolutely, before Billy Roy came heaving up and laid a ham hand on me and said that it was time to go, this joint was getting like the Dripping Springs Reunion on Saturday, these old boys and girls would be a-fighting next. He got Razumov, who was passionately preaching something, I thought maybe arguing, with some of the doublebreasteds, to wave our driver to us, and we left without the double or triple agent, never to behold him again. Singh, who had sat in total silence in the corner posing as a quiet American, got out of there with us.

In the car I said to Billy Roy, "You'd leave me alone, in jeopardy of my life with that terrible spooky guy with the black hat and cane, the head of the Chechen Mafia for pity's sake, but come hot-footing over just the moment I start to talk to an attractive woman? Is that how Miss Lily told you to take care of—to guard—me?"

"You got that right," said Billy Roy.

"I had an idea, suddenly come to me, in there," I said to Singh, huddled in the back seat of the car as we glided through the Russian night.

"Oh no," said Singh. "Much too late for ideas, now."

It was for sure about two in the morning, and H. Rose full of Stolichnaya, but I told him my idea anyway. It made him shrivel up into a little ball beside me.

I TOLD THEM I was terribly sad for Russia. At the party R. arranged for us, some of the more reasonable ones praised Robert Strauss, the Dallas guy, he'd been ambassador right at first, wanted to help, was on the right track. Surely reason must prevail. I was even prepared to argue that "Primo" might be partly right, mixed economies were needed to raise up Russia and China, all the beleaguered Asian places.

"Oh no," said Singh, "mixed economies stopped usefulness 'bout twenty sparky years ago. And this other idea you have, Prince, let us call

Lily so she can expose your hot idea to the ice of her logic, is simply, like, I mean to say—"

"Crazy," offered Billy Roy. "Crazy as a dog with twenty ticks."

"See what they say. Leave it up to them."

"Who? Lily?"

"No. That fellow, Osama. He's a player. He has millions in investments, it's in his interest to be in the club with T-Rex, with 'George,' with the others."

"Listen," Singh said, "I must tell you, Mr. Chambers reports that George is now leery of us, of the King of Texas, worried about our turning foolish—dying and whatnot. In terms of our present relationship G. K. Chambers says, Mr. George in terms of our fishing together has cut the bait."

"All the more reason to do something bold, bring us all together, get some leverage on this thing, before Russia turns Communist again, or more likely, having seen those fanatic dudes, fascist. God, talk about the Religious Right. And the Arabs and Muslims all united in Holy Wars against us for what's happened in Bosnia etc. and for no good other reason than that we exploited and embargo'd and humiliated them and we are the Other."

"I do not think that reason, those reasons, for Ducky sakes, is the sober principle that should operate here," muttered Singh.

"Them sand niggers ain't capable of it," opined Billy Roy.

"Watch that," sharply said H. Rose. "Bin Laden is a capitalist. I think we can appeal to him that he should be in the club. He was a patriot, that is why they are sheltering him. My father is from Michigan, I'd go to visit him in Dearborn. He was surrounded by Arab neighbors there. We got along just fine with them. I think I can relate to him. Haven't we ever been in touch before? Okay. So what does Mr. Chambers think?"

"He is in the Secret Place," said Singh. "Working on the books. T-Rex Fund is a little shaky, I think. He would think it's foolish. Let us call Miss Lily."

"She said Prince here was in charge, just do it and get home," said Billy Roy.

"Let's give it a go, see what happens," I said to him.

"Okay," he said. "Blind hog."

"Okey dokey," Singh says, going in to access his satellite phone. "I have the bloody number." Then he popped his head back in my dimlit room. A bleak dawn was coming up over Moscow. "I must tell you, I refuse to go."

He got hold of somebody there wherever it was where they had *their* satellite phone in Afghanistan, and they said, sure, come on, they knew of T-Rex, and the terrible revanchist throwback King of Texas, they would furnish transportation, come ahead but there are no guarantees.

"What does that mean?"

"Well, I guaran-dang-well-tee you, it ain't good," said Billy Roy. "I reckon, they mean, gettin' back."

"Surely they mean no guarantee of seeing him, old Osama, in person. Though why wouldn't he?"

"They said his former secretary, who works now in a dry cleaners in Texas in Arlington, the Dallas suburb, vouched for us, said we were real," said Singh.

"That is amazing," I said. I thought it was. The world was very small. Surely much could be accomplished for the good of all by personal interaction.

"Surely, surely," muttered Singh, the popinjay.

As we drove to the airport he said, "If you are not delivered back here by tomorrow evening I will call Lily."

"Call my daddy," Billy Roy laughed. "Tell Daddy Bob to get Uncle Tom Ping and the family and come rescue me."

We went to a designated runway and boarded a lean black jet piloted by a Kuwaiti and hosted by a bearded gent in black pajamas who served us tea. I have no good sense of direction and always had trouble finding my way back the way I'd come, even finding my way back to Texas. From that moment I had no idea whatsoever where we were, except later, as we landed, it was of course Afghanistan and mountainous. It was the country I'd read about in Michener's glowing account of the Afghan rebels bravely, firecely fighting off the Russians. It did not take long, and then we landed and were blindfolded and put in an all-terrain vehicle and bumped a long way to somewhere, going mostly up all the time to where the air was very thin and, now, piercingly cold. Luckily I had on the great yellow Shearling parka Lily had bought for me, the coat worn in W.W. II by the U.S. ground personnel stationed at Dutch Harbor in the Aleutians to protect against the bitter cold and wind coming in off the Bering Sea. Oh, that was a blessing, yes it was.

THIRTEEN

"Oh, there's more pretty girls than one . . . more pretty girls than one . . . Quit rambling all around . . . more pretty girls than one . . ."

Billy Roy kept sing-songing, half under his breath, as we bumped along. It irritated me, disoriented as I was, blindfolded. He was repeating the same refrain, out of tune. Instead of telling him to shut up, I said, "You have a girlfriend, Billy Roy?"

"Got a wo-man I idolize," he muttered. "You know the one. But she is a princess, I am just a common boy . . . ."

"Well, seems like a fine figure of a fellow like yourself should maybe find himself another gal, maybe even settle down. As Saint Paul says, 'It is better to marry than to burn.' And, also—"

"He is a charlatan, that Sa'nt Paul, a traveling salesman, made up another whole Jesus. He was old Saul, faked a encounter on the Damascus road."

I was amazed at this revelation about Paul, with which I rather agreed, being myself something of the type, from the lips of Billy Roy Crockett.

"I am pledged to Miss Lily for life," then he said, in a loud clear voice, the wonderful burly romantic misled loyal boy.

We bumped along. "I'm just driftwood on the riv-er, floating down the stream of life . . . ," he tunelessly, tonelessly began to sing, or mutter, then over again . . . .

Actually, H. Rose's thoughts were crowded and I paid little real attention to him.

"Arakajeezysoo," or some such, Pashto I presumed, a shrill voice from outside said as our vehicle stopped and the rear door was pulled open and we were blindly pulled out of it. Then we were prodded but withal paraded gently up and down, not too far, somewhere and left to stand there. "Where are we?" I said aloud in case someone was with us as we stood there still blindfolded. This reminded me of my fraternity initiation in those dear forever gone days of American youth.

"We are at Nine Springs," said a disembodied voice in clear good English out in the cold ether from us. Ah, I thought, Nine Springs, the nether region, the end of somewhere, nowhere-land, Nirvana. Then the blindfolds were removed and Billy Roy and I saw that we were way up on a mountain looking over to other mountains and down to rugged hills. It was cold as bloody ho-ho and about noontime, I imagined. A cool red sun sat in a gray sky.

It is hard to stop and reflect and describe this country, but it is important, now, as memory, as memorial. I thought I saw down on the hills below a pack of golden animals that might be lions—or might be longhair mountain sheep or goats turned gold by the cool pale sun—or might of course have been O-Sam's own Afghan hunting hounds running in a pack, heading up the hill toward us. They were a lovely image, I did not stop then to consider whether toward. Billy Roy jerked his head, saw them too. Nervous, he began to half-whistle an old Ernest Tubb. A fellow in pajamas standing with us with lots of cartridge belts over his shoulders touched him lightly with his rifle. B.R. looked shocked, stopped whistling. I thought he must be cold. He wore his hat, jeans, boots but only one of those Colorado sleeveless ski tubes around his massive upper body. He gave me his mean Marine look, like, that harem-legged, scraggly-beard Muslim dude touch me again I will, Prince, hand him his gauzy ass on a fucking plate. We were unarmed and not in propitious position to call the shots, but I knew Billy Roy felt his strength was as the strength of ten for his heart was pure and his Texas was getting a tad riled. The very clear voice off to my left turned out to be embodied in a very old man in black pajamas and a black head scarf who lightly said into my ear that we were on a plain at 14,000 feet above most of the mountains, that we were at, or somewhere like, the Sari Sangar, or some such. I whispered thanks for this information and looked around again. It looked like descriptions of Tibet to me. All I really knew was that we were way up there and to the west must be Iran, to the east Pakistan. For a moment I thought of my Pakistani friends in Dallas in the dry cleaning-laundry business, how far they'd come for a new life, how they spent their money and holidays going home. Another lean customer in black came up the trail and nodded to us and we were led down a ways and to the mouth of a cave. He motioned me to enter. The skinny-ass one put his rifle across Billy Roy's chest, stopping him.

"Stay, pig," the fellow in black said.

"Goddamn," said Billy Roy.

"Take it easy, Billy Roy," I said. "I mean."

"Okay, Prince." But he was standing stiff with tension when I went in.

The fellow seated on carpets in the somehow electric-lit interior of the hillside looked like the representations of him we have in the media—scarf, loose pajama-like garb, thin-faced, bearded, holding an automatic weapon—but he may or may not have been really him. Articulate as he was, he may have been some lieutenant who from his clipped accent might have gone to Oxford or to Harvard. I heard later that Osama had a pad in Kabul, that he headquartered there before they took away his satellite phone and he skedaddled, that it would be unlikely to find him here in the mountains. But then we had reached him by that phone, and also later heard that that was exactly where the fellow was, planning the terrible events to follow, that August.

It did not go well from the start.

"I am Henry Rose," I said, "representing—"

"Yes. You look small and pitiful. Not my idea of being from Texas, you know?"

"Take a look at my buddy out there, he's a better example of the breed. Actually we come in all sizes."

"What is your message?"

I said that it was my earnest hope that the T-Rex Fund might do some joint venture with him, a carefully chosen global venture of possible benefit in the world to the people that concerned him and the people that concerned us. That surely religious differences or past antagonisms should not separate us or make us automatically hate or distrust each other in this small, tragic world, this fragile planet. That—

"You care for no people but yourselves. Only you care for profit, money. You do not fool me."

I persisted. If he would just give a listen. For example, as a native of Kuwait, he must realize our joint interests there. If we could all go together we could make the desert bloom—

He laughed. I realized he wondered who I thought was fueling the undermining of the Kuwait state. Yet I persisted, trying not to sound so fuzzy, trying to find a chord.

"Yes," he said, his eyes hot as young Razumov's, this strange old bird, this hybrid of his fanaticism and our folly, "that will be nice! I wish to blast all imperialists from our region, from Asia, Africa and Central Europe. We want to establish the Faith. I have heard of this little T-Rex

Fund. Where have you invested? In the corruption that is Russia? Yes. In Baku, for the oil? Shame! Would the T-Rex like to invest in explosives with me, for the warning, for the cleansing?" He laughed.

"Listen. Don't you have a guy, your former secretary, in Texas, in Arlington. Surely—"

"Yes. A good man. Go home and tell them he is innocent."

"Well, sir, I just thought our fellow, Mr. Chambers, our investments officer, might get together with your representative, and we might figure out—"

I heard yelling from outside. "Excuse me," I said, and went out there. I had no thought that old Sam, if that was him, would shoot anybody not coming at him.

Billy Roy was dancing around with about five guys hanging on him. "I just tried to come see about you, Prince. Get your hands off me, you Goddamn sand niggers," he bellowed.

I heard the old clear-voiced guy in black, a tiny man, sharply catch his breath, *Ah!* and then say something clear and distinct above the hubbub.

"Let go of him!" I shouted; but they hit Billy Roy in the head with rifle butts and all stood pointing their guns at him as he fell and lay there on the rocky ground. A little light snow began to fall. I went raging back inside the cave and I reckon would have caught one, or a burst, from the old boy on the carpets except several Afghans caught up with me and pinned my arms and choked my neck and took my legs out so I found myself suppliant on a red rug before him. "Let – him – be –" I said.

"You are a fool," he said. "You need a lesson. You confirm me that you people—all you—need a lesson. Fool!"

In my Bible, for it had been on my mind a while, it says never call another a fool—Raca—was on my lips; then I got my own butt to the head and stars came shuttling and streaming over the mountains and I was out.

I AWOKE with a pain in the center of my head, thinking I'd had a very bad idea, and worried about the stars, then saw that it was black dark night and they were really out, and managed to roll over and get up to a sitting position. It was terribly cold to my face but luckily I still wore the amazing yellow fur-collared Shearling parka. I felt a small stabbing finger of pain in my left hand where my next-to-last finger with the Prince of Dallas silver star-onyx ring on it had been, and tried to stand but could not yet and put the fingers of my right hand on the already healing soft little spot where they'd clipped the finger off from, and found that it, with the ring, was truly gone. I felt numb with hatred, stupidity and loss.

It was so dark, so black, I could not see around me.

"Billy Roy," I whispered. "Billy Roy," I said. *"Billy Roy!"* I screamed.

There was no answer for a while. Then he said, "They got me hanging over here. I'm all tied up. It's not a tree, it's like a gallows. But they—they ain't hung me. They—"

"Dear God," I said.

"They—keep cutting on me—" he said. "Ever' oncet in a while they come and—whack off a little piece— They took my clothes—"

"Dear God," I said. "Oh, Billy Roy—"

"I'm sorry, Prince. It was me, Henry. I never should have said it, called 'em that. Oh my. It made me mad. I lost my cool. I don't blame these fellers—much— Oh— "

I heard a thud, a *thak*.

"There went my— Oh shit, Prince— " He began to laugh, and cry a little.

"It's so cold, I'm frozen. It don't really hurt that much," he said.

"Listen," I said, trying to stand up.

"Oh, don't try to do nothing, Henry, they'll hang you too. I reckon they want you to go back and tell about it. That's good. Just keep me company, Henry, if you will . . . Let's talk a little, buddy, about Texas— Oh Lord, how I do love Texas . . . . "

Terrified, I couldn't think of anything to talk about, and he began to hum, and sing, in that tuneless singsong way, "Oh, there's more pretty girls than one, more pretty girls than one—"

Then: " . . . gave up my wife, I left my home, when you promised to be mine alone—" he sang. " . . . now I'm full of mis-ery . . . may you never be alone like me . . . "

He hummed and sang, hanging over there in the darkness not too far from me. In a little while I heard a rustle in the darkness and a whack and actually saw the glint of a blade in starlight as they took another piece off him.

It made him moan, but then he said, "This reminds me, Henry—I thought you were kind of a s.o.b. but then when I learned you was there, at the Dripping Springs Reunion, whenever I rode the perimeter when I was a boy . . .

"Reminds me of a strange thing I seen—out in West Texas, little town—   See, they would have—drawn—a checkerboard on the square—and then ever' year bring in a fattening hog and let it onto that checkerboard, and place your bets, you see—and where that hog shit, that was the winning square—"

He laughed. "Ain't that a funny thing to do?"

Yes, I nodded that it was.

"Only do something like that, you know, in Texas . . . ."

In a while I heard another sound, the slight rustle of a movement, of softshod steps, of clothes. I stood up. My bright yellow Shearling coat gleamed in the darkness. There were the stars, like pinpoints in the sky. I was adjusting and could see a little now. I saw the fellow. I could make out the lump suspended, a pale lump, that was Billy Roy. The figure, in black, went to him.

"I can't take no more, I don't believe—" I heard Billy Roy say softly. Then: "Prince. That you, man? Tell Miss Lily—I—was—That I was pretty brave, considering—"

He kicked at the figure approaching him. It had a scimitar blade in the starlight. "Say there," I said to it.

It turned around, fluidly, almost politely, as if to inquire what I might want of it. I'm sure it could see me gleaming in my great yellow coat before it. It held the scimitar half-poised. I thought I might hit it the one quick lethal blow to the chest that with the blow to the bridge of the nose and the blow to the throat they had taught us as we went off to that "police action" in that other cold, rocky, terrible place and that I had thought that I would never use. But it backed up, seemed to murmur something, I think bowed, and disappeared into the darkness.

"It's all right," I said to Billy Roy. But he was quiet, swinging from his altar now. I believe his heart had stopped. It was a good one, too.

On the ground in the dark I found the blade below Billy Roy and cut him down with it. No one else seemed to be around. I did not know whether we were near or far from where we'd been, but we were still up on the mountain. I took off the great yellow coat and put it over him. I would like to say I scratched out a shallow grave and buried him, but I was not capable of doing it. At earliest light, freezing in my damnable pinstriped suit and slipping in my fine English shoes, I set out going down what was from time to time a path among the rocks and shrubs. I comforted myself thinking I carried his soul along with me like in a jar, cradled in my left arm, clutched by my hand where it now throbbed newly missing a finger.

By daylight I was in a village, halfway down. I sat on a bench on a street of stones and people came and looked at me, and then a kind man brought me a jacket and a kind woman some bread and tea, and later some of the fellows in black came and I thought I was a goner, but they blindfolded me again and put me in a car. After a while I was released to sight and put in a hotel room in some small city. No one spoke a word to me the whole time. They did not take my wallet. They put iodine on my finger stump. I stretched out on the bed in the room and slept a long time. Then I just stayed in there. I drank from a pitcher of water with things floating in it and had no hunger, almost no feelings. I was numb, like that patient etherized upon the table, like the leopard frozen at that altitude, like some creature laid out deadened in a zoo. I dreamed of being in that horrible octopus' tentacles, of its terrible eye looking into mine.

When the door opened I sat up, numb but accepting, ready. When I saw that it was T. J. Mackey I got up off the bed, rubbing my hand where the ringed finger had been.

He looked at me, old T. J. Mackey. "I work for her, and do what she says, and she wants you back," he said, his gray eyes deadlier than the hot eyes of Razumov or than whoever it had been in that cave. "If it was just up to me, I'd kill you now and get it over with." He felt in his pocket for the sweet assurance of his knife.

"Please do," I said.

FOURTEEN

Dallas is a beautiful city. Its buildings sit and shine in lovely glass and metal colors on the prairie, beautiful all lit by night, beautiful touched by the Texas sun day by day. Each building sits separately but in tune with the others like a statement of our faith. Heat shimmered over the city, it was a hundred degrees or more; but I thought I had never seen anything more clean and beautiful than this place. I bathed for days and did not drink a drop. The missing finger fascinated Lily, and aroused her, even in her sadness. Oh, she was not sad for poor Billy Roy. "He was a good boy," she said, and looked lost, sunk, kind of like an old society dame when I told her, just murmured, that he wanted her to know he'd been brave, considering . . . . "He did his job," she said, this Lily, Princess of our Texas, Queen of our Shining City. By the same token, she did not blame me, for Billy Roy, for my awful mistake in judgment. "You were in charge," she said. "You did what you thought best. It was perfectly logical and honorable that that old Islam might want to get on board our boat, go West. Well— Fuck him, Henry, fuck him! Talk to Mr. Chambers. I have sent Mr. Singh back to India, may he languish there, he was a wreck when he came back from Russia, the very idea of him setting it up like that, so we had no control."

"I told him to do it, Lily."

"What? You want him back? He was some son of an old boy that Daddy knew in India—"

"No. I don't want him back. I agree with you completely."

"Of course you do! Dear Henry. Oh, what are we to do—"

No, her sadness was not about Billy Roy—she decreed that no mention be made of his death, no notice given, no memorial service. In the circumstances of this game, he must just disappear. Nor sadness for the mission failed in Afghanistan, or most probably failed in Russia. Her sadness was for Daddy, who had not recovered well, had declined in our absence. As a matter of fact, he lay at home mute, immobile. It looked like, as we say in Texas, Daddy was dying.

I had thought she would be furious. I'd thought the game was up as I flew back in to DFW on a charter jet with T. J. Mackey. I thought she'd moan and mourn for her obedient servant Billy Roy. But she met me grandly at the plane, queenly, warmly, kissed my hands and vowed her love and said we'd get the ring, if not the finger, back, cooed at me, and took me to her castle, now guarded by another chap in the rifle tower, led "home" to bath and bed. It was the damnedest thing. Lily was real nice then. Nor did I fathom, in the moment, why.

I'd returned to Dallas at end of July. Texas stayed in vise-like heat and drought. The markets got shakier on fears of Asia and South America, Japan, China, Korea, Hong Kong, Mexico, Brazil, everywhere going dry if not belly up. Billions in crops and livestock burned up in Texas while the vengeful Texas and U.S. Republican Guard kept their relentless single-sight on Buddy Bill. On August 7 bin Laden would deliver his "warning," bombing our embassies in Kenya and Tanzania. We would bomb them back, firing cruise missiles into Afghanistan a little later in the month. I was piously grateful to have gotten out of there.

Lily had carried on as if nothing had happened or was happening in the world, as people, even princesses, tend to do. I had thought she was fully in charge and on top of Daddy's business, Daddy's money and its uses, but now I wondered, beholding again her cracked cat's eyes and vague girlish smile, her wrinkles and her long lean languorous body, the grace and vapidity with which she greeted me, whether she actually knew even in general the state of T-Rex and our national and international affairs. I saw G. K. Chambers just for a moment as he departed her pad; he gave me a short little Pecksniffian look and nod. I asked her to keep T. J. Mackey away from me; she admonished me gently, saying hadn't the fellow come and gotten me? Yes, I said, mostly to myself, and get me again no doubt he would . . . . But Lily—Lily of the cracked blue eyes and trembling frame and ice-cold Squeakers—icy vodka shots—which I began again to share with her—had been going to meetings and receptions and social affairs, planning this and gracing that, the Crystal Charity Ball, the TACA Auction, Texas (Solar) Plexus, and so on, jealous of her dear friend Gloria who'd got her photo not only in the *Morning News* "Low Profile" section but also in the *Park Cities People*—and she did not even reside in the damn Park Cities! Why, Gloria had just cornered the poor witless photographer, forced him into shooting her! Why, Gloria was the only person Lily knew who could corner you in a round room!

Lily did have a new look, or style, she'd adopted since I had been to Russia and other terrible parts. It was a Chinese look. Lily arranged to slant her eyes and walk a little like her feet had been bound in childhood and to murmur "go into garden now" and such as that while looking really mod-Beijing in green or blue silken Chinese gowns. I was scared to death, thinking where my next assignment for T-Rex might be, but then Wing, Lily's new "coordinator/assistant," drifted into our—Lily's—wing—Lily was caring for me in her very own part of the house, bedroom, bath, den, solarium in her Bluff View castle—and I saw where the influence was coming from. Wing bowed a lot and was very pleasant and smiled and her eyes flicked around at you from behind oval glasses and I figured she was a spy, an assassin, and would come drifting into our connubial bath one evening and drown us both. Don't be such a silly, Lily purred, Wing was highly recommended by Dr. Delftman, the rector. She had come over from China, and married badly, and split from the guy. She was full of wonderful decorating ideas and gave Lily support, encouragement and adulation as needed. She was also, Lily admitted, trained in martial arts and was a good woman to have by your side in a pinch. So in a way Miss Lily had on some instinct already replaced poor Billy Roy, even as he had met his fate, by another liegeperson.

The new fellow in the guard tower functioning as our security was an associate of T. J. Mackey. Mackey assured Lily the fellow had been in Texas for a while and was loyal to it. He was a shorter, blanker-faced version of Mackey. His name was Nathan Pitts. Mr. Pitts, like Mackey in his gray, wore the same outfit daily, Navy blazer, red tie, gray slacks, cordovan loafers. His shoulder muscles rippled under his blazer when he stood at ease. Having walked up to his aerie one afternoon for exercise, I asked him whether he had gone to Yale or Virginia. "I did not go to university, sir," he said. He had a strange accent.

One evening about a week after my return, after Lily had returned to her castle having visited Daddy laid out in his, the inert Texas Rex on life support, she invited, or commanded, me to a banquet in the formal dining room. Lily was quite an Orientalized Beauty in green silk and jade, dressed by Wing as Princess Lily of the Valley of Love. Wing had set an exquisite dinner table, with rare china and special dishes and plum wine, the Feast of the Returning Lover—never ask me what delicacies, birds, sweetbreads, fishes, meats and sauces lay there before us, for I was a little bit blurred already as I sat at my end of the table. Lily, I believe, was drinking vodka from a flute. She raised it to me as Wing hovered in the wings. I raised my plummy wine to her. She looked, again, to me like a great glittering jeweled snake, a gem-encrusted anaconda.

"O Henry, dear," she murmured/hissed, "I do love you so. You gave your finger for me, for us!"

I nodded, rubbing the ossy stub. I had done so, and it was beginning to make me, as I recovered from total numbness, a little angry.

"Billy Roy gave more. Let us drink to him," I said.

She looked upset that I had mentioned him but tossed it down.

"I know you said no memorials, no memory of him, but I do think, Lily, that we should do something." Sap that I am at heart, I began to lightly hum.

"Why are you singing that? Why, Henry?" Anger or jealousy flickered in her eyes.

"What, my dear?"

"That—that old tune. 'More pretty girls than . . .' "

"Oh. Why indeed?" I stopped, saw him hanging there, a lump of flesh, saw the large whole fish on a platter set before me on the table. "A bell. A small concert hall. A study room. Something more than Bunky's bench."

"Bunky? Oh—him—"

"I mean, you see, just something, honoring Billy Roy, at Highland."

"Oh. At the college. Certainly, Henry. We can do that. Nobody will even know it's him. Nobody will ever know it's there. A nice—statue— or something. Eh?"

"Yes. Good. A little herd of mustangs . . ."

"Terrific! That is very thoughtful of you, Henry. You are a kind, good man. Now—!"

She had coiled up and spoke so loudly that I jumped. She had been all day, before visiting Daddy, at a women's symposium put on by Regina Singh at Highland U. whose theme was "Empowering Women to Assume Positions Traditionally Taken by Men." "Yes?" I said.

"This is a special dinner, Henry. You know how I love and adore you. You are the one man . . . Oh my . . . I may cry. No! I won't. But you alone make me happy, Henry Rose. I want us to be married."

Oh. My.

"Rex Ranch will be yours! But not right now. We are going to have to wait a while. I know you'll understand."

I smiled my assurance at her. For some reason Wing came and took the fish. Perhaps it had grown cold.

"Henry," Lily said, leaning far over her edge of the table, brandishing the flute which Wing had refilled for her, "besides marrying me—or carrying me off in a fit of passion I know you are so capable of— Henry, tell me: if you could be one person and do one thing in the whole wide world right now—if you could have your absolute heart's desire—who—what—would that be?"

"Oh, Lily, thanks for asking. You know I've been through a lot just now. I think that—oh well. Right this minute, dearest, I'd like to be a bass player in a jazz combo in a nice dark place, yes, kind of anonymous, backing up the piano. Oh yes—do ba, ba ba, da da, boo—"

She looked shocked, like a teacher with a dull pupil, like she might get up and come around the table and bop me. "But I will settle just to be here with you, now," I started to say.

"That is not it at all!" Meaning the jazz thing. "Oh. I see—your crazy sense of humor. No, Henry. The answer is, you would more than anything like—love—to be the King of Texas! Right?"

"Why, Daddy is the King of Texas. There is no other King of Texas."

"Daddy is dying, Henry. Don't be dumb. We have to carry on."

"Carry on? Dear Jesus. Surely when Daddy dies? The game is not going to survive Daddy, is it?"

"I thought you had learned, it is not a game, Henry. It is very Goddamn fucking real. We have many billions—invested—pledged—hedged—at risk—at work—in the T-Rex Foundation and the Fund. Ask Mr. Chambers how many. He tried to show me the books, I told him you would go over them with him soon. We have managers, a network, everywhere. Political candidates who are going to count on us. There has to be a King. When Daddy—goes away—there must be a successor. There must be—a King. I mean, the King of Texas. He must exist. I have groomed you, Henry. It's quicker than I thought, but here it is, buddy boy. Comin' at you, Henry—"

"Rose," I said.

"I am not Rose. I'm Lily."

I don't know why I said "Rose," my name, the name of the woman who walked with me in San Antonio; I know I thought of the nice wealthy woman with the house in Taos I might have chosen instead of this Lily, this incredible, megalomaniacal Lily.

"Yes, I'm Rose. But you, Lily. You. It's got to be you. When he—*dies*—it's you, his very daughter, you who believes, you who must be King."

"No. This is very good, by the way." She had settled back in her chair, was picking at the food. "Have you tried the eel? I cannot be, of course, the King."

"Well, be the Goddamn Queen, then!" What was this, primogeniture? No, not that. I seemed to be a bit mixed up in my mind.

"I will excuse you, Henry. Nor that. There cannot be a Queen, there must be a King. There are those we deal with who will not recognize a queen . . . ."

Balls, said the Queen. If I had two I'd be King! I laughed a little. She smiled, seeing me loosening up, regaining my senses. I'd had, she knew, a terrible time.

"You mean, a king on the books, eh, Lily? Someone pro forma, someone like me, that you can run . . . ."

"Of course I will *help* you, Henry! You do know that! All of us will *help* you—and you will be *wonderful*! Oh, I know it! Because you are so honest, because you are so true! And you really, really, really will be it! I promise you. Oh yes, I know you will be fine! I am so glad this is settled now! Wing, will you clear this mess off, for the love of God! Dr. Rose—the kingly Mr. Rose—and I are retiring now. Did you bring me that herbal passion powder? Oh good. Thank you so much, Wing."

We retired to enact the sexual fantasy of "The Wounded Swallow Returns from the Valley of Nine Springs." At the climactic point of the return of the swallow I thought or felt that Wing was watching. Later Lily got up and dressed, in black karate clothes. Going to a window I saw her let out of the house by Mr. Pitts and be driven off in her Lexus by T. J. Mackey. I slipped downstairs to my own room and set the alarm clock there for early, 5:30, and arose then and shaved and showered and was very awake and dressed and ready when Lily, dressed all in yellow, appeared in the room where I was sitting meditating at seven.

"Daddy died during the night, Henry," she said, composed. No tears. Makeup perfect. "He passed away peacefully."

"Well," I said. "How about a cup of coffee? I'll help you make the arrangements."

"That would be nice," she said.

She gave me that lopsided smile and gave me a hand hard as iron and pulled me up from the chair. As I got up and put my arm around her waist with the Swallow's knowledge of its softness and we walked together, of a height, I had to think, actually, this was quite a kid, to be so serene having just dispatched a father.

We went separately to the funeral. Lily was the greeter, and indeed the last member of the McIvey family of that name left standing. I stayed in the background with Sam McGee, who picked me up in that boat of a white Lincoln Town Car. I joked that there was some little white-suited millionaire in McMurtry who slept in his Town Car up in a parking garage. Sam said he'd gotten used to the car, it wasn't too different from the Crown Vic he drove for work. He remarked that I didn't seem too upset. I wasn't, I said, about Daddy but showed him the hand missing my ring and finger and told him a little bit about Billy Roy and Afghanistan. So this is real, he said. Yes, in its own strange way it is, I said.

Daddy passed away a minor figure in Dallas. Lily wrote a long obituary, the one you pay to run, for the *Dallas Morning News*. She extolled him as a father, a wildcat oil operator, one of an almost vanished species, a rancher whose Rex Ranch was well known in Texas, and a generous man, a philanthropist who had contributed to many causes. She said he had a great love for Texas. She said that those close to him knew him as a lovable eccentric. She said nothing about the King of Texas bit or about the T-Rex Fund or international business transactions. The paper did not run Oliver McIvey as a story in the obit section, instead that morning using a story about a former schoolteacher and one about an oncologist who had passed. Lily used a photo in her paid column of her father when he was about thirty-five. He was ruggedly handsome then, no pouches that later made him seem so lizard-like. Clear eyes looked straight at you. He looked quite sane. No age was given. The piece gave the haunting impression that McIvey had always existed in Texas.

St. Cuthbert's was a small church. Even so, it wasn't full. The remnant of the old oil guys in their blue suits and two-tone shirts came. Colonel Luther McLuther and some of the people from Rex Ranch flew up for it. A few other ranch folks. Some people from the church, some from Lily's groups. George W. Bush did not attend, nor did any representative of the State of Texas, nor Kay Bailey nor Phil nor old Armey whose district McIvey had been in. The local Congressman sent a greeting since it seemed old Oliver had been a Ranger in W.W. II. Rt. Rev. Dr. Dudley Delftman presided in monk's robe with a tassel and we read together from the Book of Common Prayer and then read the Prayer of Confession on our knees: *We confess to you, all-knowing God, that we are afraid to admit what lies in the depths of our souls. We know we cannot hide our true selves from you. You know us as we are, and yet you love us. Help us not to shrink from self-knowledge. Raise us out of our guilt into the freedom of forgiven people* . . . . It moved me, and I grieved. Oh, not for Daddy—for myself. For old Oliver, Dr. Delftman proclaimed, as if he knew: *Non nobis, Domine, non nobis, sed nomini tuo da gloriam . . . .*

Going out into the horrible heat I spoke to Tex Flatt, though I had to grab him by the arm to keep him from going by without a word. He looked at me, like, nasty boy, you have done wrinkled the coat arm of my twelve hundred dollar suit. "Been on a trip, I hear, or something, gubuddy?" old Tex said.

"Yes. I would like you to meet my colleague here, Tex, Professor McGee, head of our new department of Ethnic Studies at Highland University."

"What the hell is that?" I knew that would get him.

"Black and gay literary and social theory," Sam said, smiling, showing that gold tooth.

Just then Lily came up with Wing and called Tex "Uncle" and gave him a hug and a kiss and introduced him to Wing. He might not relish black or brown but he seemed to like Asian pretty well. Lily whispered to him, several sentences. He cut his old eyes to me, obviously, for an instant, shocked. Then, all back together, he came back to me and held out his leathery hand. "Let me know if I can be of he'p," he said.

I smiled and said I surely would.

"So what's up, I mean, really, my man?" Sam McGee said as he drove us away from the church.

"I'm the new King. I mean, like, there has to be one, and I'm it."

"No shit?" Sam laughed. "Be damned," he said. "So what you want us common folk to call you? King?"

"Henry Rex," I said. Actually, though Sam laughed again, it had a pleasing sound.

Back "home," Lily kissed me lightly on the forehead, told me again I would do fine, because I was loyal, good and true, and went into her own apartment, leaving me alone downstairs. She stayed there and fasted for a week and for all I knew mortified her flesh. I saw her in passing a time or two, barefoot, no makeup, looking lined and old and now, without eating or drinking ought but water, gaunt. In a week she emerged in shimmering summer silk of a vibrant blue. Wing disappeared, where to I never knew, that phase for Lily over. She was outgoing, cheerful, radiant and insatiable. I thought of getting some Viagra. She set up a long day's meeting with G. K. Chambers, who came from the Secret Place, wherever the hell that was, for me to see the books, get a sense of the whole operation. I was amazed. T-Rex had investments everywhere. Old Oliver, dear old Daddy, really had been manipulating billions.

In the time that followed, I took my responsibilities terribly seriously. That month of August in the heat of Dallas was the happiest time of my life. Playing out the King thing, manipulating people and money, gave me energy I never knew before. I would not wear Daddy's garish gold, diamond and ruby Texas ring, except at the Levies—Lily said we had to go every fortnight to Daddy's manse and keep up the Levies, which she coordinated, people had signed up for them months ago—but I felt as if I truly was the King. I held myself straighter and came to believe that I was taller, like Hussein. Even Sam McGee, my constant attendant (not to say bodyguard, driver and wit for all occasions, I came to love old Sam) said that I came to look more significant.

"How did I look before?" I said.

"Kind of like a con man not quite sure what the game was, man."

"Well, that's about the same," I laughed.

But it really wasn't. Really was not, don't you see.

I took an office in the Renaissance Tower downtown. I liked the ring of it. Put a small gold nameplate on the door: *H. Rose. T-Rex Foundation.* Got a secretary, a techno whiz, Mrs. Fortifer, ugly enough to please Lily. Got hooked up, on-line, every which way. Began to talk to distant spots, to George, to the hedgehogs, others. It was strange: I began to get civic invitations. Suddenly I was put on several boards. I bought new pin- and chalkstripe suits. People would come to see me, or call, with the idea that I wanted to buy things, like properties, like buildings or airports or small towns here and there. This happened by osmosis, it seemed to me. And it was ludicrous, the idea that I had money. I had nothing. I was tenured at the university but drawing no salary there. Lily paid my memberships and my charge cards and gave me an allowance every week. Sometimes I wondered why she did it week to week.

Yes, life as at least the de facto King became vivid, engaging, even continually amusing. Compared to King, Provost was prunes. As someone once said of another matter, compared with playing the game at little Highland U., moving on the King's board was like moving from a "museum into a fancy-dress ball." And besides that, I grew tender towards Lily. I'd had already my ups and downs with her, but it looked like we were going to be together here, in this incredible caper, shouldn't I give it a try, try to figure the old gal out, look into her heart, try to understand, skip the Viagra and make a try for true tenderness? (Not that anyone ever knew or could know another heart—or his own, either.)

"Lily," I said, "my dear girl."

"Yes, Henry dearest . . ."

We were in her pleasant book-lined den in the Bluff place I thought of as her castle. A pleasant cocoon of nubby chairs and polished floor and soft-hued rugs, gentle lamplight, abstracts on the walls. Lily had not been painting lately at all, her fierce feminoid monster women embracing, attacking men: she said her life was fulfilling her, presently. She liked the air conditioning high, forbade TV: a cool cocoon, so that I wore an old tweedy jacket, about the only time now I dressed and looked like I used to look: H. Rose, Pro-fessor.

Lily was reading, or looking for the x time at a large-sized, slick local society/fashion/celebrity journal/mag festooned with images of young pouty skeletal models with bared belly buttons wearing costumes no usual woman would or could even in imagination don. Lily had given a tea someplace benefiting something and the sheet said she had mastered "the intricate majesty of the English afternoon tea." That pleased her. "Little do they know," I said, and she stuck her long prehensile tongue out at me.

Also the rag had two pics of her, one at the tea with the dear friend she called "Tawdry Audrey" and yet another at another snazzy function posed with three middle-aged dolls named Laurie, Jeanie and Janie. I had taken *The Princess Casamassima* from the bookcase and was once again skimming it.

"Did Daddy—your father, bless his memory—just drift into this King thing? I mean, there is no background or reason or sanction for it. It's not like someone who is of an old royal line whose positions don't exist anymore. I mean, it's made up."

"I beg your pardon, dear?"

"The King of Texas. It's a myth—not even a Texas myth. A metaphor. In Oliver McIvey's mind."

"That's right, dearest. He was crazy. That's a nice way to put it. A metaphor."

She looked up from her glossy sheets.

"My brother died, the little punk. He always disappointed Daddy. That changed my life. I was a cowgirl then. I loved the ranch. And I'd go to Santa Fe. Oh, we must go there, Henry! I have a place—one of my 'kingdoms' you haven't seen. I love the shops up and down Canyon Road. Daddy was going to buy me Santa Fe, if I would just get married. My sister, Heather, lives there, now. Sometime you'll meet her. We keep her there. She is retarded but wants to be sexually active. It is a problem. All my life has been problems, Henry, caring for—others."

"When did your father decide he was the King of Texas? Et cetera."

"He was in the CIA. Did I tell you that?"

"No."

"Yes. He was in the Army, a colonel in the Rangers. Then he was in the CIA, just when it was getting going. All those crazy guys, and a lot of Texas boys, all those guys at Yale and so forth who believed in America and the kind of 'New World Order' they had going then, were in the CIA. Luther wasn't, but he was decorated a lot in Vietnam. It changed Luther, he doesn't like to leave the ranch. Daddy was the opposite. Would you like a cigar, Henry? I have some fine ones from Havana, Daddy and I would enjoy one together occasionally?"

"Oh, yes, indeed."

I cut the ends of our cigars and lit them. It was very good. Soothing. Hadn't had one in a while. Made me feel like JFK or someone really important, which right then I was. Lily let out a puff of bluish smoke, carefully edged her ash into a green jade ashtray. "Daddy said never to smoke one more than halfway down."

"My father, Aaron Rose, told me exactly the same thing."

She smiled at this rapport. "You do have a lot of Jewish names in your family."

"Like Henry?"

"Sure. Henry is faux Jewish. Right? Moses and Aaron."

"Rose is French, from the French. Old Moses fought with Napoleon."

"Not very hard, I bet. You were asking about Daddy, his turning point. Well, he took the money he inherited—we have lots of oil, you know, it's so damn depressed now, but it will be fine again as soon as there's another war—and the money he made, and he started to make a bunch of deals out of Texas, over the world. He loved Texas, but he avoided it in terms of business. He said Texas was for developers—they own Dallas, Houston—and he was not a developer. Also, he liked to sit behind the screen. Daddy just loved *The Wizard of Oz*. He would watch it again and again. He has a big screen in his house, you know, and he would like to watch World War Two films over and over, and fantasies. He would laugh and laugh when Dorothy and them found it was that little man behind the screen manipulating everything. He said Hitler and Mao and all of them did the same. Reality is what is perceived, he said.

Luckily Daddy was not political, he despised political involvement."
Puff.

"Luckily?"

"Yes. If he'd gotten serious about Texas seceding, being independent, he might have been able to do it. That would have been stupid. The U.S. needs Texas, needs its image, and Texas feeds off that. These new nuts that want to secede now—oh not McLaren and that bunch—are fanatic in their own way, and it's dangerous. Ethnic."

I looked at her. My cigar was about to go out. My tongue tingled from the tobacco taste.

"Hispanic nuts," she said. She looked at the two photos of herself in the fashion mag, deciding which one she liked better or if she liked either. Then she tossed it on the rug, stubbed her cigar and said, "You're really getting into it, enjoying yourself, aren't you, dearest."

I said I truly was. Her eyes shone. When she was happy most of the wrinkles went away. She said it may be metaphor, Henry, but remember that a myth is a sustaining belief, and this is our little sustaining belief. It's more fun, she said, to be the King than to be merely a damn old CEO of the T-Rex Fund. Or of McIvey Enterprises, or McIvey-Rose. Anybody could do that. She said to remember what Daddy always said, keep your eye upon the donut and not upon the hole. I said I thought, since G. K. Chambers was basically an accountant, I might need a little help, like they'd had Mr. Fuad and Mr. Singh. Sure, she said, just check it out with her. John Woodcipher, at Highland U., was who I had in mind, I said.

"Isn't he a liberal? I had a course from him. I got the feeling he's a liberal, Henry."

"That was because he was for the Loyalists in the Spanish Civil War. Wouldn't you have been, against Franco?"

"Sure. I guess he's all right. You're King, my little man, my dearest. Just check all your moves with Mr. Chambers. And with your Lily dear, of course."

"Of course."

She came and tousled my thinning hair and pushed my specs down on my nose and kissed me and said this had been nice, she thought she'd go to bed by herself tonight. She felt nice and young tonight, she felt like she had been talking to Daddy, like when they used to smoke cigars together and have their little talks.

"Yes. Fine," I said, tenderly.

FIFTEEN

The very next morning Sam McGee drove me in the large bulbous Lincoln we had dubbed "Dishonest Abe" to Highland U. It lumbered around corners, yawed on the straightaway but had a strong old rearwheel drive, a lot of horses. Those leather seats, all bad memories notwithstanding, were heavenly. The prairie sun, on the edges of the great tall city, was lost in a dark morning haze.

"You find out anything about our buddy T. J. Mackey?"

"He is some smooth piece of ice. How you think he got in there to get you out, from Afghanistan?"

"Who is he?"

"Nobody. Like, it's a name. You know? I checked it for a file with a brother in the FBI, but there's no file. But in the CIA, man, there's names. A lot of people, from the Fifties, Sixties, on, a lot of guys have been 'T. J. Mackey.' Like, there's some DJ on a channel, they call him 'Charlie Black Dog,' he moves away and the name stays on. So there's no 'Charlie Black Dog' except he is whoever there is 'using' the name. So who is 'Mackey,' who knows? You reckon he remembers? He is just a killing machine for hire, man. Also, he turns up in our files, Henry, Dallas Police, 'T. J. Mackey,' back at the assassination time, more'n thirty years ago. That would be another 'T. J. Mackey,' of course."

"Of course."

"May be you could ask Miss Lily to let that boy go away, to some other job, some other hemisphere. I would hate to have to try to— You know. We come up against him one day, my friend, I will be runnin' like a turkey. I ain't a killer. I'm just a cop."

"We have a rendezvous with destiny, he and I, I think. I hope not you." I could feel it in my bones. *T. J. Mackey*, uh? "And Nathan Pitts? Who is he?"

"Don't know. Another of 'em, I suppose. What you think that accent is?"

"Sounds kind of German, Austrian, to me."

"Yeah. I thought so too. Hell, who knows? There are a lot of deadly guys out and around in the world just now, hiring on, making their way."

Highland University, as we cruised upon its grounds, was looking good, even in the heat looking better for Daddy's benefaction. In the middle of the campus a row of oak trees had been planted. The buildings looked less shabby, there were new directional signs in Highland's gold and blue. The new Flatt Tower while not tall or impressive was not half bad. It had bells in it, or a carillon, which rang incessantly as if thinking itself at Oxford. I had no sticker on the boat so we parked illegally in the Chairman of Trustees space, old Tex would not mind, and walked the paths to the Humanities Building. Students were going back and forth. We found John Woodcipher, now fully returned to teaching, in his bookish lair.

"John!" I was glad to see the suave and burly fellow. He was talking to a perfectly gorgeous young Latina.

"Well, here is the man himself," he said to her in indirect greeting of me.

"Dr. Rose? Oh my goodness! My uncle sent me here, I'm going to be a first-year in the fall, and I been looking for you. Why aren't you ever here?"

"On leave, my dear." With dark and flashing eyes. "Your uncle?"

"Yes. Ray Rodriguez. He said you fought in the war together."

"Oh. Sure. We were engaged in the same conflict, anyway. Good to see you. I am sure Professor Woodcipher is being helpful. Did we give you a scholarship?"

"No. She just walked in," Woodcipher said, obviously intrigued with her.

"My uncle, my old great-uncle, he is famous, I am sure you have heard of him, in New Mexico, is paying for me. 'An investment in the future,' he says. Andrés Vigil?"

"No," I said.

"Yes," Woodcipher said.

"But I could be on scholarship here—anywhere—if I applied. I was salutatorian at North Dallas High. Thirteen-ninety on the SAT."

"Bravo!" said Prof. Woodcipher. "Well, Miss—"

"Rosie Rodriguez." She pumped his hand, then mine. She wore jeans and a red silk blouse and cowboy boots.

"Here is a number where you can reach me," I said, handing her a T-Rex card. "I won't be teaching in September, but you should go say hello to President Singh. She will be glad you're here. Please give my regards to Uncle Ray."

"Sure. I see him all the time. He leads the Bible study."

Rosie was a peach. She would be a blue chip in Regina Singh's plans to diversify the student population. When she bounced out, I asked who was Andrés Vigil.

"We have a file on him, in Intelligence," said Sam McGee. "Stays in a village in the mountains near Taos, there. He's a terrorist."

"An extremist," said John Woodcipher.

"Whatever. Scary dude."

"Head of a Hispanic group that wants to reclaim Texas, join it up to other states, create the U.H.S.—the United Hispanic States. Texas, California, New Mexico, Colorado, like that. Interesting concept. Not so far-fetched, given that it was taken from them arbitrarily, and with all the ethnic thinking going on in the 'New World Order' these days." The professor of History pulled his tie, having taken us above history.

And I went right there with him. We pro-fessors had a rare chance in this moment to rise up and make a difference in the world. I had been thinking and I had plans. John Woodcipher listened intently, nodding his head, while Sam McGee picked his teeth and rolled his eyes. I knew that John would share my views and want to participate. I knew, from his passionate study of the Spanish Civil War, he would love the Brigades idea. First I told him he must not laugh and must never tell, but I was the King of Texas now, and that silly and fanciful as that must seem, it wasn't. I said he could ask Detective McGee, as sober a man as existed in all Texas, if I was not King of Texas.

"If he ain't, you may kiss my ebony butt," said Sam.

"Oh," said John, pulling out a bottle of California sherry from his desk drawer, pulling the shade to the window looking out upon the campus, closing his door against vagrant hearers, "I don't care if you are fantasizing, Henry old cheese, this is wonderful! And you say you have the money? What fun! Do you think we might should let Faisal Fazooli, our bright guy in Economics, in on it?"

I said no, no one else. Lily would tolerate one, Woodcipher, no more. Old John had a pretty good idea, there, to include an economist in the planning, and I probably should have listened to him. At the end, flushed with excitement, as I rose from his conference chair and gave him a wave he looked at me with shock. "I say, Henry, old man, what happened to your finger? You did have a finger there, did you not?"

"Yes, John. It got infected. Had to take the damn thing off."

"When did it happen?"

"While ago, on my trip. Had some primitive conditions. No 'E.R.' Etc."

"You laid some bullshit on that boy," Sam said as we cruised again by the Flatt Tower, the carillon chiming three.

"We're going to do it, too! I hope it didn't upset him, about the finger. You know, I hardly miss it anymore."

"No, that was cool. At least you didn't tell him the chief Muslim motherfucker of the world done clipped your digit off. That would give the dude some pause."

We headed toward my little house in University Park so I could check on it. It was Pearly's day to clean and I thought I'd find her there. On the way we wheeled into Snider Plaza so I could run in to Eckerds there where I still kept my prescriptions and pick up my blood pressure medication. Afghanistan had not helped the old b.p. I didn't want to drop dead or have a stroke, Lily would be furious. I thought I should ratchet down to just two or three Squeakers and no wine in the evening, but she was no help on that. We were drinking like the proverbial Fish that Drank Dallas. We were in some rather pleasant truce on sex and were substituting extra drink for it, I reckoned. Since I was "King of Texas" that seemed to supplant our other fantasies.

There were just a couple of cars parked slant-in in front of Eckerds, but as Sam pulled the Lincoln in the space two big pickup trucks pulled in on either side of us, double-cabs with men in big hats in them. An immense old man got out on Sam's side and smiled and rapped on his window. He looked friendly, like he'd lost his way from the farm or ranch, big creased cream-colored Stetson, and Sam let the window down. Then we were looking into the barrel of the biggest revolving handgun I had ever seen, so large it could only be called a "hogleg."

"Howdy," this huge old man said. "I am Ranger Ping, and this fellow that is going to get in the car with you is Daddy Bob Blanton. We are from Jack Hays County, and we are wanting a minute of your time."

Sam nodded it was fine with him as Ping slipped Sam's little pistol out from his shoulder holster and held it by the trigger guard on his finger and reached and clicked the doors unlocked, and a man with a big chest and a big lined face and a creased black Stetson on his head, a chap about sixty or a little more, opened the rear door on the other side and sat in the back seat. Mr. Ping put his pistol away somewhere under his duster that I swear to God was exactly like the ones the gunfighters wear in the Westerns and stood there looking in at us not sweating in the heat. He had the face of a great bulldog. Who had mentioned that name— Ping?

"Billy Roy," the man in the backseat said. "I am his daddy, Bob Blanton. We are wanting an account of him."

"I thought his name was Crockett. Billy Roy Crockett."

"Hell, he just told you that. He was bullshitting you 'cause you was bullshitting him. Told you 'Crockett' like he was kin to Davy Crockett 'cause you told him you were kin to that Moses Rose that left the Alamo. Never was no Rose left the Alamo, that is a fabrication and you are one, too. You are not a proper Rose. God knows. Billy Roy had us to check on you, you are from Missouri, whole 'nother line of Roses, if that happens to be your name a-tall. He liked you tho', Billy Roy did. What in the-holy-hell did you allow to happen to him?"

"Well, sir, Mr. Blanton. We went over there, on a mission, for Mr. McIvey and Miss Lily, you know how he was devoted to her, and he was there to protect me, and he tried to do that, but he died there. I mean, we got in a scrape, and he gave his life. I mean, they killed him."

"What was the motive for it? Why?"

"I'm afraid he was disrespectful, to those people."

"Popped off, did he?"

"Yes, sir."

"That is Billy Roy. Damn . . . . And you simply sat there and watched it happen?"

"No. I— I stopped it, actually. But he was— His heart failed, I think."

"Wisht I had been ther' with you," said Ranger Ping, rivers of tears running down his old pockmarked cheeks.

"He died well."

"He was a Marine, like his daddy," said his daddy. "And you was?"

"Sir?"

"A Marine?"

"Well, actually, yes, I was."

"Yes. Semper Fi. He said he liked you, kindly, you wasn't the pissant you appeared to be, when he got to know you. Oh well," Daddy Bob said. "I have another son, Eddie. He is just a boy. Had him with my second wife Elma. Twenty years younger than Billy Roy. I would like to send him to you, I see you have this fellow here as a bodyguard now tho' he is not in my opinion too effective, maybe Eddie could be of some service to you and Miss Lily, now. And maybe, when the time would come, he could be on hand to he'p take revenge. For Billy Roy."

"No," I said.

"Beg pardon?"

"No." We sat there for a long minute or two. Then I said, "How old is Eddie?"

"He is twenty-one. Been four years in the service. He is a tough boy, a fighter."

"Send him to college," I said. "Make him be a lawyer. Let him fight that way, for causes you believe in. Not like, beg your pardon, sir— Billy Roy."

The massive Ranger Ping shifted his bulk. Sam McGee stiffened. "World's a-changin', Bob," said Ping.

He reached in his duster and pulled out Sam's pistol which seemed a toy next to his and handed it to him. He moved away and opened the door to his truck and climbed up into the cab. I looked from the front seat into Blanton's face as he tensed on the blue leather seat of the Lincoln. His eyes had clouded, like a rain cloud passing over a parched Jack Hays County. He shook his head.

"All right," he said. A hint of moisture came into his eyes. "His body. Can we go get it out of there?"

"No. Not now. But I buried him in a beautiful place, sir. On a hill. In a grove of olive trees. I am sure his spirit is at rest there, for now."

"All right." Daddy Bob Blanton eased out and saying nothing more eased up into his Ford 250 cab. They started their motors and backed out and slowly eased up along Snider Plaza and out onto Hillcrest and to the expressway and on down I-35.

"Jesus," said Sam McGee. "I am a native of Texas. Just not theirs, I guess. Oh, man— what you gonna do when that old hard-on decides it's time to go on over and find his boy's body in that beautiful olive tree grove you done buried him in? Huh?"

"It can be arranged," I said. "Anything can be arranged."

"Meanwhile."

"Meanwhile, if you share that Evian you have there I believe I will take my blood pressure medicine." I tore through the wrapper and into that plastic bottle like old Nixon.

Actually I was moved for Billy Roy, as I had been, stirred to my stagnant roots by my awful complicity in his death, moved by his family's loyalty.

Meanwhile I was King of Texas. Was I not? Oh yes. Oyez oyez oyes . . .

At my Levies in August and early in September some interesting characters presented themselves. A chap from Oklahoma wished to start his own country on a concrete platform between the Cayman Islands and Central America. It would accept citizens who paid to be there and would be a free enterprise New Utopia. This fellow took his name as a ruler, a prince, Lazarus, not from the Biblical one who came back to life but from Robert Heinlein's *Time Enough for Love.* I liked him, his literary side. He had a grand vision, unlike the Republic of Texas characters who believed that Texas was illegally annexed and was not really part of the U.S.A. They were a mean bunch and reportedly planning to kill Reno and Freeh with anthrax on cactus needles set in Bic lighters or some such. They were crazy and not welcome to the Levies. One ruler I heard of and invited but who was busy in California buying a fleet of Rolls Royces was Empress Verdiace Washitaw Turner-Gorton of the Washitaw de Dugdamoundya Empire out of Winnsboro, LA. She claimed a Spanish land grant from the 18th century gave her an empire comprising part of north Louisiana and south Arkansas and parts of Texas and Mississippi. She seemed a class act and I was sorry not to get to meet her.

A little fellow from Taos found his way into the Levy uninvited and I said to let him in since he was with my old buddy, my tree-man, Ray Rodriguez. This was Rosie's great-uncle Andrés Vigil, a fragile, paper-thin tiny fellow who represented a movement of indeterminate shape to form a nation of Hispanic states separated out from the present Union. It was a terrible idea, but I listened to him politely, because of Ray, who stood there in his plaid shirt in from the one hundred and five degree heat with his old straw hat in his hands. This Vigil said he'd heard we were planning an economic and political conference for Geneva in the fall for developing and forming nations and his people would be interested. I said he would be welcome. It wasn't really for unformed nations, but I figured we could handle the little fellow, afford to throw in a few nuts with the peppermint and chocolate and sugar to make the candy. He looked not only old and frail but poor as Ho Chi Minh, I believe he was wearing sandals. What the hell, I thought. John Woodcipher, standing by my side, also smiled and welcomed him.

Then the Levy picked up with the entrance of several characters who were in a contest to be the Texan most like Big Tex who was due to be hoisted up yet again—*Ho ho ho*—at the State Fair in a month or so, in

October. These were marvelous real-life characters from over Texas who drove in in big cars and trucks. They were all six-two, six-three, rugged on the outside but all heart, would not be caught dead without their boots on, tipped their big hats to a lady or entering church, hearts and laughs as big as Texas with a big Howdy to all, soft-spoken, quiet, tough, true, in short, Men. One loved his Ford tractor more than anything; another said, "Yes, sir, King, life is too short not to live it as a Texan." I told them it made me both proud and humble to behold them.

At the end of the month I took off on my travels with Woodcipher, Sam McGee riding shotgun. (I could not bear to let myself out of Sam's sight by now.) I was doing all my business at my Renaissance Tower office. I lived at Lily's but hardly saw the old girl. She came to the Levies and enjoyed them but otherwise I hardly knew what she was doing. Social things, I supposed. Our sex had now completely stopped. She planned no social functions or dinners that included me. I thought she must be watching me, seeing what I would do. When I told her I had plans to go to Europe and to Africa she nodded, said, check it out with G. K. Chambers, remember that Russia was the doughnut, Henry, she didn't understand Africa, Daddy would say Africa was the hole. I said I wanted to talk to her, tell her of my enlarging vision for T-Rex . . . . Fuck your vision, Henry, Lily said, your—our—vision is oil prices per barrel up, some of these down investments straightening out, we needed a *strategy* not a *vision*! One evening I came "home" to Castle Bluff and found her painting again, in her studio. I saw it was a small canvas and she was striping it thickly with dark colors, that cracked look in her eyes. It gave me a little chill and I went down to my quarters and had a glass of Single Malt. If I'd had any sense I would have gone back up and looked at her work and admired it and courted Lily, but I was tired and illusioned and, actually, couldn't stand the thought of being with her, on her, under her, and so just sat and poured another.

I must say, after that, they gave me fair warning.

Lily left me a note requesting I have a conference with Mr. Chambers. He came out of the Secret Place for it, or rather let me in to it. Turns out the Secret Place (I'd figured it was in New York or Hong Kong or Amsterdam maybe) was a little room just off Daddy's den where we held the Levies in Daddy's redbrick mansion on up from and behind Lily's small house on Strait Gate Way. That was where the stocky little prick was holed up all the time! The room was wired, with about ten computers with big screens set up to monitor the ups and downs of the T-Rex Foundation and the Fund across the world. G. K.

Chambers sat in a small chair rubbing his palms together like kneading a particularly troublesome booger and squinted through his bottly lenses at me. A few points of information, for me, for you, Mr. Rose, he said. You bet, I said. He did not fool with the King talk or title; I wondered if he had done so, played the game, even with Daddy.

He had heard the outline, some of the scheme of the thing, he said, from Lily.

Yes? So?

So he had fiduciary responsibility. As, now, did I, H. Rose. So. What was the purpose of this conference sponsored by T-Rex in November in Geneva?

Actually it did not bother me. Actually I had scammed the IRS too many times to let the likes of Chambers bother me.

Patiently I explained that the purpose of the T-Rex-sponsored conference in Geneva, that lovely city of peace and reason, was to encourage struggling nations to embrace new patterns of political and economic fulfillment by unbuckling from their inhibiting debts and building on their past strengths.

Oh? For example?

Well, most emerging nations were not prepared to emerge full-blown into democracy and capitalism. The U.S., within the nation, subsidized its interests like crazy. The State, in most places, must underwrite education, health, communications, industries basic to their resources and interests. Illiterate, impoverished peoples cannot just jump up and become democrats, capitalists, only pawns to the U.S. and developed, that is to say, investing nations. Investors can help, but it will hardly be good in the long run for Soros to own the communications industry in Russia; and look at the mess of pottage unbridled self-interested "robber capitalism" has caused there . . . .   And it's terrible, and terrifying, to proceed to cut off investments when things go bad . . . .

And the political implications, Mr. Rose?

Only economic bolstering and cooperation can stop the present and future horrors in the world, which are ethnic. Bombs and sanctions only breed hatred and horror. As Daddy, the real King of Texas, said, feed the Iraqis bread and candy, flood them with aid and medicine, they'll soon be our friends and allies, Saddam and George W. Bush will be sitting side by side at the Nascar 500 at the Dallas Motor Speedway. The new leader of Yugoslavia will be wanting Serbia to be a state in the U.S.A. . . .

Look at our great nation, the only superpower now, what an incredible mix of people and interests it is, that's the way it works, the way it's got to work in the world. Eh?

Well sir, Mr. Rose, this seems fuzzy, and confused, opined Mr. G. K. Chambers. But perhaps it is only theoretical, after all, merely academic, as universities gain credit by holding forums for irresponsible thinking. Were various people speaking, presenting papers, at this "conference?"

Yes. I would be speaking, also Professor Woodcipher. Others.

Where will they be coming from?

Oh, African nations. Macedonia. Central America. Russia.

Who from Russia? A government representative?

Yes. A brilliant young subminister named Razumov.

Ah. This strikes me, Rose, as not only fuzzy, and confused, but dangerous.

Sir?

He proceeded to give me a brief economic lesson, his eyes hidden behind the Coke bottle lenses. "Mixed economies, sir, are essentially fried-shoe." (Did this guy come up out of the Sixties? Where did Lily and Daddy find him?) Such economies worked, as nations were recovering, in the thirty years after 1944. Then the oil crash came and developing countries had to borrow from the U.S. to pay the oil bills. (This, sir, was when Daddy, Mr. McIvey, stretched his billion bucks to several billion and started dabbling in world interests, with, I must say, Mr. Rose, my advice.) Then came "privatization," private industries took over, laissez-faire. Etc. Corruption. Certainly now a need for regulation. "New World Order," as G.H.W.B. proclaimed it, after the Soviet bloc collapse in '89, Soviet Union breakup in '91. Choppy waters since, though lovely profits, yes. But your fuzzy notions are old, wrong, *defunct*, fried shoe! Oh my. Only an English professor, a non-theorist at that, could be so presently naïve! He urged me to visit with CEOs of Exxon and other multinational companies right here in Dallas who actually ran things now to clear my mind of these wrong, fuzzy, impractical ideas. They might indeed be interested in a co-conference on corporate and individual private international investment now, perhaps that would be a cool and progressive idea, if I was interested in meddling around. But he urged me to stay behind the screen and pull the wires we had, like Daddy did.

He urged me to cancel the fool conference, take Anonimo as my patron saint, not bring attention to us, not make things more complicated for him and the T-Rex funds.

I smiled and nodded and told him, thanks a bunch, G. K. old boy. I appreciated the advice, we'd see how it all came out in the wash.

He asked what was this idea of the Brigades he had heard Lily mention?

I said we, Woodcipher and I, wanted to form an International Human Brigade, to bring aid to starving, needful people, maybe to go further, to combat inhumanity, genocide and such in the world.

Oh my, he said. He said he would need to speak to Lily.

But I did not see her. That evening she was at a Dallas cultural event. I left the next morning from DFW for Kenya with Sam McGee. Sam was looking forward to seeing Africa.

SIXTEEN

In Kenya I could not believe I was meeting with chiefs of the Maasai, snow-capped Kilimanjaro in the distance. It made me think wistfully of being young and reading *Green Hills of Africa*, experiencing Hem's little jokes and pithy wisdoms in that paean to a once and former Africa as I lay on our wicker couch on our porch on our farm place in Ohio. But there were no little jokes or pithy wisdom there now. The Maasai, with their cattle, had long been losing their traditional grazing lands. The whole ecology of their swampy preserve and roaming lands beyond was encroached upon. The whole man and beast and natural ecology of Africa was being disrupted by chaotic peoples, systems, old and new corruptions, and by tribal hatreds and horrors. I visited five African states, planning and giving voucher assurance for the massive humanitarian aid they were yet needing just as a matter of course, of survival. I wondered what could be done in education, what broad, bold programs might be devised by a consortium of colleges and universities to bring their young people of intelligence and talent to our campuses and teach them, train them, practically and with ideas, so that they might return and build, restore their places that we in our own dark hearts had selfishly helped lead to blight and disruption . . . . Sam said shut up and drink your Mamba, buddy boy, there was something in the heart of Africa that would survive and surpass us finally. I drank and reminded him that Hem had gone there as to a newer, less corrupt place than our own continent . . . . Sam said that he and his family, with dim memories of shackles, knew that.

I met, in Ghana, a scholarly man called Elmer Dahfo who wrote poetry and epic novels in English, French and whatever it was that was his native language of the struggles of his people. He was a vital fellow and laughed and said his grandfather, who was like myself a king of sorts, had as a friend a wealthy American who was also kind of crazy.

We laughed over the coincidence and he introduced me to his son, Clarence, an ebony young man who also wrote poetry and who wanted to come to America to study classics. Classics? I said, amazed. Not computers, medicine, engineering, something practical and useful to come back and do? No, classics, Elmer Dahfo said. He agreed and encouraged his son in this, it was not folly, it was exactly what was needed now. *Harmony*, he whispered, *the harmony of the spheres*, such a lovely idea . . . Scipio Africanus. Augustine, that African dude, Bishop of Hippo, the faith, the reach, the vessel, the *City of God* . . .   And did we have a classics teacher at our Highland University? Yes, old Professor Lugash, emeritus, kept a cubicle, had few if any students—but versed in seven languages, making a new translation of the *Confessions* for the millenium . . . .   *Ah*, he sighed, and his eyes gleamed like a prowling lion's . . . .

I met my pal and idea man John Woodcipher in Geneva, where he was making arrangements at the grand hotel for our invitational conference on "The Middle Way." We had engaged some middling profs and pols from various points of the globe to discuss the state of economic and political affairs and Prof. Woodcipher himself was going to present a blueprint for working out a public/private, capitalist/socialist system for Russia, South America, China, Africa, etc. We walked arm in arm down the Boulevard des Philosophes. With arms folded over the stone coping of the bridge we watched the water of the river rush along beneath and talked of even greater ideas for our energy and T-Rex's money to take hold of. John spoke of forming, beyond the Human Brigades for humanitarian aid we envisioned, an international brigade able to go here and there for peace-keeping, to squash a Mladic or a Milosovich, commando-style. If Perot could go in and get his people out, why couldn't we go into trouble spots and do the right thing, above or below the random rule of nations, relieving the poor U.N. and our bully nation of the burden of responsibility? Soon, John predicted, anyway, corporations would surely be forming their own armies, not that they did not pretty much control ours now. Cuidado, buddy, be careful, I told him, looking at the rushing water. T-Rex's funds were not unlimited, but that work was, and dangerous. John shrugged. I saw that under his placidity he was a fanatic. He was in love with the idea of an armed International Brigade for the world. This ain't Spain in the Thirties, I said. The whole world, now, is Spain, he said.

I said I would not be against the use of strategic commando force to get rid of bin Laden. In that beautiful, peaceful city I spoke to him of my sorrow for Russia, dismay at the Serbs, pity for Africa. Like John, I felt a deep professional urge to "fix" things.

It seemed as if all was well as I returned to Dallas. Ross Perot had hosted a dozen Russian law professors for dinner at his Circle T Ranch outside the city, toasting FDR and Lincoln and giving them ten-gallon hats and letting them bestride his Longhorns, and we got in the act by having Tex Flatt host Gorbachev, who was passing through seeking further Texas investments in his crapped-out nation. I heard Tex and Gorby got along real well, Gorby admiring mightily Tex's prize bull out at his spread in West Allen. But Lily greeted me, in our cosy "home" place, sullenly, scarcely stopping her painting of the leaping naked women of yore, her hair a bush, clad in a ratty old kimono, no makeup. She refused my invitation to dinner at the Riviera and to bed, respectively, and told me we were meeting with G. K. Chambers in the morning. I gave her a little peck on her lined, sullen cheek and called for Sam to bring the car around. I stood on the front stoop at that fortified "castle" on the hill, glancing up the driveway where the white Town Car was parked around the curve, wondering what in hell was eating Lily here in the moment of my ascendancy, my approaching triumphs, when I heard the explosion.

It was a terrific blast, like the whole house had blown up. But it was just the Lincoln.

It was a mass of flames and shattered nothing when I walked, unbelieving, in shock and horror, up the driveway to behold it. Just a roar of flaming debris, scattered, scattering—*Smithereens*, foolishly, was all that I could think—

Then: Oh God, no! Sam! Jesus! Sam! Bunky! Billy Roy! Now Sam! Oh Jesus God, I did not think I could bear it—

When Sam came running out the front door and up to me.

That gold tooth. Those rolling whites of eyes. That ugly cheap suit. That ring in his ear. Dear God, yes. It was Sam.

"It was Pitts," he said. "Oh holy Jesus— Poor little fellow! I was on the 'puter, getting the email for you— he said he'd bring the car around for me—for you—"

Lily came down the driveway in her skimpy kimono, barefoot, staring at the flaming car, at us. T. J. Mackey came from the tower or wherever he had been.

"I called the fire department," she said. "Keep the police out of this, okay, Mr. McGee?"

"Listen, ma'am. I mean, that should have been—supposed to be—me— There has got to be an investigation, anyway. My God, Pitts! Mr. Nathan Pitts was in it!"

"Plastic bomb," said T. J. Mackey.

Lily shrugged and padded back down the driveway and into the house. We heard the sirens coming.

How had she known, from her studio, to call the fire department?

That evening, among the mail in my office, I found a package from abroad, from Paris. I asked Miss Fortifer to open it as I stepped out for a moment. When it did not explode I returned and undid the string-tied box within. Inside lay my—it must be mine—withered, blackened finger with the small onyx and diamond ring of the Prince of Dallas on it. I quickly put it in my desk drawer, not showing Fortifer.

I was getting more messages, signals, than I could manage this day, and I did not wish to be with Lily either, and I was still jet-lagged and just a trifle terrified, and so had Sam, who was considerable shook-up himself, drive me in his Crown Vic to my little refuge in University Park. Sitting outside in his car, I told him to cut bait, get out, go back to the DPD—and keep an eye on me. He said he believed he would, and would do. I thanked him for his many kindnesses and services, and let myself in. It was eerie to be in that little house, with its small, tacky furniture and dusty shelves of books, like another life, which it had been. On the dining room I found a note from my loyal maid Pearly. *Hey, Mr. R.*, it said, *somebody been in here goin thru your things. Real neatly But I can Tell.*

I spent the next several days there, anyway, out of touch, mostly drinking. I missed the meeting with Mr. Chambers, but Lily let me be, did not send Mr. Mackey after me. I slept a lot, or sat in a stupor. Never in my life had elation and high purpose turned so quick to fear and dread.

On the third day, I recall now it was that red-letter day of September, I came out of my fog and turned on Channel 52, the CNN news. The world, it seemed, had collapsed. The financial world, at least. The Stock Market, to be exact. The great damn Hedge Fund. Meriweather. My God, could his name be *Frank* Meriweather? All American? We'd had dealings with the various hedgehogs, I knew. 'Twas not merry weather. Dominos. Down they were coming . . . . Haywire. Staying tuned, I heard even Bill Gates had lost a billion or so. From what I knew I figured, into the next day or so, that T-Rex must be down a couple billion . . . . I figured I had better get it up and go see darling Lily. She would be upset.

"Upset" is not the word. "Fury" comes to mind. And it was not just the Market which had collapsed, it seemed, as I presented myself to her and the ubiquitous G. K. Chambers. I had collapsed, also. In her mind I was wiped out completely.

"You have ruined us!" she screamed at me. Her vivid blue eyes looked not only cracked but had yellow flecks in them, like froth. Her great McIvey mouth was a quivering gash. She raised her fists at me. "You bastard! You poor stupid little prick! You—"

"Not quite," murmured the bottly little Chambers.

"What?"

"Ruined. We are not, quite—oh, far from—ruined. But, sir, Rose, you have broke the rules."

"I 'have broke' the rules?" The grammarian in me could not resist.

"You—terrible—little—*professor!*" Lily screamed. "Oh, Daddy knew, he warned me. 'Pro-fessor—' And Billy Roy, he knew! Oh, Jesus, what a fool I was to trust you—love you, you worm! You piece of dried-up goatshit! You moron—"

"The first rule," Mr. G. K. Chambers said, "is that we must make money, there is not philanthropy without a profit to it. Everyone knows that."

"We told you that! Henry? My God, can't you *listen!* And I gotta tell ya—Henry, you *cretin*, the second rule is not to meddle, not to fool with things, not to fuck around in things. My God, we have been getting bills—   Based on your extending credit line, your fucking *vouchers*, Henry! Millions, Henry, for aid to fucking countries *everywhere*, just *giving* it, my God, no return on the buck a-tall! And that Woodcipher— Remind me to kill him, Geoffrey—asked us for millions for his fucking *brigades!* Jesus—"

"Whoa," I said, afraid that she would really kill him. Dear God, where was Mackey? Afraid that she—he—would kill *me*.

"You were the heir apparent. We gave you all our love and faith and trust. But the heir cannot be *apparent*. We told you to lay low! So the whole world knows now that T-Rex exists, and has heard that you are going to have a public thing, a conference, to stir up trouble in the world—"

"Lily. Listen. Please."

"Your conference has been cancelled," G. K. Chambers, Geoffrey, said. "Every detail of it. Void. And Mr.—Dr. Woodcipher—"

"Leave him be," I said.

"Your allowance is cancelled, Henry," she said, her rage spent. "And your credit cards, and accounts—whatever . . . ." Dully.

"All right. I'm sorry that we—that you all—lost money. I know I committed a lot, but I was going to check it all out with you. And it wasn't just that, you have to admit the whole thing, the markets, are down. Lily? Surely you know that. Lily? Dearest?"

"I hate you," she said. "I can't stand to look at you. What in God's name—was I *thinking*—?" A scream again.

"Okay, kid. Sorry you feel that way. So—what the hell. I abdicate."

"*What?*"

"As the Goddamn King of Texas? You know? That little game we were playing, and Daddy died, and I was the King? Remember that?"

"I told you," she said in a voice like ice, "it's not a game. Oh God, Henry, if you only could have believed, realized it is *real*."

"That is what I did. That's, I guess, the mistake I made. Believing. Putting myself, my all, my own ideas, into it." Spoken piously, like a martyr on a cross. Sadly, for my great personal loss of her. (Which I was feeling just a twinge of, really.)

"You are a shit, Henry," she said, "a hypocritical, manipulative insincere . . ."

"It wasn't me, Lily. I was the fly, not the spider. You know? Really, old girl. Lily." I stood there rubbing where my finger had been so she would notice, and remember, and respond. She was staring at me in a way that made me frightened, truly, for my life.

"You can't abdicate," she said.

What? As opposed to what? Dying in office? Jesus.

"It doesn't work that way," she said.

"Like hell," I said and with a nod and a finger-less salute to Geoffrey, left.

SEVENTEEN

I did not really think that they would kill me. Part of me even thought her anger would die down and we could begin again, sweetly, reasonably. But I went over to Highland, to the campus, thinking it would be harder for them to whack me there. I slept in my office there, afraid to go back to my little house. Also, I got chilled thinking about the car blown-up and the finger sent to me, further rotting away in the desk drawer of my office in the Renaissance Tower, where I was afraid to go, also. The danger was not just from Lily, probably not from her at all. Surely she would get hold of herself. In a day or so I called the office downtown to talk to Miss Fortifer; the number had been disconnected.

The Fall semester had started, was a month underway, in the heat. Already some of the new trees planted on campus were suffering from oak wilt. I skulked between my office and the library and the student center and the gymnasium, wherever there were people.

I told John Woodcipher everything was off. He had a strange reaction, like he was miffed, mad at me. Poor dreamer. Should not have got his hopes up. He would turn away, look out his window, whenever I went by his office. Good God. What did he want? I had meant it; I thought we were on the way to great and noble things. *He* was let down? Mercy. I did not tell him I was in danger, and he might be also, if reason did not seize Lily. I chuckled a little when I thought of that. Fat fool. I knew he drank wine and brandy secretly in his office. So did I, i.e., Scotch whiskey. In fact, I took to drinking quite a bit and once or twice caught myself staggering across the campus. I would take straight gulps from the bottle, toasting myself as the King of Texas, which I still was, according to Miss Lily. Day to day the conviction grew in me that she would straighten out, see the light, that the T-Rex Fund would climb, that she would look up and see me coming and smile. Then I would have the dream, or see the vision, of the horrible gray octopus and its cold eye,

again, and be sick physically, thinking of being in her embrace, in her
clutches, her damnable claws again. Then I prayed she'd just forget me,
leave me alone, find another "King." What did she mean, I could not
abdicate? Oh God! She was right . . . . I was a hypocrite, a fool, all my
life merely "apparent," a player at this and other strange and foolish
games.

But Lily, surely she would come around. Lily could be lovely,
loving, even likable . . . .

The whiskey went down smoothly, just like mother's milk.

I knew they knew where I was. I looked among the students
walking or on bikes or motorcycles to find T. J. Mackey in disguise. I
recoiled upon passing Arab and other such students, agents of that other
power that wished me dead. I dreamed in my fitful sleep, as often day as
night, in my office chair of T. J. Mackey, his cold, cruel eyes gleaming,
as he prepared to kill me. I was strung out pretty good, Fernando.

Often feverish, seldom sober, I began to itch. My wise great-uncle
Sage Rose had been a homeopath. When everything was out of whack,
he said, the dislocation of your spirit and body would manifest itself in
the dread Itch. My feet itched. My hands itched. The Itch began going up
my legs. My left big toe twinged. Dear God. I prayed, don't let me get
the gout or shingles. My father Aaron periodically got shingles, ring
around his body, terrible pain. My grandfather Henri suffered from the
gout, I remember him with his foot wrapped softly up on a pillow, of
course he drank. With care and some fascination, sitting in my little
office there, I took my shoes and then my socks off to see if there was a
rash or if this was mostly mental. It was not a rash exactly on the smooth
white skin of my thin feet and ankles but there were several hundred
small round red dots clustered there, and on investigation, on my wrists
and lower arms. (Pediculae, I later learned to call them.) I reshod and
walked down the hall to Woodcipher's cubicle. He looked up then
looked away when he saw me, though obviously engaged in nothing
more important than stroking his silk necktie.

"John," I said, "do you have a doctor, a physician that you go to?"

"No," he said. "I heal myself." Fool. Right then he had a weakening
heart and didn't know it. Later he would topple over and die from a heart
seizure in the act of quaffing a flagon of Texas cabernet. I was sad then,
for he was a man of style and points, I suppose my best friend in the
university, or anywhere.

Regina Singh gave me the name of her doctor, Dr. Ashkubar, but
warned me that he practiced West and East. That was fine, I said, either

would probably do fine, I just had these little red spots here and there. Probably you are acidic, she said. I notice you have been drinking quite a bit. Drink some bicarbonate of soda in a tall glass of water and lay off the booze, Henry. By the way, when are you going to end this unusual leave of absence and come back to teach for us? Your quite popular course "The Myth of the West"? Spring. I hoped to be here in the spring. And how was Miss McIvey? Lily? Our wonderful benefactress? Fine, I said. Miss Lily was fine as wine in the summertime, pure as the driven snow, hot as a pistol, busy as a bee. Get some rest, she said. You know better than to be drinking on the campus. Regina had become right presidential. She had fired that old bat of a secretary and had a young male secretary. That was a good thing Lily did, to make Regina president. On my way out I passed by my old office and waved at the new provost sitting in it, Dr. Rosemary Contreras-Harrison.

Dr. Ashkubar took me right in, no wait whatsoever. He was a trim little fellow with enormous black eyes and a friendly, snappy style. "Hey, man," he said, "what's got to be wrong with you?" I showed him the pediculae.

"Hey, you been drinking a lot of vodka, gin and tonics?"

"Whiskey."

"Okay. Come with me."

He walked me down to a lab where they drew some blood from my arm. He stood by me whistling a little Mozart while they checked it out. He looked at the lab sheet. He murmured into a cell phone. Then he took my arm. "Okay, Henry, Professor Rose, friend of my friend and patient Dr. Singh, she is a sweetie, come with me, man, you got a little problem. Walk with me slowly, you understand, and don't bump into anything. Okay? We don't want no—any—scratch, no cuts, no bruises. Just glide along with me, man, you dig it, over to the next building here."

The next building was the hospital. He took me carefully, keeping hold of my arm the whole way, whistling, up the elevator to the fifth floor and into a private room.

"Okay," he said. "You stay here. Don't do anything, okay? Don't scratch or brush your teeth or floss or force a bowel movement. If you start to bleed in any way, just push the button."

"What in the world?"

"You lost your platelets, in your blood. You have almost no platelet count. You can't coagulate."

"Sir?"

"You are in danger of spontaneous bleeding. You could bleed to death. Okay? You sit here and don't do anything, man."

"How can this happen? What causes it?"

"Beats me," said Dr. Ashkubar. "Who knows? I'm sending you a specialist."

He departed. I sat very quietly in the chair, trying to fathom this development. When I thought I'd burst if I didn't pee, I sidled into the bathroom and approached the toilet tenderly, scared it would pour out red and I would ooze out blood from every pore and die there on the spot. I was sitting in the room in the chair by the bed, unmoving, when Dr. Fitzgivens, a breezy old man, one of those doctors who exude assurance and authority though they don't know the first thing, or anyway the second thing, about your malady, and his team of specialists arrived.

They called it I.T.P. Idiopathic Tricky Pullulations. Unknown-funky-blood-pustulations, Plateletum Nunc Dimittis, the Idiot's Disease. I had never heard of it. I knew I had red cells and white cells but I don't believe I'd ever heard of platelets. My little plates. Oh boy. They had a list of possible causes, including alcohol, insecticides, any poison to your system. There was no way of being sure, of knowing, what had caused it. I was terribly tired and drinking too much; that was enough for me. There was a pretty narrow curve for curing it, getting back the platelets, too. First, a big dose of steroids, see if that would knock 'em back in place. If not, they could always take out my spleen.

This was wacko. It was a mis-signal. The protectors against the outside bad guys that might get in your blood were coming like zappers out of the spleen and getting the wrong idea that the platelets were the bad guys and eating up the platelets. Whoa!

After taking out the spleen? What if that didn't work, eh, Fitz?

Then? Don't worry about then, Mr. Rose. I mean, my friend, that better do it, chuckled Dr. Fitz.

So for several days I sat in there high as a kite on steroids. Every morning and evening the "vampire" came to take my blood, count the count. I stayed about 180,000 platelets down. I had so few I decided to name them and talk to them, tell them to hang in there, surely help was on the way: Andy, Lucy, Betty, Bruce, Moses, Dave, Bunky, Duanne, Molly, Billy Roy, Sam, Eddie and the Cruisers . . . . I meditated quite a bit. It was very strange. I felt wonderful, terrific. I felt like I could fly out my window over the parking lot below and off to—Arabia Deserta—wherever I was going next. I felt like I could run in with the torch and take part in the Olympics. These steroids were a kick. Every morning I got totally dressed, and then I sat there and tried to read (Julie or Jamie, one of the nurse's aides, brought me a magazine all about how to manage my money) and to think and not think and to try to lift my mind out of my body, through meditation, but it was stuck there, in the body. Dr. Ashkubar brought me a copy of Bill Moyers' *Healing and the Mind*, and I read a bunch of that. When the phone rang on the third day after so much total silence it made me jump from the chair and crouch around in a circle in the room. The damn thing rang again.

"Hello," I said.

"Would you like to know, exactly, how many million your 'projects' and your assurances have cost us—are still costing us? The record is being kept. Oh yes—"

I hung up on him. It rang again. Like a snake pretending a mongoose could not kill him, I put it to my ear again.

"You are responsible for this. You and your associate, Woodcipher, have bled us—"

I hung up on the ill-chosen metaphor. He did not call again.

In the morning the count remained low, and good old Fitzgivens talked of removing the spleen. I told him if 'twas phlegm or choler I would part with it more easily. He did not get it, was not tuned to old Ben, it did not seem humorous to him. Nor to me, alas. They took me carefully down to have a physical in anticipation of the removal of the spleen. They wanted me to go down in the dinky gown, but I went fully clothed and changed in the exam room and then dressed again. I felt better, more like a human being with a chance, in my suit and tie and pebbled loafers.

Coming back up Nurse Nancy handed me the form about the operation from the surgeon. Under "possible complications" he had written, in red ink: *DEATH.* Reading it I passed right by the room, then did a doubletake, and peeked back around the door jamb and beheld Lily in there! She was kind of prowling around the room looking at everything in it, and something long and thin and glittery was in her strong, purple-veined, wrinkled hand that could be so soft and could be so terribly hard.

She picked up Bill Moyers and slashed at him, slashing through the book. I heard the slash, the pop of the book being cut, the pages rip. I popped my head back but had seen her face: contorted, vengeful, horrible, seized of passion, hateful, terrible, manic, mad –

It was a long knife—a long thin thing of flashing green and silver, of jade and steel, a beautiful and terrible blade--

Full of energy, steroidal, I got my mind and body out of there. I told it, Go, old Henry! Holy Moses, I would settle for the platelets that I had—

I CAUGHT A cab letting someone out right out front. I had money. I had forty one-hundred dollar bills in my wallet and in the moneybelt I had taken to wearing since Russia and Afghanistan. I did not see her henchman, Mackey. Wing! Was that Wing I'd seen going through the lobby? Had she furnished that Chinese assassin's blade to Lily? If it was Wing, she had seen me go. No one in any form of Lexus seemed to be following us.

At DFW I scanned the departure board. Not thinking clearly, I had gone to American. Anybody in Dallas would first check at American. The plane to LaGuardia was full. There was one in a couple hours to Anchorage, Alaska. I knew Alaska. I could get lost there, maybe. I booked for Anchorage. Kept changing where I sat, kept my eyes peeled, sweated heavily in my tan Brooks Brothers suit, started trembling with the fear and steroids.

She would have cut me. Just a slash. Watched me bleed. And bleed. Oh Lily, dearest girl. What passion, what a vital force! And how many had she killed, or had killed, by now, in her fine ripe mature old middle age?

It had never occurred to me that she would do the job herself. All my dreams, in bleakest black and white, were of T. J. Mackey killing me. If she had come in the room as I was reading or meditating there I would have looked up and smiled at her.

I went in and out of the smooth, rounded urinal room with the men's symbol on it a number of times, sometimes peeing, sometimes just passing through. Coming out I bent to the water fountain, let the chilled water caress my numbed mouth and teeth, and came up to see, again, the small bar space across the way. I'd been wondering, tempted, if I might have a little drink, a shot of Scotch or vodka, anything.

A small man in a blue coat and a Yale tie stood at the outer edge of the bar space with a glass of something, gin or vodka, in a short glass with olives in it. When he moved from side to side in a kind of hopping motion as he drank from it his shoulder muscles rippled under his coat. He was about to look straight in my direction, catch my eye as I stared at him, when there was a shattering sound just by him like an explosion. A beer bottle had fallen or been pushed off the nearest little table. A big man with a gnarly face in a red plaid shirt who must have also been heading for Alaska slouched at the table. "There goes another one," he said.

A short woman with a beehive hairdo who ran the bar came quickly with a broom and a pan and said something to the man, who was pretty oiled on beer he hadn't spilled. The short man in the blue coat and rep tie went over and waved his glass at them like it had gotten glass in it. The big guy turned to him, they exchanged words, and the plaid shirt shoved the little guy as the waitress stepped back. The short guy put his drink down on the little round table and hit the big guy one time, hit him so fast you could only guess it was in the stomach. The plaid guy gasped and broke in two and sank to the floor, and the little fellow looked down at him, then slowly looked up, but I was steroid-high like an Olympian already running zigzag away from where I was, and off to the right and through a revolving door exit, and down into the blistering heat shimmering over DFW, this New Jerusalem on the baking prairie and onto whatever bus was standing there, wherever it was heading, and away from the American gates and to the North airport exit, and as it happened hooking a right and moving through the "reaches of industrial prairie" between the two cities, and on the highway to the nearer one, Fort Worth.

Only sitting there, cooled by the bus's air conditioning, mesmerized by the ugly road, numbed with the steroids, fear and exhaustion, did I articulate it: that was Nathan Pitts. Mr. Pitts, alive, having a toddy as he paused a moment, doubtless in his search for me. Why else would he be there? He was alive. The terrible little shit for whom we had not mourned but been glad it was him and not us was alive as hell! He had not been blown up in the white Lincoln Town Car in Lily's driveway! So they—*they*—had blown it up—to scare us, to cause us fear and trembling. Already then Lily had been turned against me.

I got off the bus in the Museum District of Fort Worth. I walked by the Amon Carter, not for a moment thinking of going in to see the Russells and the Remingtons, the cowboy and Western stuff in there, and to the Kimbell. I went in the Kimbell to be cool. There was an exhibit of many exchanges of ideas and techniques of the lifelong dialogue between Matisse and Picasso. Many strangely wrought women. I thought, my God, this is crazy, this is Lily's meat, Lily might be here! Then began to see her on the walls. She was here, in many pictures, fluid, female, lovely, grotesque, angled, Lily with her glittering eyes, her façade of ordinariness, green and blue and red, in the Romanian blouse.

After wandering around with my head in the Matisse, the Picasso, wondering what it would be like to have such talent, to have such a friend, I sat and drank tea and then, with proper change, made a call on the pay phone in the lobby with some lugubrious old courtier blackening on the wall staring at me out of little round black-rimmed eyeglasses. Then I sat and drank more tea and wondered what my blood count was, if the platelets had gone up or down with this excitement. I felt scared, that is, terrified, deep within but on another level, calm. I had no idea what to do. I knew that they would find me. I would not have been surprised, just taken another sip of the Earl Grey tea, had I seen Lily coming down the walk through the trees to the museum, to smile horribly and slash me; or Mr. Pitts, or T. J. Mackey.

But it was Sam, my man, my fine friend Sam McGee who came for me in a marked Dallas police car, parked it right in front of the Museum entrance, came in picking at his tooth, sat down and had a cup of tea.

EIGHTEEN

Sam had the Dallas police go to Lily's and arrest Nathan Pitts, or T. Izru, and turn him over to the INS for extradition back to Turkey, where he was wanted for a few murders and other crimes. I am sure he went slipping through the net and is engaged in some terrorist activity somewhere for someone and some cause even less logical or necessary than the King of Texas. Mr. Mackey Sam could not deal with or account for: he was a non-person and, now, a disappeared one. Miss Lily McIvey expressed concern and amazement to the police that she had been harboring such a being as T. Izru, who came to her with perfectly good credentials and references as a butler and security person for her art and other valuable collections.

I spent a couple days with Sam McGee, then stayed a week with my friend Pearly, who kindly took me in. She was gone doing day work from early morning to late afternoon, and I became deeply meditative. I had seen the picture, from a painting by George Catlin, of the mystic Native American medicine man Old Bear in Moyers' book and I became Old Bear. I sat in loincloth barechested on a rug of freedom Pearly's grandmother had woven years ago and willed my spirit to be strong and my body to be calm as the steroids went away. I willed myself to be Old Bear and my platelets to come back to him. I had a vision to go to Taos, that my destiny was to be met in the Taos mountains. It was very clear and beautiful that I must go there, to the quaking aspens, and find peace.

Sam urged me not to go anywhere, but to stay where he could keep an eye on me, and to go back to the doctor for a blood count. I promised him both things, as I made preparations to go. Pearly said that I was crazy, where was I going to stay, in Mexico? I said that I had a friend there I could stay with.

It took Ray Rodriguez a couple days to finish up a pruning and trimming job he was doing and to get the tires and coolant checked on his old red Ford 150 truck before he could drive me out there. He said it was a pretty good time for him to go, he was glad to do it for me and $200, as Mrs. Rodriguez was going to visit her mother in Beaumont anyway and he could pay his respects to Uncle Andrés and visit his son Aaron while in Taos. I was Old Bear but I dressed like Ray's twin brother in old jeans and a work shirt and a straw hat and old boots. I thought whether they were still after me or not—I told Pearly and Sam I didn't think they would be but deep in my core where the blood still bubbled I knew that Lily wanted me, my self or my blood, 'twould be the same to her—that this was as good a way as any. We left early one morning right after Pearly left her house not knowing I was going, or exactly where. I left her a stack of hundreds on her kitchen table. She was a lovely person and a pal.

We reminisced, going out of Dallas and along up to Wichita Falls in the still-heat of early October, of Korea, of the jobs he had done for me, of buying Mrs. Rodriguez her anniversary ring. Ray spoke with pride of his niece Rosie, who was now enrolled in Highland University. All afternoon, then, on the way to Amarillo, he told me about the Bible. When we stopped, just past the cattle pens at a little motel on the rim of the world, he was at the Acts of the Apostles. It stormed beautifully that evening as we ate thin steaks in the little place's restaurant as a family of Indians from New Mexico at the next table talked of training ponies, racing horses. It thundered and lightning lit the sky, and it poured, then cleared to a pink and violet twilight. I talked of mundane things with my old friend Ray whom I had never really known; Old Bear inside, knowing I was heading to my peace, my fate.

It was the first rain out here on the dome of the earth. Elsewhere, too, in Texas, the Dry Rock had cracked. A month ago the rains had come heavily for weeks up and down the eastern part of the state, flooding of course, the ravaging water claiming lives and homes all over the south and east, immoderately. Old Bear did not live in Texas. His heart was in the mountains. Old Bear did not know the King of Texas.

I rubbed the red knobby place where my finger had been as we drank coffee in the little place and looked through the windows at the purple-violet sky, but my companion did not notice it. I wondered where the withered finger with the diamond and onyx ring on it had got to when they shut the downtown office. Still locked in my desk drawer, stored somewhere, or had Lily taken it, put it somewhere? Sure, probably on an altar . . .

We slowly took the narrow lonely road through the escarpment and grazing land in the morning to Las Vegas, and made our way down through Ojo Sarco and the villages and then down U.S. Hill into Ranchos and into Taos in the afternoon. It rained as Ray let me out at the Sun God Motel, where I told him I was staying. Thanked and paid him. After he went rolling off in his red truck, going up into the mountains somewhere to see his kin, I walked back along the road teeming with vehicles, some ancient, and into the Sagebrush Inn on the highway there and roused the bartender and had two margaritas and called my friend. He said he would come get me when he had finished working, and I had otras margaritas, and when he came we sat and talked and had a couple more, plus a beer or two. I told him I had become Old Bear and he laughed and said, damned if these old Indians don't drink, and we had another and he took me home, looking to Taos Mountain, where fierce angry geese guarded his vegetable garden, and he got back to work and I tapped out on the bed in his back room and slept for a day or more.

When I awoke it was afternoon, a cool, sunslant day. The great mountain with its cap of snow lay at a distance from us in the valley, like a centering presence, like God. (In Mabel's yard by her lovely, rackety house sat a great cuneiform stone that was said to hold fast the spirits emanating from the mountain.) There was a feeling of great calm and uninterrupted human and natural history at my friend's place, looking to the mountain. I pushed out through the screen door and stood looking far away, the clouds and space and icecaps far off, then at the earth and the remaining squash, beans, tomatoes and stuff still in early October in his garden. The geese were calm and did not scream or peck at me. Marty came around from the shack he wrote in. We went back into the kitchen and he heated up the coffee he kept in an industrial pot there. We put lots of sugar and a little whiskey in it.

"You ever read this, Henry?" he said, pulling a small volume from the kitchen shelf.

"I believe so, along about in the eighth grade."

It was the *Communist Manifesto*. "I believe I'm pretty much a Marxist already, now," he said.

"Well, it's gotten to be a small club recently. You are probably one of the few around here, anyway."

"Oh, I don't know, brother. You'll find 'em over here, next door, in the Big House, man, and up in the hills, the *raza* people, it's alive with collectivists up there. You got them, what I guess you'd call old-fashioned socialists, and then you got these crazy-ass folks want to be entrepreneurs, own everything, take back all the land, even take *our* land, form their own nation."

"From what I hear you have such people in the Pueblo, who want to claim everything, all the water, the land, the air. No?"

"Sure." He smiled. He had a cocked eye and was missing considerable teeth. Marty was a Pueblo, and lived here at the edge of the pueblo in his own house, as did many who had not lived in the actual pueblo for generations. He went in to do dances for the tourists in the evening, but he was a serious poet and writer of brief plotless stories about this and that that he published through his own small press in Taos. His gnomic Indian Zen-like poems were like lovely little pieces of polished something whose use you could not imagine, but years ago his *El Solo on the Mountaintop*, a crazy, surrealistic, Kerouwacky "novel," had been picked up in paperback nationally and was yet a cult book among college kids and still brought him bread. He was one of those anomalies we hide in certain locked-in, locked-out sections of the nation, successfully unsuccessful, unsuccessfully successful, happy. He lived in the old tradition and outside of it. He liked to fish a lot, and to go up into the mountains.

"It is so strange," he said, "this town, Taos, is so full of people now. Not just tourists but new people, rich people who come here to stay all the time, pushing up against us. So I go up. You know, Henry, I can go up there and follow trails, go high, and find what is left of the wild life and the old flora and the purity there, and I can walk around up there for days—and never encounter, never see another person . . . . Still yet now I can do that . . . . "

Marty went off into town in his ancient truck for his gig at the Kachina, leaving me with the *Manifesto*. So I sat there, numb, vacant, Old Bear with no feathers in his headdress, wondering about my blood, drinking the strong coffee, waiting to drink more whiskey till he returned.

Towards evening a boy came pedaling on a bike into the yard. He was a Pueblo boy, brown and Chinese-looking, black-haired, chubby, out of breath.

"Martin says, mister, go hide!" he told me peering at me over his handlebars. "Get going! They are asking about you, all over town. They asked him. They asked him wasn't he your friend? Martin says, they're scary, man. Okay? He's not going to come back here, lead 'em here. Okay? So long, mister."

The small envoy turned and rode his bike away, the geese cackling, having a shit-fit in his wake.

Well, that didn't take long, did it?I thought. He's good, my old buddy, I thought, if it's him. About as good as you can get, I supposed. Or maybe it's the boys in the pajamas, that bunch, the finger-boys still on the trail. Could that be possible? They had let me out, let me go from there . . . . No, it was him. It was Mackey, damn his soul. In my bones and blood I knew that it was him . . . . Lily, oh Lily dearest, can't you relent? Oh Jesus. I took a heavy wool plaid jacket from Marty's coatrack and a Watch cap and bundled up and headed off across a road and a field, going by a small herd of goats and streams and always to the foothills, and then, towards dusk, hours later, up.

I found the sign, the trail, that said Bear Lake. As I climbed I saw a red-tailed hawk circling above me. I came to a little jewel of a lake. I lost my wind and got it back. It was cool, then chilly with the wind, then very cold, cold but beautiful up the mountain. I pushed on into twilight and could see ravens in the treetops below me. I came to a rocky place, a ledge, and sat there looking down, winded again, sore and aching, on a great fallen, rotted tree. When I got up I felt them all over me: ticks. I shed my clothes and picked off what I could, then put the clothes back on. The ticks would suck my blood out, the good blood and the bad. I would get Rocky Mountain Spotted Fever—I would revel in it—I would rejoice if that was all I got! Turning I almost walked into a great steaming pile of bear manure. Piping hot bearshit. I looked around. Dear God. It was becoming dark. I was numb with cold. I was Old Bear. The only trouble was, I was not really Old Bear, not at all, or any part of him . . . .

Turning again, I saw the most beautiful vision, or reality, and realized, for the central fact, I was nothing. Oh, at most, a carbon-based, air-breathing helpless human dude.

It was a big bear, all gold and chocolate, so beautiful, standing not too far from me looking at me, a real bear, looking at me standing by her minutes-ago poopoo, shaking her large lovely head as if saying, *Tsk, tsk,* H. Rose, I didn't expect to see *you* up here: and I so in awe thought back to her, sorry, so sorry, your majesty, your very real highness, just passing through, so sincerely do not mean to intrude . . . . Longest, most real moment of all this vexing narrative . . . Until she kindly, wisely, in her power, ordained that I might live a while longer, and shook her head from side to side, and with what seemed a strange little grin turned and ambled off. As she turned she seemed to change color and become black. Or perhaps it was the deepening tinge of evening come upon us.

Tick-ridden but numb from cold, I coiled up and passed the black night on that ledge in sleep and fitfulness, slept on that smooth stony place, stony like Korea, like that Afghanistan. Dreamed of Billy Roy hanging, singing, there, in the terrible darkness.

The next day, or maybe more than one, remains a blur to me. I know that from cold and fear and hunger and pain and itching I hallucinated more than once. I believed I came upon a frozen leopard as I came even farther up. In a mountain meadow full of gold and green and quaking trees I came upon Myrtle Springs, decked out in her sunny Sunday best. What in the world, Henry, she said. Do you know what you are doing? I saw Lily grinning from behind trees. In a burst of lucidity I headed back down, gasping. The altitude was too high, my blood too thin. I fell and fell again and gashed myself but did not seem to be hemorrhaging, just gently bleeding. Looking down from a vista I beheld all the little Bear lakes, counted as my vision cleared and I was calm, seven, eight or nine of them. Found a glistening lake down what seemed to be a trail and thought I remembered it, that I had been to it before, perhaps with Marty. That there was an ancient kiva site on the ridge, about halfway down, that he'd showed me.

Bloody, dirty, ripped and ragged, hollow, I found the site, stumbled to it and sat there on the sacred ground, looking down into the kiva hole, playing with a shard, a piece of something. I remember colors, the yellow of aspen leaves, golds and reds, the scarlet of sumac on down the hill. I sat scratching sacred ground with the shard, the sun beginning to warm me gently, when T. J. Mackey found me there.

He came gliding into the kiva site quietly, his eyes flat, his angled face like a piece of sculpture, in fatigues and a cap, a rifle with a telescopic sight on a strap over his shoulder. He sat on a rock across from me, expressionless. "I spotted you in my binoculars thrashing around up there. Thought I would let you come on down a bit." Matter-of-factly.

Then he added: "You little pissant. Henry Rose."

He slipped a long thin knife, merely a shimmer in his hand in the sun across from me, from his boot, and caressed the blade, and further added: "Miss Lily sends her regards."

I did not reply, not wishing to give him any more pleasure than he was already deriving from my company.

He said: "You don't know how I have waited for this moment. Some marks are not just professional, you know what I mean, Rose?

You are such a— Let me just say, you I really do not like. You unnastand?"

I nearly did reply. I thought I did know how he'd waited. I'd sensed it, dreamed it, foretold it for so long.

I thought just maybe if I could rise and he came toward me I might whack him, across the nose, or in the sternum. Just maybe, try anyway, though I had no doubt . . .

Like a robot he did stand up and sighted me along his blade as if it were a gun. I stood up too, Old Bear no more, just H. Rose, waiting for the blade. For a moment I got the impression he was going to throw it, that might be a trick he had.

Then we both, my old buddy and I, heard a *clop clop* sound and I realized, divined in some odd separate compartment of my mind, that it was the lazy sound of horses' hooves.

Mackey bent and slid the knife back in his boot and unslung the rifle, fluidly, like the soldier, the mercenary, that he was. Looked around.

"Put it down, señor," came a voice from our perimeter. "I assure you we have your ass covered, man."

We heard some more *clops*. Looked. Three horsemen looking down at us. T. J. Mackey put the rifle down.

It was a prudent thing to do. It probably saved his life. I know that it saved mine.

Mackey, ever the pro, said something fluently and at length in Spanish, intuiting correctly. It ended with a questioning note, offended, as if he were being caught hunting deer out of season, but what the hell, come on, you guys. In answer, about five more guys, all in camouflage suits, like real soldiers, came out and unarmed him, knife, Glock and rifle, and led him away.

"We are the Army of Liberation of the United Hispanic States in Exile," said the horseman to him in español as he departed. "You will be treated as a prisoner of war."

Then the young fellow leaned down from his mount and extended his hand to me. I took it, sensing I should, battered as I was. "Soy Aaron Rodriguez," he said. There was a star on the collar of his camouflage. "My father speaks of you, and recommends you. ¿Qué no? If you can ride—" A horse was brought beside me. "—we will go to our Presidente, who wishes to see you otra vez, to confer with the King of Texas."

I thought he was a bit off the mark there but did not wish to mention it in the moment. Sorely and with help I mounted and let the nag carry me along behind Ray Rodriguez' son.

The old man, Andrés Vigil, received me in a cabin somewhere in those mountains. It reminded me of a meeting I'd had with a rebel leader in such terrain. He reminded me of his attendance at my Levy not too long ago in Dallas. He thanked me for my kindness in receiving him then unannounced and lamented that our great conference on the hopes and problems of emerging nations had to be cancelled. He was a very polite, formal, scary and crazy old man. Sensing I thought so, he murmured that we should take them seriously, the United Hispanic States, they had movements in New Mexico, Texas, Arizona, Colorado, California and elsewhere. One day these states would secede and would form a new rightful nation and acknowledge Mexico as their Mother but be independent also of Mexico as in history they had begun to do previously in a natural progression and they would return this tier of land which was wrongly taken by the anglo U.S. to its true people and be a vital entrepreneurial separate nation unto itself, that is, señor, if the coming Wars of Water might be won.

Meanwhile there may be complications on this road between the states as they existed now. Old issues must be cleared up as much as possible. Vigil produced a document, imitation parchment so I thought I could see light through it and through his sere old hand holding it. It was a quitclaim to any part of northern New Mexico ever held by or claimed by Texas. I remembered that Daddy, old McIvey, had indeed proclaimed that a slice of New Mexico had once belonged to Texas. If I, Vigil said, who still in the present muddle of things presumed to be "King of Texas" and had economic resources behind me which would cause this claim to be taken seriously by himself, Andrés Vigil, Presidente in Exile, if I would be so good as to sign this document renouncing any such claim, why, all would then be mighty fine and I could say adios and be on my way back to Texas and they would wish me well, as long as I never spoke of them or their movement or of this matter to anyone in public or in private, which transgression would of course, señor, result in my immediate demise. Muerte.

So I signed the thing. Lily said I could not abdicate. I daresay old Daddy was squawking in his grave. One day when all this absurdity had turned to a new reality, as often is the course of history, when Texas had seceded alone or in concert with other states and entities (which I as a stout Missouri Union man prayed would never happen), it might turn out to be a real renunciation. ¿Quién sabe?

I bowed to El Presidente viejo y un poco loco and let them clop me out of there, and down to Taos, and to a hot bath at my friend Marty's.

"The spirits of the mountain told me that they were watching you," he said of my miraculous return. "Hey, that one guy, that guy that came looking for you, he was scary, man. What happened to him, Henry?"

I shrugged, as if I did not know. Nor did I tell him of the great and real golden bear who changed into a black bear who spared me. It was nothing to put words to. Marty had his own mystical moments, he did not need mine. T. J. Mackey? As I said, they took him away. I do not know what they did with him. We never saw him again. Of course, some version of him will come again. Until we have some sanity and genuine reform in our world, there will be T. J. Mackeys in it.

Ray Rodriguez had visited his son in his mountain stronghold and paid his respects to Uncle Andrés and was hanging around town hoping I would need a ride back and would lay another two hundred dollars on him so he wouldn't have to strain his stomach muscle with another big tree job too soon.

"You shouldn't have tried to give us the slip, Henry," he said, driving along. "That was foolish. Hell, we knew where you were every minute."

"I'm glad," I said.

"Well, you nearly outsmarted yourself," Ray said, giving me a pat on the shoulder, "going up the mountain like that. Lucky for you, man, that's like being thrown into the briar patch for us. You know? You are pretty lucky you didn't run into anything dangerous up there, they got cougar up there, mountain lion, you know, even bear. Last time I was out here I saw a big old bear, came pretty far down, swat a big old dog, kill it with one swipe of its paw."

I didn't respond. I was grateful, that is to say, alive. But as we rolled along towards Texas I nearly reached over and strangled him a time or two as he regaled himself and me with endless examples from the Bible of people who had outsmarted themselves.

"Remember, Henry, you can never outsmart the Lord," Ray said. "He always knows who the hell you are."

I nodded, and shut my eyes on the endless country, and even thought about it.

NINETEEN

I cannot tell you how happy I was to be back on my lovely little campus. Highland U., with the rains that had come to the prairie, looked fresh and new. Regina Singh was vigorously battling the wilt in the new oak trees and was planning a formal dedication of the small but stately Flatt Tower and a party to celebrate the first fifteen million raised for the "Campaign for Excellence and Diversity." (Changed from "Campaign for Excellence" by Regina.) (That was ten mil of Daddy's money, with ten more lurking in the background, with Tex and a few others ponying up the rest of "phase one"; but who knew that besides us chickens? To the media and the public it seemed a great success.) I idled about on campus waiting for the spring term when I would actually teach again and "helped" Regina and her provost and her inner circle devoted to our old goals and her new goals engineer Daddy's dough towards library holdings, scholarships, a few new faculty known beyond the Trinity River, and such. Regina even kept one foot on Bunky's path, setting up a computer and software system, as every place must do in these days as we hurtle towards the Millenium, say I as I scribble this on a pad with pen gripped lightly in my teeth. Ho ho.

I walked among the students on the campus, listening to them speaking that peculiar language that they speak, living in their mental world of "like." "I'm like—" "She's like—" "Oh, man, I like reached in the 'frigerator and found the sandwich and threw it at her—" I walked along behind a group of young women: "I only, like, like other students, you know, who are smart and cool—" My worlds, returned to: the books I love, and this other young, warm, vital approximation of reality. "And I'm like, listen . . ."

I stop and look across at Humanities Hall, our oldest building, going on six years old. At the base of the building's steps stands a group of students of various colors and garbs listening to a young man with flowing hair and a brown beard who looks like Protestant pictures of Jesus speaking and holding a sign: "Free Tibet." A bright-eyed young woman dark of hair holds a similar sign next to him, waving it and jumping up and down in her excitement. I recognize her as Rosie Rodriguez, Ray's niece, now with us here. Free Tibet, indeed! Free Texas! was what she meant. On the walk by the library some other, straighter students are handing out literature flakking the inevitably coming presidency of George W. Bush. Cut it left or right or down the middle, the campus is juicing up.

One day when I arrived at my office cubicle a very black young man was waiting for me. Politely he extended his hand and asked did I remember him, he was Clarence Dahfo, son of the poet-novelist and sage of his country Elmer Dahfo, we had met in Africa? Oh yes. Oh my. He had come here to study Classics. I took him by the arm and we went by to wake up old Professor Lugash snoozing in his office and then had young Clarence and the old boy and Regina for tea and sherry in the small dormitory apartment I now kept on campus.

When, in November, Daddy Bob Blanton and the massive Ranger Ping brought Bob's boy Eddie on campus to enroll for the spring term, as he was getting out of the Marine Corps and wished to go to college and on to law school as I had suggested, I thought on first spying them walking toward me in their large hats that they had changed their minds and come to kill me after all. Eddie was a big, strong boy, Billy Roy's little brother. His daddy said he had graduated high school with no sweat but did not have a natural affinity for reading books. I said that if he would try we would admit him and would attempt to make it interesting enough for him to read 'em. Daddy Bob said that was fair enough. Eddie nodded. His uncle, Mr. Ping, growled that Eddie would be the first in the family to go to college and he damn well would do well. Bob Blanton asked how the King business was doin'. I said it had sort of faded into oblivion what with removals of fortune and all. He said that sounded about right, he was always sorry for Billy Roy to get tied up with that crazy old man, McIvey, but that Billy Roy always just did adore that Lily. How was Miss Lily, he inquired. Pure and sweet as ever, I replied.

We marched over to where I suggested we build, one day, a memorial to Billy Roy. It would have to be anonymous, but we and a few others would know it was a tribute to him, and everyone would be able to sense his spirit in the group of four bronze mustangs we proposed. I had set aside a little money from Daddy's largesse for it; it would be right here at the edge of campus where it gave off to the world outside, to remind our students to harness up the energy and be ready. The Blantons, utter stoics, did not this time shed a tear but seemed pleased at this prospect.

I was glad to have them here, Rosie, Clarence Dahfo and Eddie. Quizá, they could work it out.

Regina Singh, our leader, had her celebration party for the Highland U. campaign at Tex Flatt's and invited everybody, and not a few attended. It was a pleasant, sunny, fairly windy November day. The Lexuses and Lincolns, the Cadillacs and Infinitis, the Jaguars and Mercedes rolled into Tex's driveway in significantly greater numbers than before, including a pale green Lexus SUV I recognized though the dark tinted windows hid the driver. Regina had spread our net more widely, so the wealthy and the wise, the queens and the worker bees, the mayor and the owners and the managers and some bat boys and girls all came. Some Basses came from west of us, and some Trouts swam in from the east. Some Hunts came from Dallas and some Hunters from Ozona. Our brand new Highland band played loudly on the grounds something indistinguishable from the noise of horn and snaring drum. Regina had a contest going to name the Highland teams and to choose a mascot for the school. They had summarily dismissed my suggestion of the "Highland Flings." We had no teams as yet, but Regina envisioned, I believe, volleyball, soccer and rowing as a start, though where we would row out here on the prairie was a matter of concern. The band, pumping away, was wearing, I feared, something terribly close to the McIvey tartan (but with a splash of gold in it). I was reverted back to my old Buick, which still ran, and parked the fine old artifact myself and strolled in to Tex's abode. He flicked an eye of scorn at me as I walked past him but did not snake out his hand. He'd known me as a failed provost and now I was a failure as a king. I smiled at him but he truly did not notice, I was "history" (meaning burnt toast, old brisket, dried-up goat turd) to him, as he darted his lizard hand in and out of that of the CEO of TDS and then the CEO of TxS and the COO of APR. The CEOs of XLT and RSV and P.com were also at Regina's party at old Tex Flatt's familiar place.

I passed through the rooms of the sere mansion and came upon John Woodcipher tasting from three different bottles of Texas Cabernet Sauvignon and nodded to him and passed on out to the back where the long rectangular pool lay, its water now skipped with wind, reflecting cirrus clouds above. As if she planned it, I saw Lily standing in what seemed the same shimmering blue dress, or something mighty like it,

across the pool's length from me. I almost bolted back to Woodcipher
and his dark goblets but remained standing there looking at her. She
waved an arm but not at me, gesticulating to the short, chunky fellow she
was speaking to. I recognized him as a minor poet from another local
university and felt I should run over—maybe swim across, if the water
was not actually a déjà vu illusion—and warn the fellow. But how could
you warn a poet, a spinner of words and images, of such evil? How could
I have been warned? Anyway, I surmised he would not last long, if
through this party; he was a head shorter than our Lily.

Susy Crabtree, Regina's new V.P. for Development, came up to me
and looked across to where I was last looking. "Do you know Lily
McIvey? She's fantastic! She's a *major* donor, you know." Susy was not
yet in on our little secrets.

"I met her at our last do here," I said. "My God, can it be five
months ago?" Startled by my vehemence, even perhaps frightened, Susy
left my side.

Back in the long yard beyond the pool, where the high adobe wall
bounded his place, old Tex had erected himself a new monument, I saw.
I strolled over the new green rye grass to behold it.

It was a brassy bronze, red-brown replica of a huge old Longhorn
steer with great horns making his head hang low, the horns curving out,
way out so it looked like it could turn its head a bit and scratch its tail
with the tip of a horn. (I had read of this, of course, in Dobie.) It was a
fantastic, near grotesque replica.

For some reason, maybe he was pleased I had noticed it, stuck back
here along the wall, Tex Flatt came up and stood by me. "That is Old
Champion," he said. "Had the record horn span, ever. Nine-foot horn
span. Twenty inches at the base of each horn. I had Tom Klause cast Old
Champion in bronze for me. What you think, gubuddy? Damn
impressive, eh? Rose?"

I nodded.

"It is a symbol," he said, for my elucidation.

But not of you, I thought. You were never a rancher, were you,
didn't you come out of the black dirt of the East Texas oil fields as a
wildcatter? Did you know that Daddy, old McIvey, had the actual horns?
I did not say this because suddenly I sensed what a sad old shell of a man
he was.

Tex cut his eyes at me; I could feel but not see it. "What's all this I
hear about your great-great-grandad, someone, was Moses Rose, the

fellow that left the Alamo? That you brag about being kin to Moses Rose?"

"Why would I claim to be kin to a coward who ran away from the Alamo?" I said, turning and smiling at him.

Tex shook his head and walked away, leaving me looking at Old Champion and his nine-foot span of curved longhorns. Maybe we should just plant a tree for Billy Roy, I thought, a nice live oak that would grow large . . . . No, it probably would not grow well out here on the hard black waxy. Do the mustangs, sculpt the wild little ponies. Bronze and brass grew best out here.

I went back in and had a glass with Woodcipher, fairly red of face by now, then drifted through the rooms and into the library room where I had these months ago encountered Daddy, the piebald old King of Texas, and his daughter Lily, and the amiable Billy Roy, and Mr. Fuad and Mr. Singh. It seemed again, all leather and lamps and books, a little red Turkey rug, a lovely room. I turned in a circle, remembering them, where the old boy had sat, his crazy eyes and smile, his toad-like skin, the large diamond and ruby and gold ring of his illusion, his strange majesty. I went to the book shelves and looked along them and found and pulled out the volume of *The Princess Casamassima* that Lily had taken down and leafed through on that afternoon. I wondered had she read it. Had it somehow helped to build up her own illusion? Certainly her cause was not the "people," not "democracy." But had she seen herself as such a privileged Princess, me as a "Hyacinth?" Ah, here I went again.

And there she was, dear Lily, having watched and waited for me to come in this room. Beautiful, shining, shimmering Lily, all in blue, with her large green-blue cat's eyes alight, her long lithe form erect, looking youngish, radiant, serene. She moved to me as I shelved the silly book. I looked to see if she held a blade. My platelet count had come to normal somehow through the adventure in the Taos mountains, but still one could bleed quite easily when put to the test of a keen Chinese knife. She came and stopped before me. We were of a height exactly and looked into each other's eyes.

"Henry," she said.

"Lily."

"I always loved you."

"Well," I said.

We stared at each other. It was as grand a moment as two old college acquaintances coming upon each other in the aisle of the supermarket. She cocked her head at me, and a bit of the old cracked look came back into those eyes.

"You ruined us. I have hardly a penny. Well, a few. But I forgive you, Henry."

Her eyes said murder and forgiveness, both: come back into my web and— It was not up to me to forgive her. And still, she terrified me.

"You know," I said, "I really kind of miss your daddy, that old bullshitter. I really kind of did like him."

"Poor little Henry," she said. "You could not hold—a fucking candle—I gotta tell ya, Henry, a candle *wick*—to Daddy—!"

Then thank God she turned and swept away.

On my way out I encountered Doris Waltenburg, the sweet little woman who was one of the richest persons in Texas, standing in a circle of other wealthy folks. She clung to my arm a moment and said that she hoped I would be lecturing to their group again soon and she said she had her little villa in Taos and maybe sometime, she knew I liked it there, it would be so pretty there soon with snow on the ground . . . .   and I patted her slightly humped shoulder and thought with my damn luck it would turn out she had buried three former husbands on the grounds there and picked me for the next, and murmured that sounded lovely and I looked forward to seeing her again but as for now I had just returned from a lovely stay in Taos.

I made it to the great oak door of the Spanish-style mansion before Miss Lily McIvey, like a girl at a prom, came racing up and caught me by the arm, and, giggling, whispered in my ear, "I have your finger, Henry!" and went running back to her new friend the poor little unsuspecting poet.

The wind had picked up as I went out and the sky had turned a shade of slatey-gray and that strange blue-dark green and I thought a norther might be on the way.

Back inside, that was about when old John Woodcipher collapsed dead with a seizure gulping a last great swig of the Texas cabernet.

LILY, OH, LILY! What passion, what loyalty, what—Godforsaken— strange—fierce—love! ("Ambivalent, eh? Ambi-valent, eh? A professor, eh? Valens! Be strong! Be dubious! Hello, Cronkite, I'm Dubious! Vaudeville, eh, Pro-fessor—")

I dreamed of her, successive nights, of my sweet Lily and I enacting the fantasy of "Love Lost But Ne'er Forgotten" in which after the frantic, fevered coupling the woman becomes one of the grotesque figures, all loins and flying limbs, in Lily's paintings and goes howling through the glade whilst the man cowers, missing parts, in his grove of trees . . . .

I will dream it more, I know . . . .

SOMETIMES I walk the now more lively campus and think of Bunky, stop by his bench, and of Billy Roy, those I was responsible for, and of the old Afghan fellow I was somehow spared from killing or being killed by.

At times now, living on the campus, I grow restless. Sometimes I'll go off campus to have coffee at the train station or the courthouse with Sam McGee and talk of various adventures we might have together. For a flash we were excited about going up to Alaska and joining the fight for the ecology there. But I did not really want to go back to Alaska. I couldn't think, actually, of any place I really wanted to go, just now, or anything odd or heroic I wanted to do, dear Lord, I had created enough adventures for myself, riding that dragon-horse of Texas mythology, to last a while, hadn't I?

Instead I go to the Rose Room, I had named it for myself, the rare book room of our library here on campus and fondle the old leather and other cracked old dusty volumes that are kept here locked away. Just now I reach in the cage and take out a rare copy of Doughty's *Travels in Arabia Deserta*, much admiring the passage that I find in perusing it:

"I asked some nearby man of them, who came to me trembling in the chill morning, how he looked to accomplish his religious voyage and return upwards in the cold months without shelter. 'Those,' he answered, 'that die, they die; and who live, God has preserved them.' "

Deftly I slit that page from the book and slip it into my notebook and steal away with it through the alarms and out of the building. It is a small adventure, but for now it suits me fine.

THE END